The Laughing Robot

The Laughing Robot

Julia Ross

A

First published in 2024 by Arena Books

www.arenabooks.co.uk

Julia Ross
The Laughing Robot

A CIP catalogue record for this book is available from the British Library.

Paperback ISBN: 978-1-914390-33-3
Ebook ISBN: 978-1-914390-34-0

Thema: FBA; FDB; FLP; FQ; FXL; FXS; JKSN; JKSG; JBSP4; MBPN; 5LKS

Cover design by Arena Books

For my grandchildren
Daniel, Ben, Logan, Sam and Kya

He said, "You become. It takes a long time. That's why it doesn't happen often to people who break easily, or have sharp edges, or who have to be carefully kept. Generally, by the time you are Real, most of your hair has been rubbed off, and your eyes drop out and you get loose in the joints and very shabby. But these things don't matter at all, because once you are Real you can't be ugly, except to people who don't understand."

The Velveteen Rabbit by Margery Williams 1922

Contents

Chapter 1

S am the robot, was a tiny, white, and very shiny robot with a
screen for a chest. His bright, alert expression and large, shiny
eyes made him seem like a small, friendly, and curious child – even
more so when he held his head to one side when asking certain
personal questions. He gesticulated expressively with his long
jointed arms and excessively extended digits. His voice, coming
from his small letterbox mouth, was high and metallic. He had
indents for ears on either side of his face, and a slight bump in the
middle to indicate a nose but no nostrils. As I watched him move
and respond, I wanted to touch him but didn't want to offend.
How human was he? He could hear, and talk, and see, but how
real was he? Would he be able to recognise me the next time he saw
me? His lack of nostrils would make smelling tricky and yet surely
smelling was an essential criterion in the work he was to do; in the
care of the elderly, little accidents are inclined to happen often and
unexpectedly.

October 2018 was the first year that Sam the Robot attended
the Annual Social Services Conference. It was also the first year that
robots started talking to each other in their own language. At least
that's what was reported on Facebook. It was also the year when,
having been worn down by the endless nagging from my daughter

Evelyn, I was beginning to think that perhaps I should start using Facebook myself.

"Mum, it's not like it used to be, it's a way of making arrangements and booking things … Even *I* don't use it for family photos and catchups anymore."

I knew this wasn't entirely true. Curiosity had led me to sign up to Facebook and a nudge now popped up whenever she posted a photo of our grandchildren. To understand the possibilities for robots, there's nothing better than watching children play. Evie had two children, not robots, Matilda and Hugo, but our son Stanley didn't have any. He showed no signs of having any either, much to my growing annoyance.

But there was a problem with some of these robots; it wasn't so much that robots were talking, or that they were talking to each other (data scientists had been programming them to talk for years), but that they had started to create a language of their own. These clever little things could communicate with each other better and quicker when not having to go through the unnecessary rituals and instructions dictated by their over-controlling human masters. They were definitely "disruptive" (that badge of honour much beloved by techy people). They were doing just what they were supposed to do after all – teaching themselves through machine learning and AI. But their human masters couldn't understand the new language, and paranoia about robots runs deep. What were they saying? What were they planning and plotting?

And so, it was announced on Facebook, and in the press, that these robots were to be discontinued and the project abandoned. I wasn't so sure if this was true …

Some people were convinced and frightened that humanoid robots were about to take over the world. I quite liked the idea of someone or something else doing the heavy lifting. Why not work shorter hours, and have more time for leisure? Why wouldn't manual labourers or people doing boring repetitive tasks want to be replaced by machines? As long as they got paid for whatever else they could do? So where did the fear come from? As a social worker, I knew that most of my colleagues would prefer people over machines, but I also knew that they were fearful. Was it simply a fear of the unknown? Or was it that AI challenges our perceptions of what it is to be human? If robots look like us and behave like us, then what's the difference?

I'd been a social worker most of my life until one day, the whole messy business of people being people, just got to me. Looking back over thirty years, it was clear that despite all my efforts, and all our collective efforts, hardly anything had changed. Quite simply, we had not made any real difference, and making a difference was why most people go into social work. Despite all those marches, noisy trade union meetings, policy writing, and campaigns, children were still not only starving but being starved, burnt with cigarettes, locked in garden sheds, and sometimes even beaten to death. Usually, but not always, by their parents. There were still people with serious mental health problems (although we now called them "issues"), homeless people on the streets, and even food banks had made a comeback.

Disillusioned, and annoyed with the world I now belonged to, I began exploring other options. I reckoned that I had just enough time to divert into something new before I retired. Tom, my husband, was older than me, and I had noticed that he often fell asleep in front of the television in the evenings and had begun to heave himself up with both hands from his chair. His university work was slowing down and both Evelyn and Stanley were now off our hands. Since they finally both left home, I had felt a rush of energy with time to spend on myself. I bought a new fashionable wardrobe of grey leather jacket, black culottes and black polo-necks and had my long greying hair cut into a short, tousled streaked bob.

I thought it might be a good idea to make some use of the massive amounts of raw data in the NHS and Social Care archives.

In particular, I wanted to look at the developments in AI and at the potential in the NHS in predictive analytics. I had no idea where this brave new world would lead me, but shortly after I had started my own research, I was approached by someone who was looking to set up a 'start-up.' Ed wanted help with designing new dashboards for health and social care data analytics. Six weeks later, I found myself with a new job analysing health data and social care records and thinking of ways that we might improve integrated working and care pathways across the system. AI and robots came later.

Ed, my new boss, came from Silicon Valley. He had an uncompromising crew cut, button-down shirts, and walked around in a waft of after shave. I never saw him wear a tie. I never heard him laugh or make a joke. The only time he became animated was when he was eulogising voraciously about the latest Ted talk he'd watched on YouTube.

"See here Anna, watch this and you'll understand."

I didn't. As I watched yet another corporate video on Happiness and Mindfulness, I began to see that Ed loved the logicality and the intensity of technology, but that people were a complete mystery to him. He proposed, at one of our mini-board meetings, that we should all talk to our families that evening over dinner about what had made us happy that day and then report it back to the next board meeting. Inevitably, it was excruciating. Our American colleague, Wayne, told us in mind blowing detail exactly what had made each of his three children happy in school that day, and relayed to us how impressed they'd been by his new sale that day worth $50,000. Money matters. I laughed and point blank refused when my turn came.

Thankfully, Ed was more successful when focusing on his passion for making money. For him, money was the sole purpose of business. Money and profit defined his success as a man. His friends and acquaintances were all working in business or finance – and of those, the venture capitalists were the elite. Ed's ultimate aim was to create a company over which the VCs would vie, and that one of them would ultimately take it over for huge sums of money. One of my first tasks for Ed was to do what's called an 'elevator sales pitch.' My pitch was, with hindsight, naïve, "We can revolutionise the world with better data and improve lives for so many people. Especially if we help people understand how the NHS, and social care, can work better together."

Ed's response was to sigh and say, "That's a good pitch, but can it meet the bottom line?"

He would no doubt make money, but I couldn't see how his business would ever be taken over by the big VCs. Common sense told me that good ventures need passion to drive success.

This was the last year I would attend the Annual Social Services Conference. I had been a faithful attendee for the past 20 years, first as a social worker and then as a social work manager. But now that I was officially a 'techy person,' it was time to move on. The conference always took place two weeks after the annual autumn round of political conferences. I was expecting this one to be both crowded and noisy since the government had yet again avoided making any future commitment about funding social care. People like me, the Baby Boomers, were living much longer and costing everyone, especially our poor children, a fortune. Who was going to look after us and pay for it all?

I had booked into the Cumberland, one of the better four-star hotels in Bournemouth. It boasted a spa, which of course turned out to be closed for the winter, but at least it was along the seafront. In the past, I had regarded the annual mingling of Directors of Social Services and politicians, and the inevitable feeding frenzy of gossip and politics, an essential part of the system. Now that I had moved on, its sheen had diminished. The Cumberland was slightly more expensive, but that mattered less now that I'd found myself the private sector.

I was beginning to separate myself off from my colleagues and paying extra for a sea view and balcony was worth it; not because I was expecting much sun, but because I've always loved the swelling vastness of the sea – the powerful sweeping back and forth of the waves over the soft sand. I ordered dinner in my room; a classic "Cumberland Burger" with fries and a bottle of Merlot (which I told myself I could finish over the next three days). As I opened the glass door out on to the blustery balcony, for a little fresh air before dinner arrived, I noticed something odd. There was a strangely shaped bundle sitting on the old-fashioned slatted wooden seat of the bus shelter on the far side of the road. It was about a hundred yards away, too far away to see clearly, but the bundle was upright and about the size of a small person bracing itself against the wind and rain. The bus stop, despite its peeling paint, offered some shelter. Then I heard a knock on my door announcing my dinner and forgot all about it. I turned on the TV and two hours later, I was surprised to find I'd drunk most of the Merlot.

Next morning, when I pulled back the grey green curtains, the bundle was still there, but I was too busy to think about it as I headed out to the conference. I had forgotten my makeup bag, so left early to pick up the essentials in a local shop and I managed to squeeze into the main auditorium just in time for the first keynote speech. Cllr Kathy Wright was a former trade unionist and now the feisty chair of the Local Government Association. She was something of a celebrity in the Labour movement and I knew we were in for a fighting speech as she strode onto the platform in her grey trouser suit and black boots.

"Women are still living longer than men by about two to three years. Good news that," she began in her gravelly voice as she peered over her granny glasses. The audience laughed, "But under this Tory government, there are disturbing signs of a slowdown in life expectancy, especially among women. Why is that?"

Her speech went on to cover the crisis in social care and then to the use of robots in Japan. My neighbour whispered above the applause, "I'm not so sure about robots though, maybe okay for the Japanese, but I can't see them going down over here."

As Councillor Wright's speech closed, I wanted to ask my neighbour why she thought the Japanese would like robots more than us, but I lost her in the crush of people leaving the auditorium.

Each political side was blaming the other for the growing NHS waiting lists that older people were having to endure. Creaking hips and knees were hardly a priority. You're old, put up with it. Never mind the pain, the inconvenience, the indignity. A childhood song about knees and toes, knees and toes that I had sung to the grandchildren, Matilda and Hugo, came into my mind. I hummed it as I moved up the escalator to head for the coffee stand – not so much because I wanted coffee (I'm a mainstream tea drinker) but I confess the wine-drinking had left me a bit hung over. I mustn't do that again. I needed to wake up because I wanted to check out an unusual session run by a district council that would be featuring Sam the Robot. The council was from one of the loneliest places on the planet, and surely one of the most unexpected councils to be foraging in the world of new technology; I was intrigued.

I turned up for the session expecting it to be packed out, and it was. A big wig called James Hillingdon, Senior Vice President of Capital Homes, was the chair. James was one of those sleek, smooth men, always beautifully dressed in a three-piece, pin-striped suit – the sort I wished I'd been able to persuade Tom to wear when we went out. Tom had always refused, preferring his university rumpled cords and jerseys instead. James Hillingdon was a good speaker with a strong voice and a self-deprecating style. He introduced Kevin from the district council, a burly and smiling middle-aged man who proudly presented 'Sambot,' the first robot to be programmed for social care. Kevin was evidently Sambot's self-appointed guardian, but surely not a social worker, I thought.

Next to me, a motherly-looking social worker whispered, "How on earth do they think that machine is going to be able to help frail older people? How could it do all the washing and feeding, let alone changing incontinence pads?"

Meanwhile, Kevin continued to beam with enthusiasm and something close to affection for his ward, "Sambot is our first robot , and we hope he is the first of many. We think he's the future for care services. He's 120 cm tall and retails at £2,000 and he comes here today all the way from Japan with the help of a special academic research license."

He continued, "I took him home with me for several months, until the wife got fed up." Pause for laughter and with perfect timing, he went on, "I taught him the basics so he can speak and answer some questions. He can move too, but only slowly. He can't go upstairs, but that will come. Otherwise, we can programme him to do anything you like – well, within reason." He added hastily.

I put my hand up. "Can he talk back? Hold a two-way conversation?"

James looked towards me and gestured me to join him on the podium. He held his hand out to help me up. His hand was warm and friendly as he gestured me to approach the robot. Kevin said something quietly to Sambot and, as I reached him, Sambot's face rose slowly up to meet mine. I felt driven to crouch down to his level. His bright, shiny eyes stared back at me. With his head cocked enquiringly to one side, he seemed to want to get to know me. It was ridiculous but I could now understand how the burly Kevin might feel affectionate towards this little creature. I reached out and took Sambot's bony hand in mine, intending to shake it, I suppose. Unlike James' hand, Sambot's metallic fingers were cold, hard, and brittle, despite being encased in white net bicycling gloves. I jumped back as the tiny metal fingers twitched slightly in my hand. Or I did I imagine that? Touching is one of our five senses as humans, but presumably he couldn't *feel* my hand, or could he? And what about taste? Surely he couldn't taste – he had no tongue. I laughed to myself and noticed James was watching me closely as

Kevin focussed on Sambot. I blushed slightly.

Sambot blinked in a very disarming way and began talking in a hard metallic voice which was strangely impelling.

"Hello, my name is Sam. The Fourth Industrial Revolution is dawning."

"We have Sambot visiting our care homes to work with older people with dementia," Kevin interjected, addressing the audience. He pointed at Sambot's front screen and invited me to tickle him, "They really like to interact with him – especially since we introduced the tickling screen."

Feeling a little foolish, I scrambled my fingers on the screen and there was a loud cackling sound as Sambot rocked back and forth.

I jumped back in alarm, but Kevin smiled down affectionately and said, "The old folk really like that – they like being able to interact. And that all helps with whatever the next steps might be."

The audience, now crowded, was made up of a mixture of young techy men and middle-aged female social workers. Many of the women were looking sceptical and one or two nudged each other with raised eyebrows as I made my way back to my seat. Kevin, blissfully unaware, continued to smile benignly as Sambot nodded and carried on in his stilted, tinny voice, "One of the areas I am looking forward to working on is the Reminiscence Group."

Kevin picked up the story. "Sambot sits with an older person and listens to them talking about themselves. Then, he asks them about it the next time they meet. It's why he's called a 'companion robot.' He's been very well received, with one exception, at our old people's homes – they see him as a child-like creature who they can talk to."

"What was the exception?" One of the smart young men wanted to know.

Kevin hesitated. "One of the residents screamed when he came near her. She wouldn't have anything to do with him. She wouldn't say why, and we still don't know." He shook his large head sadly.

9

The feel of Sambot's steely strength, his cold, hard-as-iron digits that could have crushed mine in a moment, had certainly taken me by surprise. I could easily imagine becoming nervous around him.

The audience was clearly struggling with the idea that this little creature could be a companion, let alone a carer. I watched as James Hillingdon nodded at Kevin to close the session. I definitely wanted to hear more, so I signed up for the Robot Network Programme on Kevin's clip board on my way out.

Back at the hotel that evening, I googled Sambot, and robot programmes in Japan. They seemed to be way ahead of the game there, despite being such traditional and family-centred people. Then I read, 'Sambot's affability should not be mistaken for something less innocent.'

What on earth might that mean? Less innocent? I read on, 'The 120-cm tall robot must not be taken off the owner's premises or be used to harm humans.' Other clauses included banning owners from using Sambot to send spam emails, and 'tampering with its software to give it a sexier voice.' This section also warned that 'performing lewd acts upon the robot could be met with punitive action.' Unlikely that this would be a major issue in health and social care, I thought, especially given the age of the older people using services. And how would they know? Was the robot programmed to tell tales on its owners?

Later that evening as I was putting my feet up with yet another beef burger washed down with a fresh bottle of Merlot, a programme about robots popped upon the T.V. A youthful presenter was saying, "we think robots will appeal to an older age group by showing them how to keep fit and reminding them to take their medicines." Then, more robots when series 13 of *The Apprentice* came on. The deeply rumpled and wrinkled Alan Sugar, still going strong in his seventies, was asking the youthful and desperately keen contestants to design and manufacture robots for their chosen demographic – either young children or older people. The team working on the robots for youngsters immediately started playfully throwing ideas back and forth but the team working on the robots for the elderly seemed stumped.

"We think the robots should appeal to an older age group," they said hesitantly, "by acting as care companions and teaching them things like yoga." In the audience, a young-looking older person laughed, "Sounds like a nanny state! I'm not doing yoga at my age, whatever any robot says."

As soon as the programme finished, my mobile rang. It was my daughter Evelyn, "Did you watch that programme about robots?" she asked excitedly.

"Yes, loved it. I'm thinking of getting one," I joked. "What about you?"

"Can they cut the grass, cook dinner, and do the washing up?" Evelyn laughed.

"Actually, yes to the grass and you already have a dishwasher, although I'm not sure about dinner just yet. But seriously, just think, robots could be looking after us when we get old!"

"I can't see it happening Mum. Would you really want one?"

"Why not?" I was beginning to reassess Sambot. But my daughter had moved on, "Mum, it's half-term in two weeks. A whole week this time. Can you come up again please?"

I groaned inwardly. "Well, I'd love to see the kids, and you too, of course," I added hurriedly. "Let me go back to my diary. If it's the whole week, I'll need to rearrange things. Won't Andy be around?"

"Yes, but he's just lost his license, so I can't rely on him right now."

I loved our grandchildren, Hugo and Matilda, but I'd have to cancel a few things if I was going to do this. Lots of my friends complained they were permanently on grandparent duty now. Lots of them were doing a regular one or two days a week rather than the odd holiday, so I suppose I was lucky. Tom hardly ever came with me anymore; he didn't get on with Andy. The children were growing up fast. They were lovely kids – very full on, but now that Hugo was also at school, it was a lot easier looking after them both. Matilda was growing up to be a real beauty with her mother's thick, wavy auburn hair and slim build. I liked to think she took after me, but taller and somehow more confident.

The next morning of the conference, the weather had settled, unlike the politics. The driving winds and rain had stopped, and the sky was a bright blue with just the occasional scudding white cloud. I took a long look towards the sea, now calmer, and the bus stop. At first it seemed empty, but when I looked more carefully – my long-distance sight has always been relatively good – I saw the object again. It looked like a white cocoon now, merging into the white and yellow paintwork of the bus shelter. It was tightly swathed in what looked like a white duvet with a yellow hat. The hat moved, and a face appeared. Even at a distance of 100 yards, I realised it was a hunched up woman. She seemed to be staring back at me.

The hotel phone rang loudly like an alarm call, cutting across my thoughts. I picked it up and then held it away from my ear as Tom's cross voice rang out, "Where have you been? You've not been picking up your mobile?" he complained accusingly.

"Sorry, the signal's not good here. Busy conference. I thought you'd be away still. Good funeral? "

"Bit gloomy, everyone over eighty, makes you wonder what next for us. I think I'd like 'Rock of Ages' at mine, please, nice and solid."

"Okay, let's do a list of your favourites when I'm back." I didn't have time for Tom's morbid obsessions right now. "Listen, I've got a bit of a problem." I was slightly anxious about the bus stop apparition, or more accurately, I was beginning to feel a creeping sense of responsibility. I described the woman to Tom. "I'm not sure what to do. I can't do nothing! And I get this odd feeling I've seen her before."

"Don't you dare go anywhere near her or him, for that matter!

They could be dangerous!"

I laughed. In twenty years spent working with emergency mental health admissions, I had become immune to this type of fear. "Don't be daft. She's not dangerous. But I feel bad about just leaving her there."

"You mean how would it look with a conference full of social workers and one poor demented old lady camping out at a bus stop all night, while you're all tucked up in your nice warm beds?"

"Well, yes. I wonder why she's chosen a bus stop. Was she planning a journey and then something went wrong? It's such an odd place to camp out."

"Does seem a little odd, but it's not your problem."

"She's reproaching me. All of us."

"Well, why don't you go and ask at the hotel? See what they say? They must know about her!"

He was getting impatient, as he often did when something didn't have an immediate answer. As I went down to breakfast, grumbling to myself that despite the fancy Art déco furnishings, The Cumberland didn't seem to have caught on to the fashionable crushed avocado on sourdough toast craze. Old-fashioned eggs and bacon would have to do. I vowed to go on a diet as soon as I got home. I couldn't afford to lose my shape now.

On my way into breakfast, I stopped at the reception desk, and choosing my words carefully, asked, "Do you know about the person who is sitting in the bus shelter opposite?"

The young Italian receptionist was busy at her computer. She hesitated, then looked away into the back office and gestured to an older colleague. They exchanged something in low voices, then she turned to me, somewhat aggressively, and said, "She's mad you know."

"Well, I can see that there's a problem, but do the police or the doctors know about her?"

She shook her head dismissively. "She doesn't want any help.

She won't go."

Did they think I was going to insist they bring her in for a good bath and breakfast?! There were people coming into the reception, so I lowered my voice and said slowly, "I want to know if the police or the doctors have been told about her?"

"Yes, yes, they know …" And she turned away back into the office before I could ask another awkward question.

On my way back from the conference late that afternoon, I decided to walk along the sea front past the bus stop. I watched from a distance as a stream of mostly older hotel guests surged across the road and clustered around the bus stop looking at the timetable. I wondered what would happen. She was hidden from view at first. Then I spotted her sitting motionless whilst the crowd swarmed around her, pulling up their hoods, adjusting rucksacks, polishing glasses and peering at the timetable. I was surprised she didn't withdraw. After a few minutes, the crowd drifted into a disorderly queue as a towering double-decker red bus swept up and stopped abruptly. The crowd clambered on board without a backward glance, leaving her sitting there. I felt, rather than saw, her relax back into her seat.

As I drew closer, I was surprised to see that a lime green suitcase had now appeared at her side and the cocoon swaddling her seemed to have shrunk in size. She was perched upright on the slatted wooden seat. I sat beside her, being careful not to get too close and make her feel crowded.

"Hello, my name's Anna." Silence. "Better weather, isn't it?" Still no reply. I waited a few more moments and then tried again in a lower, slower voice. "I'm staying at the hotel across the road, it's …"

I stopped as she muttered something in a rusty sounding voice.

"I'm sorry, I didn't hear you," I said, tempted to move closer to hear better, but knowing this might frighten her away.

"Pandora, that's my name," she muttered.

"Good to meet you, Pandora," I replied and held out my hand, which, to my surprise, she took. She was wearing white cotton gloves on both hands and her grip was tight, almost as tight as Sambot's grip yesterday at the conference. She didn't let go and moved her hand up and down in a slow handshake for a minute or two more. I tried to look her in the face and smile, but she was looking down at her feet.

"That's a lovely name. Are you waiting for a bus?" She shook her head slowly and let my hand go at last. I massaged it with my other hand for a few moments. "Is there anything you need? Can I help at all?" She shook her head. I wasn't sure what else I could do, so after a few moments I said, "I'm going back to my hotel now. Do you want to come and have a coffee with me?"

Again, she shook her head and feeling a little silly, I got up and walked across the road, looking carefully in both directions even though there was hardly any traffic. I had tried. She had that frozen look that I'd seen before with people soon after they had been on a heavy dosage of drugs or ECT.

In my room, I googled mental health and ECT. Up popped a *Guardian* article. The article described how the use of ECT had come back into fashion, especially for older women. I didn't have time for much more, so I saved the article and went back to my emails. I noticed my confirmation of registration for the Robot Network Programme was waiting in drafts, so I pinged it off with a flourish, reservations all gone.

The last morning of the conference, a Friday, was a masterpiece of the usual attempts to keep hold of everyone for the full three days. Usually, the Minister or the Secretary of State for Health and Social Care would be there to give a keynote speech and then be heckled by the local councillors. This year, there was no-one. Probably because they knew they would have been booed off the stage. Instead, there was the same big cheese from the private sector who'd been at the Sambot session, James Hillingdon. His talk had a suitably euphoric title, "Investing in the Future for Care Homes." He must have offered a massive sponsorship deal to be a keynote speaker. I wondered if he was perhaps a venture capitalist friend of Ed's. The session was more interesting than I had expected and he ended on a futuristic note, "Our new-build, one-level villas are attracting interest for this new generation of older people with all the onsite facilities, especially …" here he paused for effect, "as we roll out our new programme for care robots."

There was silence until the first audience question caused a ripple of laughter. "All very well you putting robots into these villa things, but they're hardly going to wipe old folk's bottoms, are they?"

His reply was confident, "Of course we need to develop the technology further for the more delicate movements, but it will come. Of that I'm sure. It won't be long before everyone's asking for them. They're our future workforce – they never take sick days or holidays, and are totally reliable." He was moving away from the lecture podium when suddenly he swung back and, staring firmly at the audience, said very insistently, "You know, there are older people who don't like being touched in an intimate way by a complete stranger; they would much prefer to be cared for by an anonymous machine rather than an endless stream of different carers. I know I would."

I was expecting a tirade of objections from the trade unions in the audience, but those last comments shocked them all into silence. I wasn't sure if it was the sheer novelty of his ideas or the obvious sincerity of his delivery. I clapped along with the others, wondering how seriously this audience would take his words. Would they later dismiss him as being just a profiteer? Or too far-reaching?

Later, as I packed my bags, I took one last look out at the bus stop. It was empty, no Pandora. I ordered a taxi for the station back to London. Outside the station, I read the headline in the local newsagent, "Tragic bus Accident." The first line read, "On Friday evening, a well-known local resident died instantly when she stepped out in front of the Number 76 bus."

Chapter 2

Back home that night in our terraced house in Islington, I slept badly. I dreamt of Sambots dressed in white medical gowns giving ECT to women in an endless long queue winding down hospital corridors. As each woman reached the bed, one robot injected the woman with a tranquilliser, another held her down, the third intubated her, and the fourth administered the electrical current. The patient shuddered each time, and then sat up in a rigid movement and shuffled out as the next woman moved on to the bed. I woke in the middle of the night in a cold sweat remembering when I had been on an ECT treatment team on a psychiatric ward many years ago and wishing I hadn't been there. And I realised that I also felt sick with a feeling of dread and guilt about Pandora's death. Could it have been my fault?

Later that Sunday morning, the sun shone through the crab apple tree, still laden with bright yellow fruit, in the tiny front garden. I decided to shake off the nightmarish dreams by going for a bicycle ride along the canal towpaths. I was soon full of the happiness that fresh air and being outside brings. Later, back home, Tom and I were relaxing in front of our wood burner with the Sunday papers spread out on the floor and Aretha Franklin's "Amazing Grace" flooding through the house (my nod to Sunday church). Tom was sitting with his stockinged feet up on our brown leather sofa. His tall, lean frame, wearing creased green corduroys and a thick-knit jersey, was comfortably rumpled. His curly grey hair was getting thinner now and was falling over his collar. He needed a hair-cut.

I grimaced at the powerful roar from the street, thinking about the pollution. Two minutes later, the front doorbell rang. As Tom eased himself up from the sofa, I went through to the kitchen to put on the Yorkshire puddings. As I opened the oven door, the smell of roast beef poured out, filling the house. Stanley was coming to Sunday lunch with his new girlfriend. Ridiculously, he had driven from his rented flat only a few streets away in Camden in his new bright red Porsche. Probably showing off to his new girlfriend, Cassie. It looked completely out of place alongside my old bicycle chained to the railings on the pavement outside.

Stanley came in first as Cassie stood back, smiling. As he bent to kiss me, there was just a faint whiff of expensive aftershave, not too much. It softened his otherwise razor-sharp edge, essential for a young man working in financial services. Today, as always, my beautiful boy was well turned out with a soft light-grey cashmere jersey that I'd not seen before and recently pressed Ralph Lauren jeans framing his slim build. His sleek black hair was fashionably long. Too beautiful, I sometimes thought, as I wondered if Cassie did his ironing.

Cassie came forward with her hand held out and smiling generously. On first impression, she seemed sweet, friendly, bright, her mop of tight blond curls falling over her pixie face.

As we bustled into the warm living room, and Tom moved to serve out some pre-lunch wine, Stan picked up one of the papers. "You Baby Boomers are so Selfish!" screamed the headline. He snorted and handed it over to Cassie. "We were talking about this on our way here, weren't we? You lucky sods, the mortgage-free generation."

"I may be a baby boomer, but I worked hard all my life and I'm still working hard at nearly sixty," I said, defensively.

Stan just continued, "And there's all those benefits – free TV license, winter fuel allowances, bus passes, and all the rest of it! I bet they've all gone by the time we get there!"

Cassie frowned at him as she sipped the white wine Tom had poured for her. I'd forgotten until the last minute that Stan had said she was vegetarian. It was too late to cook anything else, but luckily I had made cauliflower cheese as well, so that would have to do.

Tom was talking animatedly as I came back from the kitchen with the roast potatoes and cauliflower cheese, his tall frame stooping slightly towards Cassie. "The papers were saying that it was all the fault of the older voters who voted for Brexit."

Cassie replied, "Actually, I think the Brexit vote backfired for a different reason; not enough young people bothered to vote. Then they got all stirred up by social media and the Corbyn lot, to vote in the general election."

She looked across at Stanley, who was frowning thoughtfully at her. From the impression that Stan had given, I'd had her down as a full-on radical feminist, so this was a little more considered than I was expecting. I was pleased. Perhaps she was actually the right one for Stanley, but would he think so too? I turned back to Cassie, who certainly wasn't much more than a millennial herself, and asked, "So, do you think all this bad feeling about the Baby Boomers is politically driven?"

"No, I'm not saying that exactly. I think there's a real problem. We're just not going to have enough to go around. As Millennials, when we hear that Baby Boomers are going to live longer, which is lovely, of course," she smiled, "I worry about how we are going to look after you all." She paused and added hastily, "I don't mean you, of course! I'm sure you can look after yourselves."

I chuckled ruefully along with her. I really enjoyed Cassie's way of talking. She seemed to be well-informed, good at building bridges and finding common ground – especially between myself and Stanley. Unfortunately, this was an increasingly necessary and difficult task. We were often at loggerheads on both political and ecological issues. He was an angry young man with strong views on making money at the expense, I thought, of saving the environment and mankind. He hadn't always been like that.

As we sat around the dinner table, my good feelings continued until, apparently from nowhere, an argument erupted from zero to boiling point. My immediate feeling was worry about what Cassie would think of us. Stanley was getting increasingly irate, "I tell you, it's going to be impossible! It's not just the Baby Boomers with your houses and pensions, at least you'll pay your way. It's also all those on welfare getting obese at our expense. Nevertheless, it's still your generation who are standing in the way of solving the biggest crisis for us millennials; the housing crisis!"

"So, what's your solution then? What did you vote?" I said, trying to sound neutral. Stanley was acting as if he was too busy gravy-dolloping (he liked it all over his vegetables, not just on the meat) to answer. But sons should answer their mothers, so I kept on at him. "Did you vote? You did vote, didn't you?"

I knew I was being inquisitorial, but when Cassie looked at him sideways and made a slight face, I began to think that perhaps he had indeed not voted. She herself was a campaigner for Liberty, so I reckoned she would no more have not voted than kicked a dog.

Shrugging me off as if I didn't get it, he said, "Mum, leave it. I was really busy at work."

"So, which vote was the most difficult to forget, the referendum or the general election?"

"Of course I voted in the referendum. But I just couldn't see the point of another general election. And before you jump down my throat, I voted to remain." Then he added sarcastically, "Hope you did too? Most of your lot wanted to leave!"

"Yes, of course, we both did," I said placatingly, as Tom gave me a warning look. "What bothers me most though, is that the press keeps stirring up angst between the generations. Obviously," I went on, "I don't like it that lots of my generation voted to leave. I heard that since Brexit, there's been a growing problem of demented eighty-year-olds being dumped at Heathrow off flights from Spain."

Tom came in, resignedly agreeing with Stan's points, "I've got colleagues who were senior civil servants retiring on pensions of £60,000 odd. Then they go off to get another job in industry!"

Cassie looked up with a shocked expression and shook her head in disbelief.

"It's true that a lot of us are having a glorious time at the expense of the younger generation," I went on, "but we're suffering now with the crisis in the care industry and the loss of all that cheap foreign labour."

Tom piped in, "You know, I can't help feeling that the real problem is yet to come." He looked at Stanley and Cassie. "Not your generation, but your children's … when you have them," he added hastily.

"Everyone seems to delay having children now. Maybe the next generation will change all that?" I suggested.

Stanley and Cassie studied their plates carefully.

Diplomatically, Tom jumped in again while tucking into his roast beef, "I read in the *New Scientist* that the rise in life expectancy has just ground to a halt. Some Professor Marmot blames 'austerity'. But I guess if it's here to stay then we're not all going to live forever, after all. Thank goodness!"

Stanley, clearly still irritated by my earlier jibe, said, "So, what's the answer then, Mum? You've always said you'll live until you're 120!"

"The answer is that we're going to retire and live somewhere nice, like the Isle of Wight, as soon as we can." I replied.

Tom looked exaggeratedly aghast. "Speak for yourself! I'm pretty happy where I am thanks very much. Anyway, what with austerity, I reckon we'll all need to work to our dying day."

"What do you guys think we should do?" I asked.

"Sorry Mum," Stanley said, "I know you worked hard when we were young – time to stop now you want to. You have my permission! Or slow down a bit?" He smiled across at me.

Cassie looked approvingly at him, but Tom surprised me by saying, "Oh, your mum would be bored stiff. Wouldn't you?" he said, turning to me. "All the research shows that if you stop, you drop."

Was there something he wasn't telling me? It's true that a couple of his colleagues at work had retired recently and got bogged down with hip and knee replacements, or worse.

Stanley came to the rescue. "It's fine by me if you two stop working – the sooner the better as far as I'm concerned. I'm more worried about there being no jobs left when the robots take over. We're already talking about it at work. Fully automated financial transactions, no more cash, driverless cars, and then we're next!"

"It won't be all doom and gloom," soothed Cassie, "I can't help feeling they'll be problems ahead, but robots can be made to be a force for good overall."

Stanley replied, looking at Tom, "The robots are moving in everywhere. They're already in the construction industry and anything to do with heavy lifting. They're saying that the new algorithms will replace predictions in the city any day now."

"Well, I met my first robot this week," I told them. "His name was Sam. He seemed like a real little person, but so hard and clinical at the same time. If he replaces difficult tasks, then that's got to be a good thing."

Stanley threw me a smile, "Well, *I'm* thinking of making Mum happy and going back to my first love." He threw me a wry smile, "Remember when all I wanted to do was watch nature programmes and chase frogs?" Then he dropped the bombshell. "Seriously, I'm thinking of a career move. Maybe retrain and restart before it's too late."

Tom looked at me and I raised my eyebrows. Turning back to Stanley he said, "If you're looking for help, then Mum and I will need to have a chat." No retiring to the Isle of Wight for a while then! Then Tom, continuing to address Stan alone said, "Why don't we go out whilst the sun's still shining and stretch our legs along the canal? There's something I wanted to talk over with you too."

Cassie and I looked at each other and I shrugged, "You can go too if you want? I'm okay doing the dishes and I've got some work to catch up on anyway."

Cassie protested, "No problem!" and was quick to look busy. "I'll give you a hand and then I need to get back home to pack – I'm off to New York tomorrow first thing for an international conference on civil liberties."

The front door slammed, and I turned to her, "So, what are your plans?"

"You mean with work? Or with Stanley?"

I wasn't expecting such a direct answer, "What about both?" I laughed.

She leant back against the draining board with the drying up cloth in her hand, "I love my work but if we want to settle down and have a family, then I'll have to stop working on the international front." She smiled ruefully.

"Will you miss all that?"

"Yes and no. I love it but it's also quite disruptive attending all these international forums. If I was more UK-based, I could move into policy work."

"So might you settle down quite soon then?" I asked tentatively,

"We've been looking but prices in the areas we want, like around here, are way out of our reach – especially now that Stan's talking about changing direction too."

"Was he serious about changing his career?"

She put the drying up cloth down and shrugged, smiling,

"Looks like it."

When Tom came back whistling from his walk an hour or so later, he was alone. Cassie had already headed home and must have texted Stanley because he went off in his car without coming in to say goodbye. I wished I could have given him a hug after hearing all Cassie's news. I felt more in touch with him than I had for a long time. All down to Cassie I thought, with a thankful sigh of relief.

That evening, Tom tuned-in to one of his favourite *Star Trek* episodes. The never-defeated Enterprise, under the command of Captain Jean-Luc Picard, was being taken over by the evil Borg for whom resistance was futile, as usual, and who was beaten by Picard, as usual. When Tom turned it off to begin a conversation, I knew it must be serious.

"I always thought I'd live forever," he began, "but it's beginning to look as though I might be mortal just like everyone else."

I laughed, "I'm afraid so, but we could still have a good thirty years or so more … at *least*," I added optimistically.

"Do you really want to retire to the Isle of Wight?" he asked incredulously. I thought you wanted to keep on working for the time being?"

"What about you?" I ducked the question. Tom was five years older than me. He loved his academic work, and the university was happy for him, year-after-year, to continue.

"Better sort the screening out whilst I'm still on Bupa, then we'll see."

"What screening?" I asked worriedly.

"I've been having a few aches and pains. I didn't want to worry you. The doctor said I've got to have some blood tests."

"Why didn't you say? I'll come with you. When's the appointment?" I felt myself going into overdrive. It was my worst nightmare. His face went blank the way it does when he didn't want to talk about something. He shook his head, so I changed tack. "And now there's Stan apparently wanting to change direction. Did you manage to chat to him about it on the walk?"

"Sort of ..." and he trailed off. "You're as bad as Stan, you know, with your soap boxes. I guess that's where he gets it from. Cassie's good news though I think, don't you?"

"Don't change the subject!" I laughed. "Well, I *would* like to slow down a bit. London's so noisy and the air pollution makes me cough. The Isle of Wight is an interesting place – peaceful – and they say it's got the most sunshine anywhere in the UK, as well as loads of your favourite, garlic!"

"Well, let's see how the tests go and then talk some more."

Tom was always a light sleeper. He would drop off quickly and then wake up in the night at about 4am and turn the radio on quietly. That night, we made love for the first time in a long time, and he was asleep afterwards as soon as his head touched the pillow. As he snored lightly away, I lay back imagining what it would be like to live on the Isle of Wight. We had family there – my cousin Peggie and her husband Edward who were both a lot older than me. Peggie had married Edward who was himself an islander. There must be lots of rundown properties in need of renovation there, I thought. Tom would love that. I fell asleep dreaming about a simple self-sufficient life on the island with a garden full of vegetables and chickens for fresh eggs. I resolved to talk to Tom about it in the morning. My thoughts tumbled into dreams.

Chapter 3

The phone rang loudly and insistently. Evelyn was in the middle of correcting homework for class the next day and called out from the kitchen, "Andy, can you get that, please? I'm busy with the homework. It's either PPI or Mum and you know she always likes a chat with you."

"Oops, sorry, I forgot to tell you. She rang earlier!" He called from the sitting room, "I said you'd ring her back – she's worried about your dad."

"Bugger, I'm only halfway through." Evelyn sighed as she picked up her mobile and dialled. "What's up Mum?" Taking a deep breath, she pulled her mug of tea towards her and rocked back in the old wooden kitchen chair.

"It's Dad. He's out at the moment, so I can talk. He's got something wrong with him and he won't talk to me about it. I wondered if he'd said anything to you?"

"No, but I don't think he would anyway."

"Well, do you think Andy would mind calling him? He might talk to him, especially if it's a man thing?"

Evelyn winced. Andy was very squeamish about anything medical, and he'd never really got along with Tom. "Okay, but maybe Stan would be better? He's more likely to talk to him. Have you seen Stan recently?"

"Yes. And I met Cassie last weekend, they came for lunch. It seems as though he might finally be ready to settle down. But he never answers his phone and I'm not sure if he'd let me know what's up – especially if Dad wants to keep it to himself. I thought maybe if Andy tried, then you could tell me?"

"So you think Dad's not well?"

"He says he's got to have some tests. Then he started talking about retirement again."

"I'm sure it's nothing. But I'll talk to Stan later if you're really worried."

"I've also been wondering, would Andy know anything about powers of attorney?"

"Sorry Mum, not a good time," she said hurriedly, "powers of attorney? What do you mean?"

"I heard on the radio that there's a huge increase in elderly parents giving their children enduring powers of attorney. The lawyers seem to be pushing it like anything."

"I guess it might make sense if you had dementia, and you were worried about the financial side of things. Why, are you and Dad losing your marbles?" Evelyn joked.

"Ha, ha. I just wondered, if Dad gets any worse, whether I might need to sign things for him. He's always managed the financial side of things until now. I guess I'm just a bit worried about what happens next."

"In what way?"

"Oh, I don't know, like dealing with car insurance, household bills, and the money we've got in shares. Stuff like that."

"Oh, I wouldn't worry about the house. Listen Mum, I've got to go. I'll get Andy to read up about powers of attorney. He'll be interested if it's hitting the headlines and there's some sort of abuse going on."

"Abuse? What do you mean?"

"Nothing, Mum, I'll explain another time. Take care and thanks again for doing half-term. You're a star! You certainly fed Hugo well last time. He's asking for pancakes at breakfast every day now!"

As soon as she got off the phone with Anna, Evelyn dialled Stanley. "Stan, have you got a moment? Mum's worrying about Dad and she's talking about getting power of attorney for the house if Dad gets ill. Do you know anything about it?"

"Not really. But that reminds me, I was going to tell you … Dad's thinking about putting the house in a Trust so that if something happens to them, it'll come straight to us. What do you think?"

Evelyn felt a rising irritation, "I bet he hasn't even said a word to Mum about it. You know she's totally against that sort of thing. She thinks people do it to avoid their nursing home fees – which, of course, they do."

"That's exactly why he was sounding me out first."

Evelyn felt the old familiar pang at feeling left out, "Do you know what Stan? I'm fed up with you talking behind my back. Just when were you going to tell me?" She didn't care if she sounded angry.

"Oh, calm down. You'd have to know anyway because you'll have to sign the papers, so will Mum come to that. The house is in his name, always has been, but she has rights as well."

"Says you."

"Listen, I don't know where or how the power of attorney fits in, but I'll give you a buzz after I've been to the solicitors' with Dad. Things ought to be a bit clearer then. Whatever you do, do not tell Mum just yet."

Evelyn remembered why she'd called in the first place, "Listen, Mum's worried about Dad, seems he's got something wrong with him and he won't tell her what's up. You can imagine how she loves that!"

"Oh, for god's sake, Evie, so what?"

"Well, she was wondering if you could ask him about it."

"Why didn't she ask me herself if she's so keen? I saw them both just last weekend, and he seemed fine. Can't you leave the poor man in peace?"

"If you picked up the phone when she calls you, then maybe

she would!" There was no point in arguing. Evelyn changed the subject, "What's this I hear about you and your new girlfriend Cassie going places?"

"Mums impossible. Nothing's decided yet, but maybe in the spring."

Evelyn heard a door slam downstairs. Andy going out for a smoke outside. "Gotta go. So you'll ask him?"

"Oh, for fuck's sake." And he put the phone down abruptly.

Evelyn gulped a large mouthful of tea, and almost spat it out. It was stone cold. She shivered and stared out of the window into the dark outside. Reluctantly, she pulled the homework books towards her. Everything was going online next term – the sooner the better. She wasn't sure how much longer she could stand this side of teaching. Andy was worried about being made redundant – not many books were being edited by real people now, and journalists were becoming an endangered species. How would they manage on just her teacher's salary? And he'd just begun talking about being a househusband. For god's sake! How was that going to work?!

What would the old family home be worth now, anyway? Mum and Dad had bought it twenty years ago, at least. She recalled them all moving in from their tiny flat around the corner to the big house on the tree-lined street. She remembered, with fondness for their younger selves, the excitement of having a garden and guinea pigs for the first time. Islington was a pricey area now – it must be worth several hundred thousand, although they'd paid something like £20,000 back then.

Evelyn reached for her laptop, looked over her shoulder to check the kitchen door was shut, and the Zoopla results came up straight away. £920,000 for the Islington house. What they couldn't do with even half of that. Then she checked their own house – just £220,000. If anything, prices had gone down. It was rural Wales, lovely views but less jobs, less opportunity, less entertainment on your doorstep. Even so, it didn't seem fair.

Chapter 4

I woke the next morning to the sound of Tom clattering in the kitchen. As usual, he brought me a cup of tea in my favourite mug. As we sat up in bed planning the week ahead, he said abruptly, "I've got the doctor's appointment on Wednesday morning."

"Shall I come with you?" I asked, tentatively, "I can easily rearrange work – I could just wait outside and then we could get a coffee afterwards?"

"What about a good breakfast? It's fasting bloods they want, so I'll be ravenous by then."

Wednesday morning came, and I held back and waited outside, as promised, as Tom went in. When he came out, his face was completely blank. Probably not good news then, although it could mean he was just dazed. I knew it was best not to push it, so we said nothing as we walked down the street to our favourite local Italian. As always, it was steamy and noisy inside as waiters shouted orders across to the kitchen and people greeted each other over the tiny tables. There was a pungent aroma of fresh coffee and baked croissants battling against the mouth-watering savour of crispy bacon. I ordered a Full English and Tom had his usual scrambled eggs and smoked salmon. He went over to pick up the *Guardian* and *The Times* from the rack by the door.

"Here you go – *The Guardian* on the problems in the NHS. Too many blocked beds. Just what the doctor ordered!"

"Aren't you going to tell me anything?"

"Nothing to tell. Just have to wait for the results. "

That was it. I knew there would be more to what the doctor had said, but I could hardly force it out of him. I had ignored his comments about 'blocked beds', which he knew was something that would get my attention. It annoyed me; older people get stuck in hospital through no fault of their own.

That evening, Tom was in the kitchen getting us both a drink while I was watching the 7 o'clock news on Channel Four. The main item was immigration. Politicians on all sides seemed to agree that it was sensible to restrict the admission of unskilled labour from the EU. The news reader began talking about a new initiative which might solve the problem of finding people to work in the fields and pick crops; robots had been taught how to pick raspberries by fine tuning their digits to apply just the right amount of pressure. As Tom came back in and passed me my glass of white wine, I turned the sound down. I noticed he was drinking a new low-alcohol beer that he'd never drunk before.

He nodded towards the TV, "That's them pandering to Brexit and the Leavers and their racism – saying we'll be alright when we won't."

I agreed, "I don't understand how they're not making the connection between Brexit and the workforce crisis in care homes. Robots might be able to pick raspberries, but they can't wipe bottoms – not just yet anyway. At the moment, almost all the workers come from the EU, or even further afield." I looked at Tom's drink feeling a more urgent worry, "Anyway, forget the EU. Have you stopped drinking wine now?"

"The doc said I should go on a health kick; eat less heavily and cut out alcohol altogether."

"Maybe I should too. Was there anything else on the medical

front?" I tried, but he shook his head. "Have you spoken to Stan recently? Do you think he's right about a change of job?"

"I can't imagine him giving up that fancy car of his. He'd be short of money for a good five years, and what would that mean for settling down with Cassie?"

"I get the feeling Cassie's got her head screwed on. They're definitely a number, as they say. Fingers crossed, I'd love some more babies around."

Tom smiled as he shook his head, "I'd be keen for us to help him if he's serious but I'm not sure he's thought it through properly."

"We'll have to be careful about being fair to Evie though."

"Why doesn't that idle bastard of a husband of hers pull his finger out and look after his own family?"

"That reminds me, I've got to go up next week to look after Hugo and Matilda for half-term." It was actually just Hugo really. Matilda, at 15, was getting a bit old to need looking after. "Will you be okay?"

He shrugged and turned back to the television.

***

I arrived at Cardiff train station cold and tired after the long journey. Evie's muddy station wagon screeched through the sleeting rain at the last minute. Even in the grey half-light, I could see she looked worn out. Her lovely thick, auburn hair was scraped back into a ponytail, and for the first time, grey streaks were obvious. Her baggy jeans were half tucked into her green wellington boots.

"Thanks for picking me up. The train was freezing."

She gave me a quick hug, "Jump in quick! It was the least I could do – the kids are so looking forward to seeing you. I'm afraid it's not much warmer at home. The oil's run out so the central heating's off. Andy's on the phone to the suppliers, but it may be a day or two before they deliver."

"Tell them you have your elderly mum coming to stay. That might hurry them up!" It was clearly going to be a challenging visit. I hoped they had something to drink. As we drove up to the old stone house, all the lights were blazing. Hugo and Malila came to the door and gave me big hugs. Andy wasn't in evidence. I remembered when they first bought this lovely house with its spectacular views. Their lives had seemed so full of promise then, with dreams of healthy country living. Evie had been heavily pregnant with Matilda, and they had agreed to allow the neighbour's goats to continue living in the garden.

Evie brought me into the sitting room where the wood-burning stove was blazing away. Andy came in from the garden with an armful of wooden logs.

"Lovely to see you, Anna. Welcome to our humble abode. Glass of wine or something stronger?"

He came back with a tumbler full of whisky for himself and red wine for me. Food, however, wasn't quite so forthcoming. After a few minutes, Evie called us through to the kitchen for a dinner of thick lentil soup and homemade bread. I made a note to check the cupboards and do some shopping tomorrow. I wasn't going to survive long on homemade soup, however nourishing.

It was lovely to see Matilda and Hugo, but I was thinking this would probably be my last "childcare" visit. As the week wore on, I spent most of my time making Hugo his favourite meals. I started each day with pancakes for breakfast and then caught up with ironing, which Evie had stopped doing altogether. The house, nestled in the Welsh hills, was picturesque but very cold unless Andrew stoked the open fire and kept the Aga going. He used my visits as an excuse to catch up on his reading or whatever it was that he retired to his study to do. I didn't mind really. They hardly watched any television anymore with both children stuck on their own screens, so there were no family get-togethers on the sofa. The week passed slowly and coldly.

I was glad to be back home again with Tom at the end of the week. He was very quiet and spent the next few evenings at his computer, so I was left wondering and worrying for another week. I knew I would have to wait for him to tell me in his own good time. Then, one evening, Stanley rang the landline. Would I find out now at last? The fact that Tom moved into the study with the phone and shut the door was a good sign. From the bedroom, I could just hear the murmur of voices as they held an intense conversation. As soon as I heard that the voices had subsided and the handle of Tom's study door open and cups start clattering in the kitchen, I called Stanley on my mobile.

My son was as direct as he has always been, "He's got a lump in his groin about the size of a small melon."

I went downstairs to the kitchen. "Everything okay?" I asked, as Tom moved about humming with the drying up cloth.

He looked at me and then went over to the wine rack and opened a bottle of red. He got out two glasses and polished them slowly with a cloth, holding them up to the light to check they were spotless. "Want one?" he asked.

"You know I never say no," I replied. He stopped humming, poured me a glass but none for himself, and slumped down at the table.

"I think we should talk. At least that's what Stan said." He shook his head as though to clear it. "He says you're worried about me and that it isn't fair on you not to talk about it."

I sat quietly sipping from my glass as we both stared down at the old wooden table that was stained with marks and worn from a lifetime of meals and intense conversations.

Tom took a deep breath and said in a matter-of-fact way, "They said that I have a lump that's stage three cancer, which could be worse but needs taking out right away. Then I have to get chemo ... and lose all my hair and probably my brain power too," he added, resignedly. He kept his eyes on my wine glass. I reached across to touch his arm, but he moved it away and stood up, turning to look out of the window.

"I'm so sorry," I said. Then, because he didn't say anything, I asked, "What happens next?"

He shrugged and carried on staring out of the window, straightening his shoulders. "I go in next Tuesday at 10am." He paused, "Please don't make a fuss."

"Of course not. What can I do to help?"

"Oh, for Christ's sake, just don't make a fucking drama out of it."

He snatched the bottle of wine and went back into his study, slamming the door shut. He didn't come to bed that night. The next morning, he brought me a cup of tea as usual and sat on the edge of the bed and said quietly, "I have to do this my own way."

***

After Tom's surgery, the following weeks passed in a fog of recovery and chemo. We fell into a routine of driving to the hospital, and me preparing meals for Tom to eat in bed. The days ran into each other. After each session, he looked frailer on the drive home. It was as though the chemo was cutting into his essential being. Each time taking a slice of him that I feared could never be put back. The last few times I just dropped him off at the hospital and he got a taxi back. I couldn't bear him shutting me out, and not talking or telling me how he was feeling. Some days he would return to making silly, light-hearted jokes about it all. Sometimes he'd burst into tears. One day, before going in for one of many scans, and evidently feeling more talkative, he described the MRI machine. "It's like going into a long steel coffin on an automated treadmill, but there's only just room for you and you can't move. Then they turn this machine on and it begins with the most terrible clunking clanking noise that feels as though it's inside your head." Another time, he came back giggling, saying, "I am Borg," and moving his arms and legs about in a semi-mechanical way. It was lovely to have those occasional happy moments.

It was late autumn now, and the sun shone on the window boxes of herbs and fading red geraniums. My mother had always told me never to put white and red flowers together because it was the sign of death, so I pulled out the white geraniums and left just red ones. One day, as we sat at the kitchen table looking at the red geraniums, he said, "There's nothing more they can do." He sat with his shoulders hunched up and fingers tapping on the table. He'd lost a lot of weight and his whole body, including his face, was bony and ungiving now.

After the exhaustion and fatigue of the last weeks, this moment felt inevitable. I felt resigned to it, and I think he did as well. Yet I felt unsure of how to respond. "Would you like a glass of something?" I offered. He shook his head slowly, so I went on – knowing it was not a good thing to do but not able to stop myself. "What does that mean? What happens next?"

Then I wished I'd kept quiet as he shook his head again, picked up the paper and began doing the crossword. After a couple of minutes, he threw his pencil across the table, got up, and left the room. I heard him on the phone in his study and wondered who he was talking to. I was tempted to call Stanley to see if his phone was engaged. They seemed to be talking a lot recently. But that was a good thing, surely? He came through after a few minutes and put his hand on my shoulder, weighing it down firmly, but without comfort. "Listen, I think we should talk about the power of attorney and all that sort of stuff. We should also talk about how to help Stan if he really wants to change career. We don't need it all and they're still starting out. Don't you agree?"

I nodded, but wasn't sure. I didn't fully fathom why anyone would voluntarily apply for power of attorney and give up control and responsibility to their middle-aged children? Most of that generation couldn't care less. But Evelyn and Stanley were different. Weren't they?

"If we help Stan, it's only fair we should help Evie too. She's struggling a bit with her teacher's salary, and I know she's worried about Andy losing his job. It's happening to a lot of journalists now with everything going online."

Tom took his hand off my shoulder and snorted, "Andy should be supporting his family. That's his job."

Maybe he had a point, but I didn't see how we could help one and not the other. So much was changing so quickly it felt as though the ground was falling away under my feet. Tom was both devoured by, and exhausted by, his anger about the cancer – and I'm ashamed to say that I felt exhausted being around him these days. I just hoped he hadn't completely given up – that would really signal the end.

Chapter 5

After the first two months of Tom's chemo, I told Ed that I needed to continue to work from home for a while longer, despite the fact that Tom had settled into a routine and didn't really seem to want me around. Whether at home or at work, it was a relief to get lost in the pristine world of high tech, where messy cancers didn't exist and algorithms didn't fall sick.

When I opened my emails again after a gap of a few weeks, I was surprised to see my membership papers for the Robot Network Programme pop up. It was almost a year since I had signed up for the monthly newsletter, but with Tom's illness, I'd put robots to the back of my mind. Scanning through it, I noticed an advert at the back of the newsletter:

Learn how to love Robots in Person.

Sam the Robot was available for the knock down price of £1,200 for a limited period as an incentive to join the Robot Network Programme. Remembering what I had read in the Japanese press earlier that year, I wondered who was behind the RNP. Google didn't help on this occasion, but the sales blurb continued:

Thousands of people have been enticed into parting with 198,000 yen (£1,080) for their own companion robot. 'Sambot' has the ability to read human emotions, hold conversations, and move autonomously. But Sambot's affability should not be mistaken for something less innocent.

Again, I couldn't help wondering what '*less innocent*' meant. Sambot's launch onto the consumer market was described as a '*baby step towards our dream to make a robot that can understand a person's feelings and autonomously take action.*' I tried to picture a soft pink baby being held in Sambot's steely grip and hurriedly dismissed the notion – the vision of the two things too contradictory. I mused that with non-physical issues, if Sambot was the world's first robot to understand emotions, then he might indeed be useful in social care.

I found Kevin's telephone number and after being passed around from extension to extension, I finally got a real person. "I'd like to talk to someone about your Sambot, please. I met with Kevin at the Social Services conference a while back and I've signed up for the Robots Network Programme?"

A careful voice responded, "Sorry, Kevin's no longer with us. Can I fix you a call with someone else next week?" I agreed, but wondered why Kevin had left. He had seemed so completely consumed by his Sambot project.

As I trawled through the rest of the emails, most of them were sales pitches for conferences, but one caught my eye. It was an invite from James Hillingdon to attend the launch of the new 'Safe Care Homes Consortium' that evening. I felt a surge of excitement and accepted at once. The launch – at one of the biggest private banking halls off Piccadilly – would be a plush affair. I bet on champagne rather than prosecco. Several big care homes had closed recently, so this consortium marked a further major shift in direction towards privatisation. The takeover process would start early next year and the financial restructuring would apparently 'put the entire care home business on a sounder footing.' There was no mention of what would happen to the people living in the homes; it was all about the money.

I left Ed a message saying that I'd be going to the launch. He'd been patient with my semi-absence since Tom's illness, but it would be unwise to bump into one of his VC friends at the launch without having told him. The reception started at 6pm. I could be home by 8pm – well before Tom went to bed. Tom didn't seem that interested when I told him and just waved goodbye without looking up from his book.

A few days later, I walked up the wide stone steps to the huge panelled wooden doors, as the light flooded out onto the darkening September pavements. A doorman opened the huge door to let me in, bowing slightly as he did so.

In the cloakroom, handing over my overcoat, I wished I had worn heels rather than boots. There were several young women standing on one leg, jiggling precariously as they changed into even higher heels beneath tight black skirts. Makeup was being applied vigorously and lipstick slicked on to fashionably full lips. I sighed as I smoothed down my black culottes and skinny black top. I fluffed up my hair that had been flattened by the rain and was pleased I'd had it re-streaked last week. Other than that, I had not worried too much what I looked like since Tom had become ill, but this evening, I put on full eye makeup and a bright red lipstick. I knew I looked good.. In the main reception hall, I ignored the orange juice and reached for a glass of bubbly fizz. Disappointingly, it was prosecco after all, which probably said something about the state of the care home market.

The vast room had beautifully polished parquet flooring and elaborate chandeliers hanging from the high ceiling. It was filling up rapidly with slickly dressed men in suits and impossibly perfect-looking women. They were mostly white, but there was also a smattering of Indian and Asian people. Many of the younger ones were in navy suits and haircuts slightly longer than necessary, all slicked back.

Casting my eye over the crowd to see if I recognised anyone, I was surprised to spot Stanley talking animatedly in a group of younger, blue-suited men in the far corner. I decided to wait and let him find me, but was careful to place myself between him and the door. Taking a deep breath, I fixed a smile on my face and approached the nearest group. They moved politely apart to make space without looking at me and continued to chat excitedly about the takeover. Although I knew a lot about the current care problems in residential and nursing homes, I knew nothing about what that meant financially – either for the care homes or for the people in them.

"How did this takeover start?" I asked when there was a gap in the conversation.

One of my new companions smiled at my question and launched into an explanation, "It was a 'welcome takeover' in the end, although there was quite a history to it. Welcome takeovers generally go smoothly, with both companies being positive about it. But a hostile one, which is how this started back in 2015, is much more fun!"

I'd never heard of a takeover being fun. "What happened back in 2015?"

He was happy to explain. "CHC was a normal care home company, but it ran into difficulty. Mainly because there were too many empty beds. It's just like hotels; empty rooms mean no income. So, it was vulnerable to a takeover or closure. That's what happened with Safe Care Homes. They bought a substantial stake in CHC, which caused the company to lose control before it realised what was happening. Then CHC's board of directors strongly resisted the takeover attempts by using tactics like 'poison pill.'

"What on earth's that?"

"A poison pill allows the target's shareholders to purchase more shares at a discount to dilute the acquirer's holdings and make a takeover more expensive." My companion was warming to his theme whilst the others, notably a rotund, red-cheeked man in tweeds who looked more like a farmer than a financier, were scanning the room in boredom. "A takeover is virtually the same as an acquisition," he went on, "except the term 'takeover' has a negative connotation. A company may seek to increase its market share by reducing its costs and, thereby, increase its profits. It's all about the bottom line."

"Isn't that a bit of a problem when you're providing care to vulnerable older people?" I couldn't resist it, "I mean, how do you cut costs except by cutting their meals or their incontinence pads?"

He looked nonplussed as the red-faced farmer turned to join in belligerently. "Vulnerable or not, the market is still strong. We're building new homes this year."

"I thought there are too many empty beds for that to make sense." I knew I was becoming argumentative and the noise level in our group was rising, causing people to glance in our direction.

The farmer-type looked puzzled. "Maybe that might apply to the run down care homes no-one wants to live in anymore, but demand is still rising in the older population, especially those with money. And they're moving in earlier now too – as long as they can sell their homes to pay for a place." He turned to his brassy companion, whose voluptuous frame was also squeezed into brown tweeds. She nodded enthusiastically as he continued. "It's all about the self-funders now. The kids are pushing Mum and Dad to take out equity. Taking out power of attorney is becoming very popular too; it makes sure the next generation can get on with organising it all themselves."

A waft of expensive aftershave announced a new arrival, and I saw James Hillingdon reflected in the large mirror behind me. He was moving from group to group like a butterfly. He smiled widely when he saw me, and his beautifully manicured hands reached out to take mine. His long, elegant fingers felt cool and light in mine as he held my hand slightly longer than was strictly necessary.

"Good to see you again. You're the one who's fascinated by the robots?"

"Yes," I laughed, "I enjoyed your speech at the conference. I guess now is the time for care homes to invest more in robots, to solve the workforce issues?"

"Well yes. The whole care homes sector is changing, as you will have heard me say."

I felt rather than saw another familiar figure coming towards me and turned to see Stanley at last, smiling easily at James. "Hello there," he reached out his hand to James and at the same time moved to kiss me on my cheek.

"Ah, you two know each other then?" James asked with raised eyebrows.

"Never seen him before in my life!" I laughed.

"Anna is my mother, James," Stanley said hurriedly.

"And you must also know each other too?" I enquired, looking from one to the other.

"Stanley and I have just started working on a special project together, haven't we Stan?"

I raised my eyebrows at Stanley, but he simply smiled again and said smoothly, "I'll catch up with you on that next week, if I may, James?"

"Yes, of course!" Then, turning to me, James said, "I'd like to hear more about what you think is possible on the robot front?"

I looked at my watch. It was 7.30pm. "I'd love to, but just now I need to go I'm afraid. We can maybe fix something in a week or two?"

James nodded and smiled, "Let's do that," he said, shaking my hand again.

Stanley looked at me curiously and said firmly, "I'll help you with your coat, Mum." He took my arm to see me to the door. When I came out of the cloakroom, he'd gone back to James' group and was deep in conversation with the buff farmer. I was feeling a little lightheaded.

The robots could wait and so could James Hillingdon.

Chapter 6

Every morning, I left Tom curled up in bed as though he was defending himself against the world. The bedroom was becoming more like a hospital ward every day, with piles of dressings on the chest of drawers and measurement charts on the walls, blocking out our pretty framed watercolours. The slight smell of disinfectant mixed with sweat was inescapable.

Most mornings, Sandra, the cancer nurse, came in before I left for work. She let herself in with the keys that Tom must have given her, calling out in a singsong, "Morning all." In the past, Tom would have avoided someone like her. She was plump, chatty, called him "dear," and said things like "Never mind, it'll be alright on the night," when he spilt something or she couldn't find a vein to take blood. They laughed a lot together, which was just as well as he didn't talk to me much anymore.

One morning, I stopped her in the hallway and shut the bedroom door. "Can you tell me about what's going to happen next? I've heard about a care pathway for the end of life. I was wondering if it might be good for Tom?"

She looked at me and, putting her bag down, said, "You probably mean the Liverpool Care Pathway. It was developed in the 1990s to cover palliative care for people in their final days."

"Would it help Tom, do you think?"

"It's been widely discredited now. I never really approved of it. It became a sort of tick-box exercise. Patients were assessed as terminally ill, then heavily sedated, and not given water and food – so the diagnosis became self-fulfilling."

I hadn't realised that's what the 'care pathway' meant. It sounded so cruel the way she put it.

I noticed that she'd parked her chatty persona as she leant closer to me conspiratorially and said, "I heard that some hospitals were given cash incentives to achieve targets for the number of patients placed on it," before adding perkily, "Anyway, I'm sure you'll agree, Tom is much better off here at home with us."

'*With us?*' I thought, taken aback. Then she said, somewhat tactlessly, "We'll make sure he's comfortable. He shouldn't be in pain if we get it right," and walked passed me into the bedroom, our bedroom, leaving me standing alone in the hallway.

I began spending more time at work following up on my earlier research into robots, but I couldn't find any mention of the Robot Network Programme. It had just disappeared. I ignored emails from James' office. Managing work on top of Tom's illness was taking all my energy. I did find myself wondering about him though.

Sometimes, I stopped at the shops on the way home – a tactic, I was aware, to delay getting home. Often, I'd only just get back in time for the Channel 4 News. After asking Tom about his day, and usually just getting a grunt in return, I would go through to the kitchen to gulp down a large glass of wine before cooking supper. Tom was no longer drinking alcohol at all, so I was surprised to see four or sometimes five empty wine bottles in the recycling each week. We'd eat in front of the television before getting ready for bed at around 9pm, although Tom was often in his pyjamas all day now.

One morning, he was up before me, and for the first time in weeks, he brought me an early morning cup of tea. I held my breath. Was there a breakthrough? Would he start talking again? Part of me still hoped he was just going through a horrible treatment and would emerge strong and back to normal again. I was finding it hard to accept that something much worse might be happening. My conversation with Sandra hadn't given me much hope. I wished I'd asked her outright if he was dying. As he sat waiting at the end of the bed to hand me my tea that he'd made in my favourite mug, I arranged his pillows in a stack so that he could sit up next to me more comfortably.

"You know you were talking about power of attorney the other day? Well, I've been doing some research and there are two sorts. The first is 'ordinary' power of attorney when you want someone to make financial decisions for you – that's if you're temporarily indisposed or out of the country. Or there's 'lasting' power of attorney which has taken over from what used to be called 'enduring' power of attorney. I waited for him to continue, inwardly relieved to see him, however temporarily, back to his old slightly pedantic and academic self. "There are two sorts of lasting power of attorney – one for financial matters and the other for health and care. I think we should do the financial one just in case."

"Just in case of what?"

"You can manage perfectly well on your own with everything, but we do need to do something about the house. You remember it's in my name?" I nodded. "I'm going in to see David Harbuckle later in the week, all being well. Sandra will come with me to act as a witness."

"Witness for what?"

"My signature and yours."

I had a flashback to when we got married and we both signed the marriage certificate together. This was different, but I still didn't fully grasp its purpose. Then, what Tom said next made numb with shock, "I'm dying. They can't do anything else. They reckon I've got about six weeks, maybe a bit longer." He then added moodily, "You'll manage, you always do," and turned to pick up the morning paper. I went to hold his hand, but he pushed me away.

I got up and left the room, tears silently streaming before I reached the door. I simply didn't know what to do. I couldn't get through to him anymore. Each day was like walking on ice. He was so angry, except of course with Sandra who was his new best friend.

The next day while I was at work, Sandra brought in extra equipment which she said would enable Tom to stay at home. I came home to find a special hospital bed installed in our bedroom, and our own bed squeezed up against the wall. The bedside table, which once held just a book and the bedside light, was now piled high with the blood pressure machine and spilling over with pills and lotions. The photo of the children was perched on top of a box of tissues. The bedroom was beginning to look like a bloody nursing home.

How could I stay in here like this? I decided then and there to move into the spare room across the hall. It was a stark room with white walls and plain blinds on the cold, north-facing window that looked out onto the back garden. The narrow single bed felt pristine and cool after sharing our tumbled double bed.

Tom and I barely spoke for the whole weekend. Then, on Monday, as I was rummaging in the drawers in our bedroom before leaving for work, Sandra arrived. As soon as she entered the room, Tom said to her, "Can you get the papers please?"

I felt a pang as she came back from his study carrying a folder with yellow post-it stickers poking out of the sides. He must have already seen David Harbuckle, our solicitor. She looked at me as she handed it over, and in a daze, without reading any of the papers, I signed on the dotted lines. Sandra then picked up the pen and witnessed my signatures.

When she had gone that evening, Tom called me into the bedroom where he had been watching the news, "Come and sit with me," he said quietly. "I'm sorry, it's just so hard." So we sat together, holding hands until he fell asleep. I covered him with the new light duvet and went across the landing to my own simple cell-like room and fell asleep, exhausted.

The next days and nights became one long blur. I daydreamed and remembered in vivid detail the day I'd had to rescue Tom when he'd almost drowned out at sea in France. Tom and I had never spoken about it afterwards. It happened way before we had children. I suppose he was embarrassed. We'd been staying in a French seaside village near Cete. It had been one of those endless days; soft balmy air gently warming our lazy bodies as we dozed on the beach. We'd been sleeping off a lazy lunch of oysters at one of the dozens of waterside cafes in the harbour, with their waiters at the curb side pulling in the passing trade. I daydreamed of oysters now, juicy and globby in their shiny wet shells. Oysters fried on toast, oysters stuffed and grilled. Omelette oysters creamy yellow, flecked with the whites and yellow yolk of the eggs – slightly cooked and warm, just enough to take away the salty sliminess. A crisp green salad and a glass, or several, of the local Picpoul De Pinet.

We had planned on a lazy afternoon on the beach. He must have thought a quick swim to work off lunch would make room for dinner; but it turned out to be a disaster. When I woke up from a beach-towel nap to look lazily out to sea, I spotted Tom clinging onto a buoy about half a mile out, yelling for help. I was half-way out to him when I noticed a boat of passing fishermen in a motor dinghy heading towards him. When they brought him to shore, he was in shock and visibly shivering. The local A&E wouldn't let him out until the next day. He never swam in the open sea again.

He died three weeks after I signed the papers, at home in his hospital bed and curled up towards the wall. I came into the bedroom one morning and sensed he was gone. I waited in the doorway and held my breath to see if I could hear breathing, but there was no sound. When I went over to see him, he looked peaceful. Thankfully, his eyes were closed. His face was cold when I kissed him and hands too, so he must have died in the early hours.

The family photo he kept by his side of the bed had fallen to the floor, face down. I picked it up and looked at the happy smiling faces. Tom's arm was around Evie and Stanley, who must have been fourteen and twelve. We'd just come back from a holiday in Canada and were bursting with health and happiness. I wondered if he'd been trying to reach it.

I sat silently by his side, holding his hand in the early morning light. I didn't cry. After an hour or so, I got up and called the GP. She came round and signed the death certificate, patted me on the hand, and said she'd call Sandra. I knew I should ring Evelyn and Stanley but there would be time for that later.

I found all the instructions for the funeral in a large white envelope with my name on his desk. Then I cried. Cried at the thought of him sitting down there all on his own, working out the arrangements for his own funeral. Cried for the emptiness. And cried in dread for the future. No love letter to me. No goodbye, no nothing. That was it. He was gone. I read his requests for the funeral, "Amazing Grace" which made me smile – all those years of him mocking my love of it, "Rock of Ages" (of course), and a poem that surprised me by an Indian poet named Atal Bihari – it was beautiful yet I felt it reproach me. By personifying death as female, it felt like the closest thing to a message from Tom. I cried as I read it … *A battle with death! / What a battle it will be! / I had no plans to take her on …* "

The grief of Stanley and Evelyn was hard to deal with. I just wanted to be alone with my own sorrow while Evelyn wanted to talk about it. When I first told her, she was irreconcilable for a few days. Stanley was different. He was quiet and solemn. He came to the house as soon as I phoned him. I hadn't seen him since our strange encounter at the venture capitalist party in November six weeks ago. It seemed to take forever for Tom's death to sink in for all of us. The funeral passed in a daze with the poem clouding everything for me. Perhaps it was a distraction. Our last weeks had been a battle for Tom, but not one he wanted me to join him in. Stanley called every day at first, so it was only after the funeral that I felt I could be alone with my grief at last.

For the first time in my adult life, I was completely alone. I found myself slipping into the past for days on end. I stopped answering the phone, and let the post pile up beside the front door. The house was a deadly, cold quiet after all the illness and pain. I told Ed that I wasn't ready to come back and I just stayed at home hardly going out and living off bread and eggs. When I did go out, I avoided all the shops and places where I might meet someone I knew. Mostly though, people would cross over to the other side of the street to avoid me. They didn't mean to be unkind; they just didn't know what to say. It made me more sad than angry.

Ed called after a week and left a message. I called my GP, and she signed me off sick. Friends came round with food and flowers but stopped when I didn't answer the door. Then I lost the charger for my mobile and couldn't be bothered to go out and buy a new one.

The recycling piled up until the bags overflowed with old newspapers that I hadn't read. The flowers people had sent me died in their vases all over the house and began to smell. I spent all my days in the kitchen at the back of the house where no-one could see me.

After a week or two, I called our solicitor, David Harbuckle. I remembered signing the power of attorney papers and Sandra witnessing my signature, but I couldn't remember what we'd agreed. David kindly suggested I come in to see him. Stanley wanted to come too, but I fixed a time without telling him. David's office was comfortably crowded and old-fashioned with mahogany furniture, chintz armchairs and heavy curtains that shut out most of the light. David welcomed me with a handshake and held my elbow briefly as his kindly faced peered down into mine. He sat me down with a cup of tea and began explaining the terms of the will. He had a gentle, fatherly manner that made me feel immediately comfortable.

I said, "Towards the end he became very difficult to talk to, so some things we just left. It wasn't an easy time. I knew he'd come to see you of course."

"Yes, it was to do with the house. Tom meant to come in, but he wasn't well enough, so I came to see him at home. I thought you'd be there but his nurse witnessed his statements. I understood that was what you wanted." I felt sick with a growing sense of foreboding. What had he done? David went on, "As you know, he's put the house in trust to your two children Stanley and Evelyn. I believe he did it to avoid future death duties and possible care costs." This took a moment to sink in. So the house was no longer mine? The house, our house, my home? The ground had gone from under my feet. Stanley and Evelyn must have known. Why hadn't they said anything? He continued in a kindly voice, "I think given the circumstances; we should have a formal reading of the will with all the beneficiaries present."

"Who else is there besides me and the children?" I stuttered.

"He added a recent codicil to his will, leaving all his books to his old college. He also made his cancer nurse, Sandra White, a beneficiary." And then without any hint of drama added, "I'm not surprised, she did seem very good."

Chapter 7

An appointment for the reading of the will was made for the following week. Evie came down from Wales but I didn't see her before the appointment. She must have stayed with Stanley. At first, I wasn't going to say anything, but then I left them a curt message, "I have met with David Harbuckle, so I know about the will and the house. I want to be left alone now until I can get my head around what's happened." And put the phone down.

Evie and Stanley were already at David Harbuckle's office when I arrived. Thankfully, there was no sign of Sandra. This time, I was shown straight in to into the smart conference room just off the reception. The huge oval table reflected the sun as it came streaming in through the tall windows. Coffee, tea flasks, and water bottles were set out on a side table. Stanley had been talking when I came into the room, but stopped when I came through the door. Both he and Evie stood up uncertainly. I looked at them and sat down on the opposite side of the table. David's assistant poured me tea and a glass of water.

David came across to shake my hand and then sat down at the head of the table. He cleared his throat, "I think we should start now if you're all ready?"

I hesitated, "I thought Sandra was going to be here?" Evie and Stanley looked at each other in surprise.

"Yes," David hesitated, "we were expecting her, but she's sent her apologies this morning as she's working. She is only a minor beneficiary so we're okay to go ahead … if that's okay with you?" he added, looking at me.

Evie and Stan looked at each other again. Stan was frowning.

"How minor?" I stuttered.

David looked serious now. "Would you mind if I read the whole will through, as is usual?" I nodded. As David read Tom's words slowly and carefully, I could feel my eyes begin to fill with tears, but I was determined not to cry. I gulped down several mouthfuls of water. Stanley and Evelyn stared at David as he spoke. Evie occasionally sipped her water. Stanley sat without moving. "Tom has left the house in trust to Stanley and Evelyn, with your rights Anna, as a secured tenant to stay as long as you wish. In other words, rights to occupy in your lifetime."

They looked at each other and across to me. There was a deafening hush. He went on, "All his other worldly goods he leaves to you Anna, apart from his desk and the contents of his study; these are left to Stanley. The silver, and the grandfather clock, are left to you Evelyn." He looked up briefly and cleared his throat, "He also left his books to the library of his old college, and £500 to Sandra White, his Cancer nurse, in thanks for her care and helping to keep him at home which is where he wanted to die."

Thank God he hadn't turned really daft and left her the house or thousands of pounds. We had £14,000 in our joint bank account, which would come to me as soon as probate was unfrozen. And that was it. It was over. My children had betrayed me at their father's wishes. It must have been greed that had allowed them to go along with it. If I had known, would I have agreed? Probably not, but not to have that choice was even harder. I felt such an emptiness. I was facing the world alone. Why couldn't they see that? Tom was always the matter of fact one and he always thought he knew best. Sometimes he did, but not this time. He hadn't thought about how I would feel at not having my own home anymore. He would have seen it as a necessary administrative act, but his secrecy proved he knew I wouldn't have agreed. No-one said anything which must have surprised David. After a pause, he simply nodded. I got up, thanked him, and said I'd be in touch about Tom's library. Evie called out, "Mum," but I wasn't ready and shut the door behind me.

I didn't hear anything from Stan for days until, on Mother's Day, a beautiful bunch of hyacinths arrived – the blue ones that smell heavenly. The note said, "With lots of love from Stan and Cassie." I burst into tears – I did miss them. Stan had never sent me Mother's Day flowers before, so I guessed it must have been Cassie's idea.

In the weeks that followed, I carried on ignoring the post and my emails until one morning I saw an invitation from the Nightingale Reunion on the door mat. Pulling the embossed card from the stiff white envelope, I was transformed back into the past — before Evelyn and Stanley, and even before Tom. The reunion was held at St Thomas' Hospital every 5 years. It was a part of my life I'd left behind, but now I felt a strong need to belong. It was the reunion of the fifty or so nurses who had started training at the Florence Nightingale School in 1963. This year at least five out of the fifty original nurses would never come again. It would probably be the last time I'd go. By next time, more would most likely be dead if not incarcerated somewhere. More importantly, they wouldn't know about Tom's dying, so I could just pretend it hadn't happened. I knew it wasn't sensible, but sometimes being sensible was just too much hard work.

***

The reunion came around quickly. As soon as I got there, one old colleague began talking about her engagement that had happened at the time when she was working on the geriatric wards. She was saying, "It was my engagement ring that I worried about the most!" I wondered what she was talking about. "When he asked me what sort of a ring I wanted, I said, 'One that doesn't come off in the wash, and one that I can keep on under the rubber gloves.'

He didn't listen, he bought me one that was sharp and sparkly, so I couldn't wear it." Her lively brown eyes and smooth face looked across at me as she smiled in remembrance. "A ring with jewels," she shuddered, shaking her head, "it would have torn through their paper thin skin like tissue paper."

Images flashed up in my mind of the thin, pale skin of elderly people as we turned them from side to side to avoid bed sores. Then I thought of Sam the Robot's thin, steely hands.

As I got up to leave, I realised I would have to make some decisions about my life. I couldn't carry on ignoring the outside world. I needed to get on with my life, without Tom, without my house and home, and even perhaps without my children.

Chapter 8

It had all happened so quickly, too quickly. I didn't want to think about Tom being dead. I didn't want to deal with the sadness and the being alone. I also didn't want to have to talk about it or have to make other people feel better. Sometimes, it felt as though the awfulness of it was going to go on forever. Most of all, I didn't want to face my children. I was still so angry that Tom had given them the house, our house, behind my back. It was such a betrayal, compounded by Evelyn and Stanley not telling me. How could I trust them anymore?

Eventually, I realised that I needed to find a way forward. So, the day after the reunion, I bought a new charger for my phone. I watched it whirl into life again before what seemed like endless messages popped up. There were several from Evelyn and Stanley – they started off kind and then grew increasingly impatient.

It was too much to think about all at once, but even in turning the phone on, I'd made a start. I decided that some fresh air and exercise would be a good idea and dragged my bicycle out of the old shed in the garden. The next morning I was cycling along the canal path towards Camden lock. Everything looked calm and quiet in the early morning light. A shroud of mist hung over the canal, and tree branches drooped into the murky green water. The red-gold leaves of winter had spread across the damp tow path like mushy cornflakes. As I rode around the puddle's edges, the smell of wet leaves and musty water seeped into my bones.

The sudden whirling of a bicycle behind me, tyres on wet ground and gears clunking, came from nowhere. As the cyclist splashed past and drove straight through a large puddle, my legs and trainers were sprayed with muddy water. I cried out, "Hey, watch where you're going!" The cyclist wobbled and almost swerved into the canal as he held up two fingers and shouted, "Fuck off!" and carried on down the path, anorak billowing out behind him.

Taken aback, I slowed right down and moved my keys out into attack mode, each one poking outwards through my fist, a weapon I'd learnt in a self-defence class years ago. Round the next corner, I was relieved to see the path was clear. I pulled my bike slowly up the stone steps into a small park where the trees were still casting shadows through the thick undergrowth. I followed the path over the grass, intending to go through the iron gate onto the road, over a small bridge, and then back in a loop to head back home. As I passed the undergrowth, there was a rustling. A purposeful rustling. Something heavy moving through the bushes. It was him. I cycled on through the empty park but I could hear the bicycle coming up behind me, the whirring wheels again and the clunking gears. I ducked under the bridge and drew back into a doorway recess, breathing in through my nose to cover my short panting breaths. The cyclist raced past, standing on his pedals to go faster, his jacket streaming out behind him. The waft of his dodgy, sweet-smelling cigarette filled my nostrils, almost choking me. I unclenched my fist and looked at the deep indentations from the keys, like bite marks, on my soft palm.

It was still only 9am – too early to drop in on Stanley on a Sunday, so I headed for home. Later that day, I made myself a mug of tea and called Evelyn to try and see if we could get back on track. She picked up straight away and called out breathlessly, "Hi

Mum, hope you're okay? Just a moment!" There were noises from Hugo and Matilda in the background. How little I knew of them anymore. I heard a door shutting and there was peace and quiet. "Sorry about that. It's pancake morning. How are things?"

I decided that I would pretend that all was normal although we had hardly spoken since the will reading almost three weeks ago. "I'm thinking of making a change and moving somewhere to retire early."

"Brilliant idea! Why don't you come to Wales? There's a cottage next door just come on the market. Then I could keep an eye on you and the kids could pop over after school every day."

I groaned inwardly but said, "Gosh, that would be nice! But you know the Welsh weather doesn't suit me. I was wondering about the Isle of Wight. Your dad used to joke about it, but I think it'd be rather nice. You could all come down for the summer holidays?"

"The children would love the beach and surfing!"

I groaned again. This time out aloud. "Evie, you'd have to come too! It has record levels of sunshine and it also ranks first in the country as a place to retire to." Then I added, as a rather maudlin afterthought, "It probably has twice the rate of dementia as other regions as well."

"I'm not sure that's a good thing!" Evelyn laughed. "Anyway, last I heard, you can't actually catch dementia."

"Do you remember Auntie Peggie and Uncle Edward? Stan used to be quite close to their son, Brian. They're retired now, of course." Brian was one of those late babies, much adored and spoilt rotten, but it would be nice to be near family.

Her voice lost some of its bounce, "Yes, vaguely. Listen Mum, I'm sorry about all that business with the house."

I ignored the house comment and lightened my tone. "I thought maybe I could campaign for wider lanes in the supermarkets for wheelchairs, free toilets. Things like that."

"There's bound to be lots of facilities – buses, health services and good social care services." Evie was putting on the mother-in-charge voice she'd acquired ever since she'd had the children. I wondered if I'd done the same. Tom had always said I was bossy.

When I called Stanley, there was no reply, as usual. No doubt he was out and about with Cassie. As I left a message for him, Tom's words echoed in my mind, "don't be too hard on them, they're still young." I left a gentler, kinder message than I might have done. "Hi guys, hope you're both well? Call me when you can."

It took him till the following day. He explained that he'd been away on business and suggested that he pop round next Sunday morning.

He looked tired and grey as he stood on the doorstep. I realised that he must have been missing his father too and held out my arms. We stood there on the doorstep for several minutes in silence. When he came into the house, he looked around as though he'd never been there before and was assessing its potential. I made him a hot chocolate – sweet and strong the way he always used to like it. He winced when he took a sip, "Gosh, Mum, haven't had one like that for a long time!"

I smiled and asked, "What happened to your decision to change careers?"

"It wasn't the right time, what with Dad passing. Cassie and I are going to settle down and start a family. What about you? Has James Hillingdon been in touch? You liked him, didn't you?" He squinted at me with his head on one side.

"Well, I like his idea of robots," I replied, evading the hidden question. "I'm so pleased to hear about Cassie and starting a family. She's lovely."

He nodded, smiling, "So what are your plans? Your message said something about moving on?"

"I had a rotten fright last week when I went out for a bike ride along the canals. Some man attacked me."

"You really shouldn't go out alone near the canals. It's not safe."

"No, well anyway, it spooked me. I'm thinking about retiring to the Isle of Wight and living the simple life."

"Sounds perfect. I envy you." He paused again, "Are you thinking quite soon then?"

"The sooner the better, time's running out." I tried for a little levity, but he was deep in thought.

"I might need some help with getting a mortgage though."

"I'll put you in touch with someone I know, Mum. Just give me a few days."

Chapter 9

Stanley's phone was ringing loudly and insistently in his jacket pocket as he let himself into the flat that evening. As soon as he picked up, Evelyn launched in, "Have you been to see Mum yet? I think she's forgiven us!"

"Saw her yesterday." Stanley replied, shrugging. "She seems okay, but she was going on and on about a bike ride. Anyway, the good news is she's definitely moving out of the house."

"Yes, she said something about retiring to the Isle of Wight. She seemed quite keen, but God alone knows how she'll do it. Rent I suppose."

"If she moves out, then we can do something about the house. Make some money from renting it out. Maybe even think about selling it."

"We can't sell it though. How can we? I mean, it wouldn't be right."

"Of course we can if she gives up her tenancy rights. It's been done before. I was talking to cousin Brian about all the options. It could be the answer."

"The answer to what? Don't tell me you're short of money again?"

"Aren't we all?"

"Welcome to the club. Just wait till you have kids. It only gets worse! What are you doing now anyway?"

"I'm working on a new project with a group of venture capitalists on care homes. It's top secret, so don't tell Mum."

"What's top secret?"

"We're going to bring in care robots from Japan. It's very big business. Best not tell Mum until we're a bit more advanced."

"I think she'd approve, wouldn't she? She loves the idea of robots."

"Maybe, but I need to keep my cards close to my chest. I shouldn't have told you."

"I keep reading about the big care homes going bust despite the fact that the number of old people keeps growing."

"That's why it's big business. But back to Mum. We need to work out what she needs to do next. One thing that's definite, she needs to make a new will."

"Stan, how can you be thinking that way? Dad's only just died. What Mum needs is just to be happy and to relax."

"You're being too naïve for words as usual. She's got to make it clear in her new will what's happening with the house. Especially if she moves out. It's her only real asset."

"You mean ours, don't you?"

"It all depends. I discussed it all with Brian over a drink. Aunt Peggie and Uncle Edward lent Brian money to buy his first flat. Then, when he sold it at a profit, he refused to pay them back. Uncle Edward was furious and threatened to sue him, said it was money they were planning to use for their retirement."

"I never liked Brian. He was just interested in getting his hands on the old farmhouse."

"Nothing wrong with that. It's called 'forward planning.'"

"Forward planning!" scoffed Evie, "greedy bugger more like! Do you really want to force Mum to move out?"

"No, no, no…. of course not, but if she's planning on moving anyway ... "

"That's a guilty 'yes' then, Stan."

Chapter 10

DH Lawrence's *The Man Who Loved Islands* tells the story of a man endlessly moving from one island to another in the search for happiness, but he never finds it. He ends up alone. I had thought how much I would love being alone. On an island you are safe, across water, unreachable if you want to be. It's an escape, and that's what I needed. I would be in good company – Queen Victoria hid herself away in Osborne House on the Isle of Wight after her beloved husband, Albert, died. And Tennyson always used to talk about the Isle of Wight as "the island" as though there was no other.

The island I remembered was from my childhood summer holidays staying with Peggie and Edward, and their huge garden centre with its rows of roses stretching for what seemed like miles in every direction. Edward was quite well known for breeding new roses. Every summer, their garden was a haven, and the scent in July used to waft far across the surrounding fields. Near Ventnor and Black Chine, it was very rural and quiet. We had hardly seen them in recent years, although I was aware that Stan kept up with Brian. Increasingly, like many of the inhabitants, Peggie and Edward rarely left the island.

Everyone said that living there was like going back to the 1950s. The islanders were relentlessly old-fashioned but also endlessly easy going and kind-hearted. The pace of life was slow and relaxed, which was what I needed. Even the weather seemed more benign, warmer and sunnier than on the mainland. The island was only 23 miles across and 13 miles long, but the population of almost 140,000 would swell every summer when the festival, and the bucket-and-spades, brigades arrive.

There was also a darker side, though. The island was home to Parkhurst and a number of other prisons. Recently, there had been headlines in the local press about the prison specialising in sex offenders and stories about them being released to work in the local communities – although some of the historic offenders like Garry Glitter were too old for anything other than the geriatric wards.

The shock of Tom's death was beginning to wear off and my anger was being replaced by missing him with an ache that became unbearable at times. I missed the children too, but in a different way. I decided that I wanted to be somewhere I could be happy by myself. No more looking after anyone, and no more worrying about being betrayed. I would be totally self-contained.

Peggie was so pleased to hear from me, I immediately felt guilty about not having been in touch for so long. "I'm thinking of moving down to the island. There's nothing to keep me in London now. What do you think?"

"What a good idea!" she said excitedly. "It can't be much fun for you without Tom in London. We'll start looking for somewhere right away." Ever practical, she launched straight into planning, "What sort of a place do you want? Somewhere modern and near the shops?"

"I don't want anywhere too remote – your place is beautiful, of course," I added hurriedly, "but I'd rather somewhere near the beach. An old stone cottage would be perfect. Is that a big ask?"

"Depends on what you're prepared to pay, and you'd probably have to do some work on it."

"If you could keep your nose to the ground, that would be

great, but I'm not sure yet what I'll have to spend."

I was too embarrassed to tell her what had happened to our house in London. I knew from friends that the attitude of banks had changed and that there was a chance I could get a mortgage using my pension. For the first time in months, it felt as though life might be worth living again. Changing the subject away from my own problems, I asked, "How are you both? Are you still baking? Has Edward finally retired?!"

She laughed, "He said he would never give it up, but then his knees needed doing — and paying for! Plus, Brian wasn't showing any interest in taking the business over. What about you? Still working away?"

"Well, I've been working a bit … and have become interested in robots! But it's really time for me to be winding down."

"I was reading about those things the other day in the *Sunday Times*. Something about killer robots?!"

I knew the *Sunday Times* had carried a supplement titled 'Granny's New Best Friend' all about the care robots in Japan. I hadn't seen anything on the killer aspect. I wondered whether Peggie was reading too much into the article – robots often made people frightened. "Have you ever met one?" I asked.

"No, of course not!" she protested. "I'd hate the thought of a robot looking after me. You know, doing anything private." I could almost hear her shuddering over the phone as she changed the subject, "which reminds me I need to pop in on our neighbours. They're getting on a bit."

"You may be a good neighbour, but people aren't always as nice – many people are so alone. At least robots don't steal from you or beat you up!"

Two days later, I was sitting on the old wooden bench in the back garden with a glass of white wine when Peggie called me back. She put me on loudspeaker so she and Edward could share the call. I smiled as I listened to Peggie talking, the way couples who've been together a long time often do, interrupting each other and finishing each other's sentences. Edward didn't even seem to notice, although I could sense a flash of annoyance from Peggie every time he ended her sentence for her. She was in full flow, "We've just seen a property called 'Pond Cottage.' We think you'd love it! It's an old stone house, completely neglected and not far from the beach. No bathroom or inside toilet, no kitchen to speak of, and the windows all need work."

"Sounds a wreck!" I laughed, "just the sort of challenge Tom would have loved."

"The only problem is the estate. They want a quick sale, so they've put it up for auction. What do you think? "

"I need to see it! I'll come down tomorrow. Could I stay with you?"

What could I afford now the house was no longer in my name? I still had the £14,000 left in the bank and there were some shares I could sell. I could maybe raise a deposit, but it wouldn't be enough for the whole purchase. It would leave me with just my pension to live on. Pity Tom hadn't thought of that. He must have assumed I'd stay put, I thought bitterly. I called Stanley several times before I got an answer.

"Stan, I've got the chance to make a bid on what sounds like a really good property on the island. It's going to auction. Dad once said that if you go in with a good bid before the auction, they may take it off."

"Good to hear you're making plans," he said absentmindedly.

"I can't stay on where I'm not wanted and I need some security, not just being a tenant, it doesn't feel right. The problem, as you know, is that I have no money."

"That's a bit of an exaggeration Mum, and nobody was trying to cheat you. Of course it's still your house to live in as long as you want, but," he paused, "it does sound like a good idea."

"You were going to see if you knew anyone to help with a

mortgage?"

"Yes, I've been in touch with an old mate, Alex. Alex Mathews. He says he might be able to help."

"Thanks, I really appreciate that." I swallowed the rising bile in my throat. "This place really does sound ideal."

Alex called me the next day. After gathering a lot of information on my background, age, life insurance and finances, he said, "Mortgage companies used to be reluctant to lend to older people, but that's all changing – especially if you've got a decent pension." At a premium, I thought, but never mind, it was a solution. Then he dealt the killer blow, "The problem you may find is that this particular property sounds as though it wouldn't be mortgageable. How much work will it need?"

"What do you mean?" I asked in panic, cursing myself for jumping ahead without thinking yet again.

"The property will need a bathroom, kitchen, central heating and everything watertight – roof and windows etc." In my enthusiasm, I had rushed ahead, assuming, as usual, that I could overcome all barriers. I was missing Tom's quiet common sense. After the phone call with Alex, I decided I wouldn't ask Stanley any more favours about borrowing money against the house. I needed to keep telling myself that they were still my children, although any thought that Tom may have had that Stanley would assume the mantle of protector when he died clearly wasn't going to happen.

I was truly on my own. Best get on with it.

Chapter 11

I packed an overnight bag and called Peggie to say I was on my way. Travelling down from Waterloo by train, I caught the West Cowes Red Jet ferry at Southampton. The weather in March is often unsettled and the crossing could still be rough. The grey skies were full of clouds on the horizon, ominously scurrying up and over each other at great speed. The ferry crossing was a lurching bumpy ride which got worse when we hit the cross-currents in the Solent.

The Solent was said to be quite perilous in the winter and so the possibility of being stuck on the island for days at a time would be an additional hazard. As I walked down the gangway on to dry land again, I felt uneasy and had an impending sense of doom. It was the feeling I have when something's gone disastrously wrong, like when Tom almost drowned at sea. It had come back once or twice recently since his death. It was a warning, but a warning against what? Being cut off from the rest of the world? In a place where nobody would know what was happening to me?

As I came through the ferry exit onto the small, crowded square, I saw Edward and Peggie sitting in their muddy land rover, waving vigorously. They looked weather-worn in their brown corduroys and thick jackets; no wonder after years of rose gardening and all those 6am starts. They must be in their seventies now. We hugged and I clambered on to the back seat. It was covered in dog hairs and old newspapers. Sandy, their Labrador, welcomed me with warm, raspy licks until I pushed him down to sit alongside me. Edward and Peggie began to talk over each other, excited about their find.

My heart sank when they showed me a picture of the house in their newspaper cutting. Pond Cottage was shaded on one side by a dark green fir tree and looked oddly lopsided. Stuck on the back was a haphazard brick kitchen extension. It looked very dilapidated. Was I making a big mistake? We drove along the winding back roads for several miles, with Edward driving rather erratically, until we came to a signpost to the village. The previous sign had directed us in the opposite direction, but I was to learn that the sign posting on the island was, like its people, charming but sometimes a little vague.

As we drew up outside the cottage, Edward parked the old Land Rover awkwardly – half on the verge and half on the road outside the back gate. Peggie looked at it, then over at me with a slightly quizzical look, but said nothing. The old wooden gate was hanging on its hinges.

The paved stone path was completely overgrown with ivy, nettles, and brambles. As we jumped out, Edward threw open the garden gate which immediately fell off its hinges. I pushed the nettles aside to see if the path went all the way to the back door and smiled with pleasure as it did.

I felt the urge to explore the garden first. When I pushed my way through the sometimes waist-high nettles and brambles to the bottom of the garden, I found a slow-running stream and an almost completely overgrown pond. There were two apple trees – the trunks covered with ivy and a couple of fat pigeons sitting peacefully on the branches. It was as though I was disturbing a secret garden that hadn't been touched in years. A light-brown pheasant flew up from one of the hedges. The male pheasant – beautiful in his gorgeous colours and long tail fan – came clucking along trying to frighten me off. When I carefully moved the undergrowth back, I found a nest of five pale-blue speckled eggs.

The rest of the garden was so completely overgrown it was impossible to see anything. I would have to wait until next spring to find out what was growing there. I reckoned there was enough land to make a vegetable patch, possibly even to become completely self-sufficient. The cottage itself was sitting in the middle of the garden wilderness, which gave it complete privacy – much more than I was used to in London. The building had evidently been built and added-to at different times. The lowest part was made of huge old misshapen stones. The next layer up had low windows and was haphazardly built with differently sized stones. Some were grey and some a pleasant pinky-brown. The stones walls were at least two feet thick, so it was a good, solid building. Local people later told me that it had started life as a cow barn, then had a roof and loft built on when the tenant farmer decided to move in. It was only years later that the final storey had been added with the large windows, a huge chimney, and a roof topped with local red tiles. Unlike the photo in the newspaper, the different levels didn't make it look uneven and unhappy; in real life, the higgledy-piggledy walls were transformed into a charming feature that made a pretty period house. I reached out to run my hand across the rough surface and felt the warmth of the late afternoon sun on the old stone. Pond Cottage needed my care, love, and attention.

The old-fashioned iron key was rusty, and the heavy wooden back door creaked in a friendly way as we went in. The kitchen extension had probably only been added about twenty years ago; this was built of red bricks with a slanting tin corrugated iron roof that clattered loudly when it rained.

The makeshift kitchen floor was laid with old flagstones. I levered one up to see where the earthy smell was coming from and there was a live worm wriggling in its cast. Inside the main house, a wall of damp hit my face like a breath of cold cobwebs. We crept silently around with only the sound of the floorboards creaking.

The front door was stuck solid and wouldn't open at all. There was a tiny hallway inside, out of which rose a steep stairway with wooden panelling on both sides. I made a mental note that opening up the stairway would make the whole downstairs lighter. Incongruously, at the top of the stairs, there was a modern plastic handle. It must surely have been added by some visiting occupational therapist when the previous occupant became frailer.

Each room smelled musty. There were dead flies everywhere, but the three upstairs rooms had floorboards about a foot wide in beautiful, old, but grubby wood. I was sure we could sand away the years of blackened grime and restore them to beauty again.

There was no bathroom at all, although one bedroom had an avocado toilet in it and a wash hand basin perched in the corner – not connected to any plumbing. As I opened each door, my heart began to sing. The rooms on the first floor with the big windows were very light – and each window had a different view of the garden; the musty smell throughout the house would soon disappear with a bit of airing.

The only piece of furniture left was an old wooden mirror in the front bedroom. It was plain, with a wooden surround painted black and set on a square box so that it could swivel up and down. I opened the lid of the box, but inside there was only dust. It would do nicely for my jewellery. But why was it left behind? I revised my idea of the previous resident being a rough farm worker, into being a woman who looked in mirrors. Did she brush her hair every morning? Perhaps she even wore lipstick when she went out?

George MacDonald, in his classic fantasy *Phantastes*, says that all mirrors are magical. Peering into the mirror, I sensed what it might have seen over the years, and I decided to make it mine. The bedroom that had at first seemed empty and blank began to come to life. The mirror and windows threw reflections onto the walls of the branches of the trees outside. Tom would have loved this place.

I so wished he was still here.

As I moved back downstairs, leaving Edward and Peggie shaking their heads as they double-checked the absence of plumbing, I heard a gruff voice call up from the back door. "Hello? Anybody there?" A tall wiry man, dressed in rumpled jeans and fisherman's sweater, ducked his head under the doorway as he walked into the kitchen. His steady grey eyes and thick ruffled hair reminded me of Tom's younger brother. "Hello, just checking everything's alright. I'm keeping an eye on the place for Rose."

I came forward and held out my hand. "Thanks, we're just looking around. I'm thinking of making an offer."

"I'm Patrick," he said as he took my hand. His was rough and warm. "You know the house is going to auction in a week or two?"

"Yes, could you tell me a little about the place?"

"Well," he began, "Rose lived here all her life until she passed away." His voice sounded as though he didn't use it that often. "Rose was the tenant farmer's daughter. She was born here over 80 years ago. When her father died, she refused to have anything done to the place. I built that kitchen myself on old flagstones laid on earth." I nodded approvingly as he continued. "There's no central heating, just water and electricity. She used to feed birds and animals – any that she could get to come into the kitchen. Kept the special scraps and seed just for that and fed them in little saucers all over the floor. Even the rats."

Was he trying to put me off? He stared at the ground and then, raising his eyes to look me straight in the face, he seemed to make a decision. "She died in hospital late last year," he said regretfully. "She was a tenant farmer, you see; the estate got power of attorney and just carted her away. They said she was a health risk with all the animals in her kitchen and that she needed to be taken care of. But I reckon they were just after the property. They just wanted to sell and they couldn't do that with her there." I felt a shock of recognition and empathy for Rose. "She minded her independence,

74

you see; she'd never have gone willingly. She thought it was her that was looking after the birds and animals, not the other way around. She was getting very frail-minded. In the end, she used to carry the coals in one by one for her fire. Wouldn't take any help."

"She sounds amazing. I hope I make it that good at her age."

"They tricked her into going into St Mary's for some tests and then they never let her out. Something to do with dolls. I never quite got it. She just got smaller and smaller until there was nothing left of her. One day when I went to visit, her bed was empty. The nurse said she'd gone in the night." He shook his head sadly.

As I heard Edward and Peggie's footsteps coming down the wooden staircase, he lifted his hand in a farewell gesture and turned back out of the kitchen, ducking his head again and walking down the stone path.

I wanted that house badly. I even wanted the risk. When I called the estate agents, it seemed that they were having trouble winding things up and preferred not to have to wait for the auction. I asked if they would consider an offer. They didn't answer straight away but a few days later I got a call saying that they had had a new offer from a company but it was lower than they wanted and did I want to make an offer now? The pressure on me to complete the purchase was suddenly real and intense.

I had made friends with one of the women in the office. The next time I got her on the phone, I asked her what was going on. She lowered her voice, "The offer is not going down well. He's an incomer!"

"What do you mean?"

"It's a man called Westerby who's only just bought another home, or should I say 'mansion', on the island. The talk is that he's using his company to buy up as much land as he can and being quite aggressive in the process."

"But I'm not from the island either!" I said, feeling a rising panic.

"Yes, but the owners know your family and they've been here for years. They're a bit old-fashioned that way."

I laughed, just relieved that I was eligible through this previously unknown rule, "Well, I'd better get a move on with completing the deal then!"

After a bit of arguing back and forth, the estate agent agreed that I could move in for a pepercorn rent, and start the improvements, as long as I signed a temporary three-month lease at which stage I would have to complete on the purchase. I had to make the necessary improvements that would make a mortgage possible. We signed an agreement on that basis; it was an unusual arrangement, but I was to find that those sorts of things often happened on the island.

I got an agreement in principle, for a mortgage from Alex Mathews. The understanding was that I would put in a proper bathroom, kitchen, and central heating. It was hugely risky because if I didn't fully complete the work, I would have to tear up the agreement and lose all the hard work and money that I'd put in. It was a race against time.

A local builder advertising in the community newsletter turned up in response to my call. Steve was another weather-beaten old man, but he seemed to know what he was doing. We went full steam ahead. I began spending all my weekends on the island and was soon camping there. One of the first things I asked Steve to do was to cut down the fir tree at the front. When that was done, the warm sun poured in through the front windows waking me up in the mornings on my sparse camp bed. I reckoned it wouldn't cost me much to live there on my own, I would need to manage the mortgage, assuming that it came through, but I had my work pension and maybe I could pick up some consultancy work on the island or in nearby Hampshire.

Tom would have relished putting in a new bathroom and creating the kitchen and central heating practically from scratch. But of course Tom wasn't there anymore. Taking such a huge financial risk would have made me feel physically sick in the past, but this seemed the only thing, the best thing, to do. I had to get back control of my life. I had to build a future or I would be at the mercy of Stanley and Evelyn forever. The family house in Islington was not my home anymore despite the fact that it had been so loved when the children were growing up and when Tom was alive. But it was not home now.

Stanley said that he would rent out the Islington house and in no time at all, he had the first tenants lined up. It occurred to me, somewhat ruefully, that I was now completely homeless. In some ways it was a relief not having the responsibility of a big house. I gave in my notice at work. Ed didn't seem too bothered; he was excited about another venture capitalist deal and looking to retire himself at the grand old age of fifty. Two weeks later, I had organised the removal van for our old bed and the kitchen table – I wasn't taking much because Pond Cottage was so small. I packed my bags, and only as an afterthought added my bicycle.

Leaving London for good, I drove fast, too fast, in my hire car but I was fleeing something that had gone badly wrong and wasn't fixable. I crossed on the same car ferry as the furniture van and arrived at the cottage half an hour later. I took a deep breath as I struggled with the lock and pushed the creaking back door open. The house still smelt musty and dusty, but it was mine – at least for the next three months.

I was safe, and I was alone. For the time being anyway.

Chapter 12

What happened next was all a haze. The hard work on the cottage caught up on me. I made a fire every evening, quickly using up Rose's remaining coals. Then I went foraging for logs in the woods and on the seashore. I loved the smell and the sound of the wood crackling in the open hearth but I soon learnt that if the wood wasn't dry, the fire would spit ferociously and threaten to set the old carpet alight with its red sparks. The hearth was tiny but when it was roaring away, it quickly heated up the whole house. All except the kitchen which I avoided as much as I could until Steve could lay proper foundations and a new tiled floor. Thanks to a friend of Steve's, the central heating and plumbing soon went in. Steve's friend was equally silent but annoyingly kept his radio on all day.

At first, I tried to work alongside Steve, painting and decorating, but I could see it irritated him so I caught up in the evenings instead. The timescales were tight and the three-month deadline loomed. As soon as the kitchen plumbing was done, and the bathroom and toilet were installed upstairs, Steve called another friend in to do the electrics. It was all cash-in-hand. Sanding the beautiful old wide floor boards upstairs was a major task. The two guys who turned up with a huge heavy machine were very nervous about breaking the old wood.

At one stage, there was a downpour of heavy rain – so heavy that the drains backed up. I was in despair. Steve explained it was because the water levels were very high around the house. He dug back through the undergrowth surrounding the back door to discover an old well. He explained that farmers often used wells, but this one had got completely overgrown, hence the problems with the drains. So Steve built a small stone wall surrounding the well and installed a temporary pump. He promised to come back and finish it off when the main work was over. Maybe my dream of being totally self-sufficient could come true after all.

Ten weeks later, I rang Alex Mathews and told him that I was ready for a visit. He sounded surprised but promised to come out the following week. With only a week until the deadline, I was desperate and was hardly sleeping at all.

The morning Alex Mathews was due I showered and dressed, for the first time in months, in my old city clothes. My work skirt and blouse hung loosely on me. I looked in the mirror and saw that I'd lost weight. I hadn't noticed this was happening while dressed in shapeless workaday jeans and shirts for three months. My face looked gaunt and tense so I added some rouge and mascara. Then I made fresh coffee and put flowers on the wooden kitchen table, adding a plate of hobnobs as an afterthought. There was a loud knocking on the front door, which was freshly painted yellow, and it swung open easily. Alex smiled and held out his hand.

"How are you?" Already looking around, he moved into the main room, touching the radiators, "I see you've got the central heating in?"

"Yes, all fine," I said apprehensively, "Would you like some coffee, or shall we look around first?"

"I'll just go ahead and have a check, if that's alright with you?" As he set off upstairs. I could hear him opening doors, turning on taps, and flushing the toilet. Whatever was he doing? Back downstairs in no time, he came through to the kitchen and nodded approval at the new sink, cooker and fridge. Again, he turned the taps on. "Everything in working order then?" he asked smiling. "To be honest, I didn't think you'd manage it on time." And then, looking at my crest-fallen face, he added, "But I'm pleased you have, well done."

I sat down heavily at the table and, feeling speechless with relief, pointed to the coffee. It was all going to be alright.

When Alex had consumed several hobnobs, he asked me to sign all the papers which, this time, I read carefully. He nodded when I'd finished. The mortgage was approved! I should have been able to relax, but I no longer knew how. I wanted to be outside near the sea – to taste the intoxicating saltwater on my tongue, listen to the roar of the waves, and gaze at the vast expanse of turbulent water stretching out towards the horizon. So after Alex had left, I took the winding road down to the beach. The road to the beach wound around the corner past high trees where rooks lived all year round. Their huge nests looked like permanent structures, dominating the skyline. I counted at least twenty. They cawed loud, insistent, almost metallic, as they swooped back and forth.

During my first weeks in the house, I settled into my new routine and began getting used to the house quirks. I would come down every morning to find glistening trails traced across the kitchen floor and up the walls. Where were the snails going alone at night? Where did they come from? And where did they disappear to? Once I came down in the middle of the night when I couldn't sleep, aiming to make myself a cup of tea, I surprised a small slug midway between the kitchen and the hallway. It pricked up its ears in surprise. I swooped to gather it up and felt the slime on my hand as I opened the kitchen door and threw it out onto the damp grass outside. It stuck to my palm, and I had to shake it hard to get it off. I was not Rose, not yet anyway. I wondered where Patrick lived. I hadn't seen him since the time he first came round. Fresh vegetables began making the occasional appearance by the back door – I hoped they might have come from him but it could have been one of the neighbours.

The cottage was not only home to slugs and snails; it was always full of creatures. The animals that Rose had fed clearly still felt it their home. Birds and tiny dormice, sometimes even red squirrels. The little red squirrels with their big bushy tails were quite rare, and the island was one of the few remaining places that they still inhabited. Elsewhere, most had been killed off by their more aggressive grey cousins. Occasionally, I glimpsed a country rat, small and plump, unlike its huge aggressive town cousins rummaging in fast food bins. Country rats who lived off the land, looked more like guinea pigs. Overnight, the spiders would weave their delicate webs across the windows, I'd watch them for hours as they captured flies with surprising inevitability. When I wandered out with my mug of tea on warm, sunny mornings, I would find beautifully intricate webs covered in dew and strung out across the pathway – not used to being disturbed. A whole army of little creatures must have been working their way through the old stone house, eating into the fabric of the walls. Over time, if left undisturbed, they would bring those walls down to dust.

I began sitting out in the evenings during the gloaming. I'd sit under the old apple tree staring over at the eaves of the village hall just as the bats began their frenzied darting in and out of the eaves and surrounding trees. I watched for the swooping of the white barn owls as they left their roosts at dusk and came back again and again, with tiny field mice for their hungry young. Once, I saw two round white faces with blinking eyes, one above the other in the apex of the village hall roof. I was careful not to mention the owls to anyone for fear of people coming to stare at them. They were my owls and their magic seemed to become part of the garden which was growing wilder again.

However, it wasn't all idyllic. Another time, I was lying in bed with the window open and I heard a strange noise, like a small child moving through the bushes. I sat up and looked out into the moonlit garden. I couldn't see anything at all so I went downstairs and outside with a torch to investigate. It would have to be an animal of sorts, probably a large animal judging from the sound of the movement. A loud bark frightened me and then suddenly, a large black and white head with a pointed snout appeared and startled me into complete stillness. As the badger and I stared face to face, I thought of his sharp teeth sinking into my leg. I was careful not to blink. I tried to work out an escape route but there wasn't one, so I waited. The loud squalling from the crows above, unusual in the middle of the night, sent the badger scuttling away, and it disappeared back into the hedge. When the rustling had died down, all evidence of it was gone. The next morning, I noticed signs of digging on the lawn, with a small dark brown turd sitting alongside the disturbed grass. The black garbage bin had been knocked over and was lying on its side, and its contents were strewn over the stone path. It was as though a teenager had deliberately made a mess and refused to clear it up. Bending down on my knees, I put the rubbish back into the bin and placed a large stone on top. What was it digging for? I must remember to ask Patrick what badgers eat.

It was at times like this that I missed Tom even more. He would have known what to do. But I had made my decision now and I must make it work. I looked at my hands. My nails were torn and rough. They had been so smooth and polished for so long. I clenched my fists and dug my torn nails into my palms. When I was a young teenager, just when I was getting my periods and having constant shouting arguments with my father, I used to cut myself. Then, like now, it hurt, but the pain was a relief. When my periods came in fully, my mother stopped my father shouting at me and the cutting stopped too.

Each day stretched endlessly. Every evening after a long walk along the beach, I would sit in the front room. Leaving the curtains open, I'd drink red wine and watch the rooks whirling and screeching above. As soon as the rooks settled for the night, the bats would begin darting all around, in and out of the eves, and then I'd sit out waiting for the swoop of the owl. Most nights I couldn't get up the energy to make a meal so I would make up a big batch of lentil soup with a ham knuckle from the local village shop. I'd eat that with fresh vegetables and herbs from the garden and sometimes a piece of toast with marmite or honey. It would last for days. Next year, I would make damson jam from the tree in the garden. This year I'd been too late, and the birds had come and picked it clean.

I got to thinking more about Rose and what had happened to her. She crept into my sleep until she was there night after night, taking over my dreams. I dreamt about a crumbling old house which was falling down, but now the outside walls crumbled away, and the roof was open to the skies and the birds, especially the huge cawing rooks, swooping down on me. People came and went. Evelyn and Stanley came as children and then as grown adults. My father appeared once but never my mother, and never Tom. I woke up in the night thinking I could hear Rose moving about the house and dreamt about Pandora, the strange woman at the bus stop in Bournemouth. I saw her walking out to sea and tried to stop her. I wondered again whether she had been mentally ill for long and if I could have saved her.

I was fearful for a long time about the strange noises in the garden at night. It took me quite a while to realise that the screeching sound at around 10pm at night and again early in the morning, weren't the foxes mating as I'd thought. It was in fact the baby owls in the village hall calling for their exhausted parents to bring them their next meal. If only Stan would have a baby soon. I would often fall into a deep sleep and then wake two hours later to watch the clock. Opening my eyes to the electronic red numbers on the radio clock at 2.03 am, I would lie there and shut my eyes for what seemed like an hour to only to open them at 2.19 am. Then, worrying that it might be bad luck to open them at 2.22 I'd lie there calculating how many repetitive consecutive numbers there were on the 24-hour clock whilst I waited for what seemed like a decent period. Counting, I worked out 2.22, 3.33. 4.44, 5.55 then quite a gap until 11.11 the next morning. Would something dreadful happen if I opened my eyes at 2.22 or would 3.33 be even worse? The sign for the devil was 666, or 999, or both, but a derivative of those could be 3.33. With my mind whirring in this way, I was always exhausting myself but couldn't seem to stop. I'd usually finally fall asleep and then wake with a start at 8.30am and wonder what on earth I'd been worrying about.

***

One evening, I charged up my phone after a long time of leaving it alone, intending to call Peggie but Evie caught me first.

"Mum, we're worried about you. What's going on?"

I sighed. I really didn't want to discuss things with Evie, so I said, "Nothing to worry about. There's a lot to do."

"It's my school autumn half-term next week, I'm coming down."

Two days later there was a loud knock at the door and there was Evie. I was pleased to see her and hugged her for a long time until she gently pushed me away and looked me in the face. "Mum, I've been so worried, look at you, you're so thin! Let's get something to eat, I'll cook." I'd forgotten how energetic my daughter could be, and exhausting at the same time. It was easier to let her take over. I kept pushing the omelette that she made around my plate until I saw her watching, so I forced it down.

The next morning, Evelyn made an appointment with my GP and two days later we were at the surgery. She came in with me to see the doctor after the nurse had taken my blood. I couldn't see how to stop Evie coming in, short of shutting the door in her face. So, I tried sitting up straight and saying as forcefully as I could,

"I'm fine doctor, just a little tired. Last time I was like this when my husband died, my doctor gave me some pills. They helped me get over the worst of it. Please can I have something again to help me sleep?"

"What's your problem right now?" The doctor asked.

I knew I was sounding confused, so I tried again, "Since Tom died, that's my husband. He was my husband. Before he died, I mean. I haven't been sleeping properly."

"She has lost a lot of weight too, haven't you, Mum?" Evelyn added looking anxiously at me.

I tried to change the subject. "Did you know Rose from the cottage?" I asked the doctor. "That's where I'm living now."

"No, I don't think so." She shook her head, "I'm not keen on giving you medication if we can avoid it," she said reassuringly as she looked at the blood results on her screen. "Your blood sugars are quite high though. How much alcohol do you drink a week?"

"I only have a glass of wine in the evenings. I don't drink any spirits and never during the day," I protested.

She looked across at Evie who jumped in, "You do have a bit more than just one glass, though don't you Mum?" I glared at her.

"Hmm, you know the recommended level is two units a week? It sounds as though you may be a bit depressed. I'm going to ask a colleague of mine from psychiatry to see you." Then she added curtly, "If that's okay with you?"

It didn't really sound like a question, so I didn't bother with an answer. Evelyn stayed behind and said something quietly to the doctor and the nurse before they handed her a prescription form. I had hoped for Mogadon, but when we got to the chemist it turned out there were boxes full of capsules with tiny pink happy pills instead.

After a few days, Evelyn went back home, and I was left in peace. Every morning, I took out the packets of little pink pills, rows of them looking up at me, and took one out and threw it away until the first package was empty. And each morning for the first week, I found a text message from Evie reminding me to take my pills and telling me what to eat that day. Evelyn had spent her evenings making meals from produce at the local farm shop and she'd left them in the freezer with a note on each one. Monday Shepherd's pie, Tuesday Fish pie, Wednesday Sausages and Mash. I counted ten of them. Did that mean she would be back in ten days? On Monday I tried the Shepherd's pie but gagged on it. After that, I left them all in the deep freeze, and went back to my cauldron of lentils, bacon, and any fresh vegetables I could forage or find.

Chapter 13

I slept fitfully through the nights, dreams full of Tom and Patrick building a boat together. They were all rolled into one so that it was impossible to tell who was doing what. They seemed to be getting along together though. I woke to the sun flooding through my bedroom window and jumped out of bed. Throwing on my swimsuit and jeans and T-shirt from yesterday, I set off for the beach. I was pretty certain there'd be no-one around. The sun was already warm, and the air was quiet, with just a few birds going about their morning singing. As I reached the corner of the road before the last stretch to the beach – the corner that I had now named 'Rooks Corner' – I saw Patrick coming towards me. When had I last seen him in person? Apart from in my dreams last night! I blushed. My memory was all over the place and I didn't want him to think I was coming on to him. I decided that treating him like an old friend was the safest bet.

"Hello there", he said, coming across the road towards me. He was carrying one of those old-fashioned wooden trundles full of new carrots and baby courgettes. "I see you've moved in then. Would you like some fresh veg?"

Realising then that I can't have seen him since I moved in, I said, "Yes, please. They'll make a nice change to my soup." As he picked out some carrots and courgettes, I took a deep breath and said, "I did want to ask you something … When I first met you, you told me Rose had been to hospital and there was something about dolls, but you weren't sure what it was?"

"That's right, they said she wasn't safe at home and that they needed to put dolls there as a precaution, which didn't make any sense, so I just thought I'd misunderstood."

"I'm pretty certain what they were talking about was one of those new laws about depriving people of their liberty. It was called DOLs for short."

He looked puzzled. "Why would they do that? She was harmless."

"Well, they may have thought she was a risk to herself."

He nodded slowly. "It was her estate who were pushing it so that they could sell the cottage."

"Well, I'm afraid children have been known to use DOLs to get their elderly parents removed from their homes – and sometimes to stop them being sent home from hospital."

"Better watch out then, hadn't we?" He laughed. "I'll leave the carrots on your doorstep if you're on your way to the beach. It's low tide, but watch out for those spring tides. They can be dangerous."

I felt at peace. It was lovely to see him again, and I hugged the thought of having a friend close by; I wasn't alone after all. The beach was quiet, and the sea so calm that it was barely moving – just gently gliding across the flat sands on the low tide. I walked all the way across the bay with the early morning sun warming my face, and then back along the high cliff grassy path. Back at the cottage, I found the carrots tied up in a piece of gardening string around their green fleshy leaves. When I picked them up, I breathed-in the sweetness of the carrots mingled with the fresh scent of the earth.

Two days later, there was a loud knocking on the door. I opened it to find Evie on the doorstep again, a small rucksack over her shoulder. I sighed. I knew she meant well, but it was peace I wanted.

"Hi Mum, I'm back!" she announced cheerfully, too cheerfully, and as I gave her a hug, she asked, "Are you ready?"

"Ready for what?"

"Your doctor's appointment, to discuss the ECT. You haven't forgotten, have you? I'll have a quick coffee, then we'll need to get going."

I had forgotten. Completely. I really didn't want to have ECT, but half an hour later found myself in Evie's little hire car on the way to the local clinic. We left early at her insistence to be there for 10am, but we arrived at 9.30 – far too early. I would have left it until 15 minutes beforehand, but it seemed I wasn't making my own decisions anymore. Evie was. Or rather, Mrs Finlay was. Evie asked for her by name when we arrived and explained that Mrs Finlay would be my case coordinator. Mrs Finlay soon padded into the waiting room dressed in a pale blue short-sleeved top and matching baggy trousers. "Morning my dear, come along this way."

As we went down the long corridor that smelled strongly of disinfectant, our shoes squeaked on the newly polished lino floor. Mrs Finlay led us into a bright white clinical room. Evie and I waited a minute or so before a fatherly man in a white coat introduced himself and asked me in a kindly way what had brought me there that day. I poured it all out. The feeling that control of my life was being taken away from me. And the feeling that all the sunshine I'd had over the past week had gone inside again. I began to cry and couldn't stop. I spoke about Tom, and somehow Rose became part of it all too.

"I think we should get you some help right away. You seem to be quite depressed," he said. "It seems your appetite hasn't picked up since last time you saw a doctor, and you still seem quite low – so the best thing we can do now is to go ahead with the ECT therapy." I hadn't remembered agreeing to this, but it seemed a done deal. He explained that I would be having a course of six ECT sessions and that my short-term memory would go. They said it was important to get on with the treatment and not wait too long. I wanted to slow it all down, but it didn't seem I had a choice. I was worried now – especially at the idea of losing my memory.

Over the next week, I began to think that perhaps I wasn't being fair to Evelyn. I had an ominous sense of being out of control, but perhaps I was being too mistrustful? I woke up the next morning and decided I'd give it a try. I knew the idea was that the ECT would help you stop worrying. I wasn't convinced it would, but how harmful could it be?

The following week, we arrived on time for the first session. As I lay flat on my back on the narrow bed, staring up at the bright overhead light bulb, I wondered again why it was all happening so quickly. The cool gel on my temples was soothing at first. There was a prick on the back of my hand and then I drifted off to sleep.

My heart starts to race in spurts like the bats dipping and darting at twilight from the blackness of the eaves of the cottage. I am shooting through tunnels inside a long steel box. It judders like a boat on a choppy sea. The drumming noise drones on and on. I hear the cawing sound of the jackdaws and see them swooping in the sky and falling, screaming, as they dive into the sea. I feel a surge of nausea in my throat and the taste of bitter bile comes into my mouth. My tongue is dry and sticks to the roof of my mouth. It feels too large and I worry I will bite it with my teeth. I am stretched out on my back, holding on tight to myself, but I can't move my arms. My arms are pinned down tight across my chest and even my fingers don't wriggle when I try. I keep my eyes closed. Better that way. I can smell the burnt offerings of the diseased cheese stall in the local market, pungent on my dead body. I am the living dead.

My eyes are shut, but through my eyelashes I can see a bright white light searing down on me. I don't feel safe anymore. The safeness has flown into the night with the swirling jackdaws. From the corner of one eye, I see a hand coming around from behind my head and touching my hand and arm – cool and clean, smelling of soap. Where is Evelyn?

Who is this new person? "*There you are dear; I'm just going to give you a little more and make you comfy.*"

My mind comes screaming back, "What are you doing? Don't touch me! Get off me! Leave me alone, you're killing me!" I try to raise my hand to push her off, but I can't move. My legs are all jerky when I swing out to kick her away, but it makes no difference.

The voice is booming now and comes on again from behind me and above. A voice that I cannot see but which fills all my space, cutting out the air and forcing me to catch my breath. The voice is trying to get control of me, and I must beat it back. I want to scream out aloud, but the bile in my throat chokes me and I cannot make any sound. "Better not kick too much dear, you'll only hurt yourself. Try and rest now. I'm going to give you something that'll make you feel better."

I see the cold white uniform and the hand turning the valve on the tall tube above my head. I feel the surge of cool liquid pouring into my arm, flooding into my body. It's poisoning me; the warm blood of the dead chickens taking me over. I close my eyes again and my mind screams, "No! No! Noo! Don't!! Stop!! Stop!! Give me back myself!"

I feel the humming of an engine dying away and then the box bursts open, and I am back.

I remember nothing.

Chapter 14

After a few days, Evie packed her bags at last and drove me in her hired car to the ferry. My plan was to catch the bus back after doing a major shop. As we hugged goodbye, she held me. Pushing back her unruly auburn hair, I noticed there was more grey, and that she had crease marks on her forehead. She must be almost forty. Middle age was creeping up on her and, no doubt Stanley as well.

"Do you still not remember anything?" She asked, curiously.

I shook my head, "Not a thing – probably just as well. Never again, honestly Evie. I mean it. I really don't want to have that awful thing again."

It wasn't strictly true that I couldn't remember anything. I could remember the sick sense of going into a tunnel and coming out the other end. And I could remember that in the days before the ECT, I had felt tired, so tired that I could hardly open my eyes. But I wasn't going to tell anyone, and certainly not Evie. She must go home to her family now.

The complete loss of control during ECT bothered me. I went back to the *Guardian* article I'd read. It confirmed that most ECT patients now are female, and more than half are over 60. Why? Are older women more depressed than older men? Or are they just more troublesome? I'd love to have debated that with Tom! And does it work? Not for Pandora at the bus stop back in Bournemouth, it didn't.

It was Sunday morning, so after saying goodbye to Evie at the boat ferry, I popped into the Waitrose in East Cowes to shop and get the Sunday papers. I picked up the *Sunday Observer* in memory of Tom, but the *Daily Mail* headlines "Robots take over Care of the Elderly" caught my eye, so I added that to my trolley. My appetite had picked up and I was beginning to feel hungry again, although the effort of cooking meals for myself felt a stretch too far. I couldn't imagine ever sitting down to the huge roasts again that Tom and I had had every Sunday. As I wandered down the aisles full of packaged food, lasagne, and moussaka, I heard a familiar voice. "I wouldn't touch any of that stuff if I were you."

The gruff voice coming from close behind startled me. I whipped round to see Patrick standing there and laughed with relief. "What a fright you gave me! How are you?" I felt myself blushing with embarrassment.

"Pleased to see you up and about again."

So, the message about my health had got out. I wondered how much he knew. But it was nice to be worried about. "How have you been?" I asked, hoping to change the subject. I noticed he was wearing the same rumpled checked shirt and corduroy trousers as the first time I'd seen him at the cottage. I almost reached out my hand to touch his arm and feel his warmth, but stopped myself in time. I was aware that my baggy jeans and an old shirt of Tom's that I'd been wearing to do the painting were not exactly flattering. I pushed my hair back, must get a hair-cut soon. We talked for a while. When we parted, we agreed that it would be nice to meet up again soon. I briefly wondered if Patrick still had keys to the house. I decided not to worry about missing keys and drove home, humming. Living on the island was very different from life in London; I didn't miss the hustle and bustle.

Back at the cottage, I went upstairs to wash and paused to stare into the mirror. Mirror, mirror … who is the fairest of them all? I scraped back my hair into a ponytail and decided that my substantial grey streaks added interest. Besides, there was no way I would start going to hairdressers again. At least my skin was glowing and healthily covered with freckles. It was time to think about getting my body into shape again. Maybe even buy some new clothes. I pictured a floaty floral dress for the summer. Long beach walks would help, but swimming would be best. I had always loved the clean cool feel of my body slicing through water.

The local pool had an advert for the annual Solent Sea Swim. The attendant said, "We're hoping to find a hundred volunteers who can swim at least 100 lengths of the pool for the Solent swim this August." I gulped as he went on to explain, "You'll need a coloured swimming cap, so you can be seen in the grey seas." So I pointed to a brightly coloured red cap and goggles behind the counter as he continued. "The sea swim is just over a mile, but the tides and the currents make it seem a lot more. It's quite a stretch." He looked at me doubtfully despite my enthusiastic nodding; it would be something concrete to aim for. I needed a challenge.

In the weeks that followed, I began lane swimming and managed to swim a little further and faster each week. I daydreamed of going on a rescue operation and saving lives at sea. I knew it was ridiculous at my age, but I knew that if I gave up on my dreams, then my life would just keep getting smaller. I also rationalised that if there was ever a need for me to escape from the island, then I could always swim across to the mainland.

Now that I was on a health and fitness mission, I went to find my old bicycle in the summer house. I had dumped it there when I first arrived and now a green vine had crept through the floorboards of the shed and wound through the spokes of the wheels. Amazingly, the tyres were still quite hard. I shivered as I remembered my last fateful ride in London.

My first trip was a little like taking a pony out in the fresh air. I reckoned I could easily make the nearest village. As I trundled along, I thought about getting an old-fashioned basket on the front. The first trip took me over half an hour, but over the next few weeks I was zipping along in 20 minutes or so and loving the rush of wild garlic-scented air as I raced down through the woods. It was good to feel my muscle strength returning.

With my new positive mindset, I began to wonder what was happening with Evie and Stan. I decided it was about time to get them both down to the island for some family time. Time to properly forgive them for what Tom had done. It would be nice to see Cassie again too. I called Evie first, "Mum, good to hear from you! All fine here, except Andy's just been made redundant."

"Sorry to hear that. But he's in a good position to find something else?"

"I don't know. It's a real bummer. But how are you?"

"Great. I'm cycling and swimming now and there's this health and wellbeing class in the Village Hall. They make you stand on one leg and shut your eyes. Some sort of Alzheimer's test, I'm sure. And I'm training to do the Solent swim next year!"

"I heard about those intense screening and fitness tests for the over sixties. Keep you on your toes for as long as possible. What's that you said about the Solent swim? You were joking, right?"

"Well, I used to be quite a good swimmer you know," I hesitated. Maybe she had a point … perhaps I was over doing it a bit.

It was so easy to lose confidence again. I tried to call Stan a few times, but he didn't answer. He could be so casually hurtful. Did he not know the effect never answering my calls had on me?

Chapter 15

"Hey, sis, haven't heard from you since you got back from Mum's! What's been going on? You said you'd call me."

"She wasn't too good. I'd thought she was just missing Dad at first, but then it seemed more than that. I'm glad I checked it out and that her GP could see her so quickly!"

"You wouldn't get that happening in London!"

"No, I know. I was a bit surprised … but if I hadn't gone down there, I doubt she'd have kept the appointment. ."

"Maybe the NHS is just better on the Isle of Wight?"

"Maybe. They were very professional, ready and waiting for her like a VIP as soon as we arrived at the surgery. The doctor and her case coordinator, Mrs Finlay, said that she should start on the ECT as soon as possible. We didn't have to wait long for the ECT appointment either … that's why I stayed on a bit longer so that I could be with her for that too."

"Just remind me. What is ECT?" Asked Stanley.

"It sounds horrible, but it's supposed to be really effective. They send an electrical charge through the brain to trigger a seizure. I admit, it does sound barbaric, like some form of mediaeval torture for the treatment of troublesome women or witches."

"Why are they doing it on the island then?"

"They're using it more now, everywhere, especially for older women, apparently. Before she had it, she was tired all the time. She'd stop in the middle of a sentence or whatever she was doing and forget where she was."

"So it worked? She's improved?"

"Yes, she perked up almost immediately the same day, and after a few days, her old energy came back. She started eating like a horse, thank goodness. But she didn't want to go back for more. They insist on the course being six treatments … "

"So, it's like a course of antibiotics. You have to finish it?" Stanley asked.

"Don't be silly, Stan, taking a few pills and having an electric shock through your brain are hardly the same thing … It was worrying! The psychiatrist said that if she didn't co-operate, they might section her – you know, admit her to a mental hospital against her will."

"That's going a bit far. I'd go down, but she made it pretty clear she didn't want to see me," said Stan.

Typical self-pity from Stan when it suited him, thought Evie. "Don't be so bloody up yourself. She wasn't exactly happy with me either. Anyway, I've asked the nurse, Mrs Finlay, to keep me up-to-date."

"I've been reading up on the power of attorney. We should do something about it."

"Power of attorney? Wouldn't Mum have to agree to that?"

"Yes, strictly speaking, but there's been a lot of changes recently. Brian says the lawyers and charities are selling it as part of the whole retirement package for families."

"So, its lawyers lining their pockets again?"

"Don't be silly Evie. Everyone wants to make money. The deal is if you get your mum or dad to sign up, then they're guaranteed to be looked after. And it stops them squandering their pensions on foreign cruises and fast cars. Whatever's left will be gobbled up by the state, anyway, like ice cream melting in the sun."

"Well, that's hardly likely to happen with Mum, is it? She hates those foreign cruises full of oldies with their Zimmer frames. Although I can imagine her going for a fast car, or even a new man ... Which reminds me, she was talking about someone called Patrick."

"We'd better check him out. But what do you think about the power of attorney?"

"Let me get this right. You're saying we get Mum to sign something to give away her rights after what we did to her with the house? You have got to be joking! She's only just started talking to me again. Anyway, how come you're so keen on this?"

"I'm working for a private equity company. They're investing in the future of care homes and they're very into getting powers of attorney into place for as many people as possible ... as well as investing in robots in future!"

"Mum will be pleased about the robots! Have you told her?"

"Not yet. On the power of attorney thing though, really, it's a way for relatives to protect their elderly parents."

Evie sighed, "You sound like you're reading from a sales tutorial. It's also a way to rob them blind. What do you suggest we do with Mum, protect her or rob her blind?"

Stanley laughed forcibly. "We're protecting her, of course! And maybe even from people like Patrick, whoever he is."

"I just don't think Mum would be happy about it now. By the way, what's happening with the rental from the house? You were going to send my share? "

"Oh, I meant to tell you. The family who were going to move in decided it was too expensive after all. So Cassie and I have moved in temporarily – just to keep an eye on it and make sure squatters don't move in. "

"You're such a wheeler dealer. Send me some money for rent then. But next time, for Christ's sake, tell me what's going on."

"Okay, I'll send you some as soon as I catch up myself. Just promise not to tell Mum. We can't afford to have her changing her mind and coming back right now."

Chapter 16

The Sunday papers continued to be full of robot stories like, 'Granny's new best Friend.' The more I thought about it, the more I realised that for me, there was something reassuringly steady about robots. They were reliable, programmed machines that were not subject to human foibles. The thought that I might be able to manage my life without having to rely on either of my children, or indeed anyone, was quite attractive. I read every robot article I came across and decided it was about time to follow up on Sambot, the mysterious disappearing robot. I dialled the number, but there was no answer. Just in case I'd made a mistake, I re-dialled. This time, there was a small click, and ping-pong, the phone was answered almost straight away.

"Hello, technology"? a bored official voice answered.

"Hello, I'd like to speak to somebody about Sam the Robot, please?" I replied.

"I'm sorry," the voice went on smoothly, "that programme has been closed down." The phone went dead. Puzzled, I went back to the link to connect with the Robot Network Programme website, but that seemed to be down too. I decided to try again in a few days.

The island's monthly bulletin was delivered every month by a local youth with a large canvas bag slung over his shoulder.

The September issue was usually in strong autumn colours – red, orange, and yellow – with a reminder on the front page not to roast hedgehogs in your bonfire. This time, the whole front page was taken up with a closeup of Sam the Robot, my robot! His black eyes stared straight up at me from the page. The headline, 'Sambot's Coming to Town,' announced that he would tour the island over the next few weeks, apparently to talk about something called the 'Caring Agenda.' He was scheduled to visit our local village hall just a short walk away at 5pm on the last Saturday of November. This was an event (unlike the regular bingo and ping-pong) which was not to be missed. It'd been quite a while since I'd last seen Sambot. He surely wouldn't remember me, would he? Or was this a different Sambot? Of course, it was …

When the last Saturday in November arrived, I opened my front door at 4.30pm to see a stream of cars dropping people off at the village hall. They came in all shapes and sizes; some with sticks and some in wheelchairs. What they all had in common were their greying heads and wrinkled faces with the occasional bouffant coiffed hair and a couple of ageing hippies with long grey hair pulled back into sparse ponytails. As I hurriedly stepped out and pulled my front door shut, I walked down the road to join the queue. The rows of wooden chairs inside were already rapidly filling up. Knowing there are always empty seats at the front, nobody wants to be exposed, I pushed forward and sure enough found a vacant row of chairs. In place of the usual bingo table, there was a stand with banners at either side of the stage and a huge screen in the centre. Next to the screen stood my friend Sambot. Seeing him anew, he seemed both familiar and yet strange. He stood with his face down and his long, jointed arms hanging by his side, his knobbly fingers almost reached the floor. Behind him on the screen, the Citizen UK logo and the council logo appeared on either side of the title "Introducing Sam, the Caring Robot."

As the hall continued to fill up, I began to feel panicky. I remembered once going to a cinema in London for a special showing of a slightly erotic film called *Looking for Love*. The four hundred strong audience was packed with largely black Afro- Caribbean men and women. Throughout the film, they had laughed, clapped, and groaned in unison at jokes I barely understood. At the end of the film, everyone had stood up and, joining hands along the rows of cinema seats, had sung the theme song. Tom and I had come to support a friend, and we were one only of two or three white couples amongst the several hundred. The Sambot meeting had the same evangelical tension, almost as though people were on drugs. I had felt excluded at that film in London, a bystander rather than a participant, and I felt the same now.

My feeling of being trapped grew, my heartbeat began drumming in my ears. I took the long slow breaths they'd taught me when I was waiting for ECT. Looking around for an escape route, I saw it was going to be difficult to find a way through such a busy crowd. Then I saw Patrick coming in at the back. I waved to him and began pushing through the crowd to join him.

"I'm so glad to see you! What a crowd!"

"Good to see you too. I thought you'd be here." He smiled.

As I sat down, his warm bulk leaning against my shoulder, I smelt bonfires and was disturbingly reminded of roasting hedgehogs. Sitting next to him I felt safe. On my other side, squashed up tight against me, was a woman in her sixties with bright brassy blond hair. She looked at me sideways and stared when I'd squeezed in between her and Patrick. Then she turned and started chattering away to her neighbour on the other side. A few minutes later, at 5pm on the dot, and just when the hall was becoming unbearably hot, the side doors were thrown open and the stage suddenly flooded with light. The demo was a slick, practiced affair, much like the one I'd seen at the conference, except this time it was a woman taking Sambot through his paces. This Sambot joined in a lot more. He beamed up at his new keeper and almost danced round her, his gesticulating arms and long fingers wafting around him. I wanted to feel the cool, hard strength of those fingers again. The woman presenter looked the sort who would bake cakes for coffee mornings – something fancy yet traditional – sticky toffee meringue or maybe a lemon drizzle. Having taken 'Sambot' through his paces (I noticed she didn't call him that), she cheerfully announced the new project, one that would be a 'once in a lifetime opportunity.' Volunteers were being sought to trial the new care robots at home for a month. They would undertake simple cleaning jobs, fetch and carry things, and remind people to take medication and do their exercises. Looking up brightly at the end, as she said, "We'll take the details of anyone who'd like to volunteer to take a trial robot, and I promise you, you won't be disappointed! "

There was a murmur throughout the audience as this information sunk in. People seemed to have been quite impressed with Sambot – and no doubt the prospect of unpaid extra domestic help – but I was fascinated, wondering how many would actually go for it when the time came.

Standing at the back of the hall on the way out, I didn't immediately recognise Kevin, Sambot's former keeper from Southend. He was standing with a clipboard, checking people's interest and taking their names and details. Close up, he was instantly recognisable, with his large frame and huge hands. I looked around to introduce Patrick, but he'd disappeared. Kevin looked down at me and smiled formally as I said, "Hi, I met you at a conference a while back. You came with Sambot?"

He looked down at me, his smile dropping, "What are you doing here?" He almost demanded.

"I'm retired now. I moved here to the island, a year or so back." He seemed to recover himself. "I actually left in a bit of a hurry. There was suddenly a LOT of commercial interest in Sambot and things got a little busy. Remind me, what's your name?"

He looked down at his list and checked my name off. It was odd that he had my name on the list – I didn't remember giving anyone my telephone number, but it was evidently there, along with my other contact details, my email address and twitter account.

As we gradually moved out into the gathering gloom, I looked up to see the ravens swooping across the skies with their loud and insistent cawing. The queue of older people waiting for their cars paused their animated chatter to watch as the birds swooped in menacing black swathes. Standing beside Kevin, Sambot seemed to be frozen and staring up at the sky. What was he thinking? What did he see?

***

Three days later, there was a loud knocking at my door. I opened it to find Kevin standing there with a big smile on his face and a lot of official-looking papers bulging out of a battered brown briefcase. He stepped back and waited for me to ask him in. I looked behind him, expecting to see Sambot, but he wasn't there.

As we went in, Kevin looked around. "Nice place! It's good that you're all on one level down here. The robot should be able to get around alright." He beamed again.

"Are you with the Isle of Wight Robot Network Programme now?" I asked.

"Yes, we're doing a lot of programming for the island. It's a huge contract. I've come to check out if you're really interested in signing up?"

"Well, I'm definitely *interested*, but what would it entail?"

Sitting himself down at the kitchen table, Kevin explained that I would need to complete an application form and that part of the application involved a rigorous medical. If I passed that, I'd then come to the training depot where I'd meet Sambot, or rather *my* Sambot, and they would train me to programme him. "A few weeks after the induction, the robot will come and stay for a trial month and we'd help you with a new programme based on your personal characteristics."

Just checking, I asked, "What, you mean? In my house?"

"Yes, of course. The programme is hoping the robots prove to be so popular that they take over quite a few things for older folk."

"Things like what?"

"Well, at the moment, the robot can remind you when to take your pills and any appointments, that sort of thing."

"Could he also help with cooking and cleaning and answering the door?"

"Yes, in time, but let's get the basics right first. We are thinking of calling it a 'companion carebot.' Does that make sense?"

"It does now. I'm fine with the idea of programming him." But something niggled me. "It sounds interesting, but I'm not sure I really want — or need a companion just yet."

"Well, if you decide to go for it, we could slip you into the next programme which starts in a few weeks' time ..." Kevin was sweating profusely even though the kitchen was quite cool. A small drop of perspiration fell on to the pile of what looked like the medical consent forms.

I wondered why he was in such a hurry. Nevertheless, despite some reservation, I heard myself saying, "Great! What happens next?"

"Let's work it out," he began somewhat pompously. "You'll be taking part in a huge research programme that draws on this new concept of singularity. It's when AI becomes so powerful and sophisticated that humans begin to merge with technology."

He took me through an incredibly detailed evaluation programme, line by line. By the time Kevin had been there for two hours, I was drained and my head was reeling. But I was also elated and excited.

Kevin beamed again. He was a great beamer. "Robots don't have much common sense and of course they've no sense of humour, so we must be a bit careful. If we give them to just anyone, it could all go horribly wrong. I heard about this programme that used robots in a factory to help with the heavy lifting and moving goods around. There was an accident with one of the boxes and a greasy mess spilled out. The robots didn't notice the mess on the floor, and so they steamed on through it and began slipping and falling over. Then they couldn't get up, so they all piled up on each other and a few were quite badly damaged."

He shook his head ruefully as I laughed.

Kevin arranged his papers and then pointed to one of them, "Can you sign here? And here, please?"

I looked at the forms and thought I'd better read them all properly. I'd learnt that lesson the hard way. They looked straight forward, but I didn't want to sign away my body for research purposes, or my home, for that matter. There were the usual insurance type forms, and a medical form that required me to generally agree to keep fit and active. I noticed that one form was headed 'Emotional and Sexual Purposes.' I had to sign that I wouldn't be using Sambot for sexual purposes. I remembered the blurb about Sambot in the Japanese press.

The last form was titled 'Power of Attorney: Sunset Clause.'

"What's this for?" I asked.

Kevin grabbed it back hurriedly, blushing slightly, "You won't be needing that one," he said and shoved it back into his briefcase.

"We'll send a car for you on the day of induction. It's going to happen sometime in the next 4-6 weeks or so. Expect to spend the whole day with us."

Blimey, they must have an endless supply of cars, but better than having to go on my bike or get a bus. It was quite a distance away, in Ryde, on the other side of the island where I seldom went.

After Kevin had left, I poured myself a large glass of red wine. For the first time in months, I would be going out into the world again. Intrigued about the reference to sexual behaviour with robots, I searched for the Japanese website, but it had been taken down. I could ask Kevin or one of his colleagues when I went for the training. I giggled. I didn't want to sound as though I was interested! It had been such a while since sex. I thought back to the last time with Tom before his illness, over a year ago at least.

I had put sex to one side, but maybe not forever.

Chapter 17

I had thought that Stan and Evie would be worried after I'd been ill, that at some point they'd want to have a conversation about what would happen when I got older. I'd actually been looking forward to it – I felt ready for these kinds of discussions now. But nothing. Maybe they didn't realise I was getting old at all? The newspapers were full of the care crisis again; stories of court cases with parents suing their children for not repaying loans, or children taking their parents to court to evict them from their houses. The local press on the island had endless adverts relating to elder care; ads for charities like Citizen UK, or local solicitors offering special deals on wills and setting up powers of attorney.

Thank goodness I was away from all that. Or was I? At some stage I'd have to do something about my own will, which was written before Tom died and named Stan and Evie as next of kin. Maybe I should leave everything to Matilda and Hugo. It had been ages since Evie mentioned me going to live with them, despite that fact that she herself had said, "You need looking after." At first I'd been relieved not to be nagged, but now I began to wonder if it was all was okay between her and Andy.

Stan was even worse. He'd rung to say that he'd had a disaster with one of the investments he had made. I thought for a moment that he was going to ask me if he could borrow some money. He always used to talk that sort of thing over with Tom and they often made investments together. Last week he actually had the nerve to try and advise me on financial matters! "I've been looking into it Mum. and the way things are going, you do need to be careful. I was thinking we should look at powers of attorney."

"You mean if I live much longer?" I asked. "Never mind, I can always come and live with you, can't I?" I added, laughing as I thought of the look on his face. The truth was that I was getting by just about okay on my pension, but I also had to admit I was always worried about the monthly mortgage payments. Island living was turning out to be more expensive than I had envisaged, despite me being quite frugal. As an increasingly popular retirement destination, prices were rising.

I hadn't heard anything more from Kevin about Sambot coming to stay, so I called him and he answered straight away, "Ah yes, I was waiting for the go-ahead. Good to hear from you. It's been held up while we did covid checks, but we can go ahead now."

So Sambot was finally going to be a reality. While I waited with some trepidation for the big day, I noticed that the new driverless cars were taking off on the island. Some clever person had set up a kind of environmental "white van man" company for automated local deliveries. The were called 'Notcars', and were all electric which meant that they were quiet and had no nasty fumes. This made a lot of sense on the island where the distances weren't huge.

One morning, I decided to get the bike out again. I pulled it out from the shed and pumped up the tyres. The exercise would do me good. There was a chance of me getting fit at last if I cycled to the shops now and then. Once I got into the rhythm of it, feeling the wind in my hair and sun on my face, I spun along feeling very pleased with myself. The road into the village was quite narrow and wound around old cottages and the occasional large tree. There were several moments where I began to doubt whether this was a good idea – when I had to get off and push the bike up a small hill, and when I slowed down too much when a car passed – but the cycle home was better. With my rucksack laden with lentils, fruit and a bottle of wine from the local village store, I free-wheeled down the hill in the afternoon sun, taking in a deep breath of the autumn air. I felt happier than I had for a long time. Maybe that ECT had done me some good after all. I was ravenously hungry and smiled as I stopped to pick some of the wild garlic leaves, thinking they'd make a nice pesto sauce to go with the pasta that evening.

I slept well that night and, feeling full of energy again the next day, I decided to bike along to the local library. There were masses of romance novels and some Joanna Trollope on the shelves, but nothing I could see that would keep me riveted. So I scanned the science shelves for robots and machine learning. There was even less of interest there, so I ordered some Margaret Atwood books and *To be a Machine* by Mark O'Connell which had a chapter titled 'Please Solve Death.' I'd started it in London but never got to the final death chapter which somehow now felt essential. His idea that you could solve death through trans-humanism felt like hope, and his anthological survey of people who believe technology will give us eternal life was both wonderful and hilarious. The best-case scenario was the version of the future in which we merge with artificial super intelligence and become immortal machines. The idea that we might be more likely to be killed by an ingenious computer program than to die of cancer or old age seemed basically insane. Or was it? I was reminded of the ECT machine. I certainly wasn't going under that again, no matter how bad I felt again in the future.

It wouldn't be long now before Sambot came to stay. Would it feel like a stranger in the house? Or a machine? Safer than a human being and not so intrusive but maybe dangerous in other ways, although I couldn't pin down exactly how.

One morning, there was a loud knocking on the door. I assumed it was Kevin come without warning. I was in the middle of using my new yellow Henry Hoover with the bright smiley face on the side. But when I answered the door, there was no Sambot. Instead, there stood a stout middle-aged woman with greying hair in one of those tight old-fashioned perms that still seemed to be popular on the island. She was dressed in a nurse's uniform under her navy raincoat and looked vaguely familiar. She smiled one of those smiles that stop at the mouth and took a step forward. I took a step back and almost stumbled over Henry. I halted as she moved forward again in a stilted dance.

"Can I help you?"

"I'm Mrs Finlay, I've come from the clinic. Don't you remember me from your ECT?" and with that same smile again, asked encouragingly, "Can I come in?"

But I wasn't encouraged and certainly didn't want her to come in.

"You see," she went on, "It's really important when you start a course of treatment that you finish it."

"I'm sorry, but I'm not sure I want to do any more sessions."

Apologising was a mistake; I knew that the instant I'd said it. She immediately became larger and more official. "Why don't we sit down and talk it through." And this time I stood aside when she moved forward. Deflated, I went through to the kitchen where she followed me and sat down on the kitchen chair. She could do with losing a little weight, I thought. I offered her a cup of tea and a biscuit which, after hesitating, she refused. Once she'd had her tea, with two sugars, she looked at me again with beady eyes and pulled out a form which she put firmly down on the kitchen table with a pen.

"This is the consent form for treatment. Could you please sign it now whilst I'm here? Then we'll be all set up for the next session. The surgery will text you, confirming the time and I'll see you there. Don't forget to fast the night before." I reached for the form which she seemed to think meant I was agreeing because she went on,

"Your daughter came last time, didn't she? There's no need for her to come again, I'll send a car to pick you up."

I nodded, thinking it would be difficult for Evie to come down again so soon anyway. But how could I get rid of this woman? Signing the form seemed the only way. So I did. At least I'd made her happy. It meant that I was booked in for another ECT in two weeks' time. I tore up my copy as soon as she'd left. They were only trying to help, weren't they?

I didn't tell Evelyn about the visit. When the nurse called me again two weeks later, I knew the voice immediately, "Hello, it's Mrs Finlay here again, I'm calling to say you didn't turn up for your ECT yesterday. You really do need to complete the course of treatment you know."

I shivered at the sound of her voice and caught unawares began apologising again, "I'm so sorry, I had a bad dose of the flu, but I'll be in touch next week to fix another date I promise."

I never did of course, and she didn't chase me up again, at least for a while. When Evelyn asked about the follow-up on her weekly call that night, I changed the subject and told her about my wobbling on the bicycle instead. "Why don't you wear your cycle helmet Mum, then at least you're protected if something happens?"

"Actually, it's my knees I'm more worried about but you're right, I'll do it." I said, while doubting that I would.

A week later, when I was cycling on the road to the village again. One of the Notcars came humming by very close, so close that I pitched sideways into a muddy ditch. The bike was okay but as I stared down the road at the rapidly disappearing car, I wished I'd taken its number. Then I realised they didn't have car registration numbers in the same way that old cars do. Instead, they had a sort of transparent QR Code on the back window. And, they were all the same beige-green colour. So it was impossible to identify it now. I decided to ring the local depot when I got home.

"What are Notcars supposed to do if there's an accident, please?"

The official sounding voice was annoyed, "What do you mean? Has there been an accident?"

"Almost, well yes." Why was I being defensive? "I was bicycling along the village road this morning and a Notcar came far too close, I swerved off the road into a ditch."

The dismissive voice said "Can you give me the time and place details please? I'll need to check the records. Normally that sort of thing would get reported automatically but I haven't been notified."

"Well, it wouldn't be reported because it didn't see me. You can't hear them until they're almost upon you. I suppose it was bound to happen sooner or later. Surely there should be sensors on to check if there were humans ahead? "

"The early Notcars aren't fitted with sensors as a matter of course but they will be in the future. They're a bit like robots in that respect."

"At least robots are programmed with 'Do no harm'" I snapped back.

"I assure you our Notcars are safe."

"What happens if they have to choose between running down an old lady and a Mum out with her toddler in the pushchair?"

"They would have to consider which option would do the least harm," the official went on pedantically. "So they would choose to save the child and its mother, thus saving two lives rather than one."

I put the phone down, still puzzled as to why that Notcar didn't seem to see or sense me. Maybe I was becoming a Notperson – invisible even to inanimate machines. Perhaps I had let myself go more than I realised.

I took Evie's advice and started wearing my cycling helmet when I went out – at least when I was cycling – although it was actually also tempting to wear it when walking to the beach past Rooks corner. One day, I decided it was high time to visit Peggie and Edward. I phoned in advance to check they'd be home and set off. The road was quiet and the ride uneventful. As I pulled into their driveway, the farm gate was wide open and dogs were rushing around with excitement barking furiously in greeting. Peggie came striding down the driveway, in gardening clothes and secateurs in hand as usual, calling out, "Edward, see who's here! Anna's come to see us at last!"

We went through to the old kitchen as Edward came slowly through, taking small steps. He looked at me uncertainly until Peggie cried out, "Well, give Anna a hug then!"

We sat around the kitchen table whilst Peggie put the kettle on and opened the cake tin to a mouth-watering lemon-drizzle cake. She cut me a large slice and chattered away while Edward sat there quietly. He had certainly aged quite a bit in just the one year since I'd last seen him driving the old Land Rover when they took me to see the house for the first time. I couldn't imagine this man sitting across the table from me, driving. He just sat there with his tea, absorbed in his piece of drizzle cake, nodding from time to time. I decided to wait until Peggie was alone before I asked her about him.

After an hour, it was beginning to get dark, so I said my farewells and promised to call her the next day. On my way back, along the same stretch of road between the village and the cottage, I noticed something moving around on the lawn outside the old people's home. Curious, I pulled across and stopped to watch a small round, dark green machine moving continuously across and around the wide grass area. It had flashing lights like slit eyes either side of what reminded me of a bulging forehead. A robot lawn mower! Sadly though, instead of moving around in straight lines and leave nice neat tracks, it moved randomly around. What would the birds think of it I wondered. I had a vision of it escaping and mowing down all the fields across the island before it was finally captured.

The weather stayed fine so the next day I took a stroll down to the beach, hoping I might bump into Patrick again. At the corner where the rooks nested high above in the tall swaying dark trees, I paused. They were building their nests and seemed to be louder than usual. Their endless swooping and swirling was building up to a frenzy. I walked slowly on round the corner and onto the last stretch of road to the sea and the beach where I knew the noise of the sea would reduce my stress levels. The sea had always made me feel stable and secure – looking at how the surface of the sea gets lost on the horizon in a flat and continuous way, had always made me feel safe.

As soon as I had passed Rooks Corner, I was met with a cadre of Notcars coming towards me. As usual, there was no warning sound, and they rushed alarmingly silently and speedily towards me. There were no pavements or even paths on that side of the road so I couldn't properly step out of their way and was forced into the fuchsia bushes on the side of the road. There were about six of them, following one after the other, identical olive-green robots on wheels. They must have been heading for some event. They were unlikely to be returning again this way anytime soon but, feeling anxious and scratched from the hedge, I decided to turn back. As I did so, the squalling of the rooks became louder as they swooped and dived all around me. At first, I thought they were attacking me and I put up my arms to protect my head but they seemed to be forming a protective shield between me and the Notcars, or was I imagining it? The Notcars, meanwhile continued past me on down the road off into the distance.

I walked back moving as quickly as I could up the road towards the cottage. I didn't run, thinking it better not to show any panic. What felt like an eternity later (although it can only have been minutes), I swung into the garden safely and the squalling of the rooks died down. Had I imagined it after all? Shaking and frightened I locked the front door, something I never usually did. I drew the curtains just in time to see the silent procession of Notcars glide back past. I decided not to mention it to anyone.

Some of the anxiety that I'd experienced before the ECT came back in a rush. Living alone wasn't always a happy thing. I loved the isolation, but now I wanted someone to talk to. Someone to touch and to hold my hand. I missed having someone on my side; the business of the ECT niggled me and needing sorting out. So the next morning I phoned the clinic. They wanted to put me straight through to nurse Finlay, but I was ready for them and said quickly, "I'm sorry, I'm in a bit of a hurry. Could you just pass the message on to her that I'm doing the Robot programme so I can't come in for the next appointment? I'll call her as soon as it's over." I put the phone down before they could transfer me.

The next morning, almost in answer to my call, the invitation for the Robot Induction Programme arrived. It was to take place the following Monday.

Chapter 18

Mrs Finlay called Evelyn, "I'm so sorry to bother you, but I'm afraid I have some bad news about your mother."

"Oh my god, what's happened?" Evelyn imagined the worst. "Has she had an accident?"

"No, but I am very worried about her. She missed one ECT appointment and now she's cancelled the next one. That means she's still only had one session out of the six the doctor prescribed." Then she added firmly, "I think she's getting forgetful and deteriorating again."

Evelyn called Stanley that evening, "Mrs Finlay, the nurse, called me. Apparently, Mum didn't turn up for her follow up ECT treatment. Mrs Finlay went on and on, saying that she must complete the course of treatment or she'll get worse again."

"Why can't they just leave her in peace?"

"Because she's obviously not well, for goodness's sake, Stan. Get a grip! Did I tell you that she was completely obsessed with those huge black birds when I was down? She said that they were stopping her from going out."

"Like in that Hitchcock movie, *The Birds?*"

"Stan, please take this seriously. They come and settle on the grass outside the back door, foraging for food, I guess. They have this way of strutting around and then looking up at you with their head on one side. Most other birds would just fly off when you open the door, but not them."

"Maybe they're just trying to be friends," laughed Stanley. "Mum said the old lady used to feed them."

"Why don't you go down and see her yourself?"

"Stop the guilt trip, Evie. But I might do that soon. Listen, we've got some good news," he paused for effect … "Cassie and I are going to have a baby!"

"Wow, that *is* good news! Congratulations Stan, I'm so pleased!"

"Yeah, me too. We'll have to think about getting married now."

"Getting very grown up, aren't we? Can Matty be a bridesmaid? She'd love that."

"Maybe. Cassie's organising it all, and she's got masses of relatives. "

"Okay, let me know. That is great news. I'm really pleased. The fancy car will have to go. No room for a baby in that!"

Stanley paused, putting his hand over his phone for a moment, and then said, "Cassie's just come in. She says hi, and she agrees about the car, but I'm not sure I do!"

"Say hi back! Listen, I'm worried about Mum. If she gets early onset dementia, she'll have to go into a home. We'd have to sell the house to pay for it."

"No, idiot, that's why Dad put it in our name. We just have to hope to Christ that they don't change the rules or something. Why don't you ask Mrs Finlay about dementia? You can get extra money if it's a health condition."

"It's always about the money with you, isn't it?"

"Anyway, I don't think they send people into care homes anymore. This new project I'm working on means that people can stay in their own home for as long as possible. It's cheaper to send in help – even robots. Maybe we should get a robot for Mum?!"

"What the hell Stan? I haven't got any spare cash hanging

around, do you?!"

"Okay, I am a bit short myself, too. That's why we moved back home. Anyway, if we have the money from the house, we can do whatever we like, can't we?"

"Thank goodness for that, then." Evie said sarcastically. "But Mum did say they're experimenting with robots on the island … "

"Let's get one for her next birthday! I'll check it out. The private equity owners were talking about investing in robots to save wages. It's big in Japan."

"Perhaps it's like the solar roof panels. They give you it for virtually nothing to get you hooked? Anyway, I thought you were changing direction?"

"Well, not right away now, with the baby coming. I'm stuck with the firm for a while longer."

"Didn't Dad lend you some money to help with the retraining? You can't just take it and do nothing."

"I guess that'll just have to go towards the wedding now. That's what Dad would have wanted. Anyway, I'll make a point of going down to see Mum soon, I promise."

"Don't change the subject. I could do with some help with the kids going to uni."

"It's your problem if you want to send your kids to uni."

"The house is in both our names, and I'm buggered if I'm going to let you just take it over. I bet you haven't told Mum you've moved back home?"

"Look, let's talk again when I've been down to see her. Don't you dare tell her though!"

"When you're there, check out this Patrick. He seems to be around quite often, bringing her carrots, she said. But he didn't show up when I was there."

"She must miss Dad, I guess."

"I can't help wondering what will happen next."

"You mean he might move in?! That would be a bloody disaster," said Stan angrily. "I'll talk to her again about setting up the power of attorney."

"Having said that, if they did live together, he wouldn't have rights to Pond Cottage, would he?"

"Depends on whether he's a tenant or whether he's just a lodger. But she could easily give him protected rights for his lifetime or even build him into her will."

"Oh god, I'm so far away. But I really can't go down again now with Andy the way he is. Go soon!!"

"Stop overreacting. She's always been independent, and she's pretty tough," replied Stanley.

"Tough she may be, but she's getting older too, you know."

Stanley said bluntly, "You mean she won't last forever?"

Chapter 19

Monday morning came around and I found myself whizzed off in a Notcar to Ryde. We pulled up to a large brick building with a new sign that said 'Robot Network Programme Depot'. As we were escorted through the building to the training room, twelve shiny white Sambots were lined up like identical washing machines in the corridor. They stood there hanging their heads down, their extra-long arms almost trailing the floor. Each one had a differently coloured surround to their screens – blue, green, yellow, purple, etc. They looked innocently calm, just waiting for us to breathe life into them.

Meanwhile, covid had struck, so we had all been told to wear masks and to wash our hands when we arrived and left. I decided not to talk too much about myself during the training and that turned out to be wise. The classroom rapidly filled up with a dozen men and women, all in their sixties and seventies, mostly looking fairly healthy. There were equal numbers of men and women, which was unusual as women usually outnumbered the men.

We were each allocated a small desk. I guessed the desks were probably a hangover from the building's sixth form college days. There was a chair which swung out to let you in and then back again to form the desktop. We all struggled to squeeze into the seats.

There was just enough room for a notebook or tablet. Most of the others had their iPads out and were looking at photos or Facebook, or doing sudoku. There was all the usual chat about being taught by three-year-olds how to use their tech. At one point, the conversation drifted off into a generalised rant about young people today and all their machines, which I thought was a touch ironic, given we were all volunteering to have robots in our homes … "You see those young mums with their phone on their ear all day and poor baby screaming its head off in the push chair …" "My daughter's little one is only three but she's already swiping the screen to see the cartoons …"

I was tempted to intervene, but I kept my thoughts to myself. I didn't have an iPad, just my old work laptop. I wondered if that would make a difference. Would I get a more intelligent robot?

The conversation died down as the man up front cleared his throat. "Welcome! My name's Zack, Zack Keeley." He gave an impossibly white, toothy grin. "I'm from the mainland, but Kevin here is an islander now." Kevin stood up and nodded, "and we're going to be your 'keepers' during this pilot project."

Keeper Zack, probably in his thirties, was slim and slight, and wearing tight black jeans and a buttoned-down white shirt. Fashionable luminous dark glasses were pushed back over his spikey hair. Kevin was dressed more casually in brown corduroy trousers over a loose checked shirt.

Keeper Zack continued, "We used to be called 'programmers' until the powers that be decided that was a bit too techy, so they changed our title to 'guiders'. But we thought that was a little too girlie, like girl guides." He laughed apologetically. "So we asked to be called 'keepers', like in a zoo!" He laughed again nervously.

The audience remained silent.

"Any questions so far? Please give your name when you speak."

My neighbour piped up. She was a buxom woman with bright blond bouffant hair who looked vaguely familiar. "I'm Jude. These robots, I'd just like to make sure I feel comfortable with mine, given I'm going to be alone in the house with it. What sex are they please?" She nudged me, laughing. I couldn't help giggling too, until Keeper Zack's affronted glare shut us both up.

"Don't be silly," said an angular man with his hand in the air who'd been buried in his sudoku earlier, "it doesn't matter! They're all the same, aren't they? They're just machines!"

"What's your question, sir?" enquired Keeper Zack, clearly pleased to have a diversion.

"My name's Pete. I used to be a maritime engineer, now I just go fishing. I had an early robot a while back – a mini robot dog who moved around the house picking up rubbish. When I put it outside, it turned its hand to tidying up the leaves ... after it learned about the pond and stopped falling in," he added. "My question is, can these ones multi-task as well?"

"That will come in time. One step at a time please!" said Keeper Zack, smiling and nodding. "Any other questions?"

"Are they all male then?" insisted an anxious-looking man sitting on the other side of me.

"Well," Keeper Zack said carefully, twirling theatrically on his heels towards him, "we always refer to them as 'it' but they are, of course, completely neutral."

"It's just that if they're going to be helping around the house," continued the anxious man, "I'd rather it was a female. I was thinking I could call mine by my wife's name, Doreen. She passed two years ago." As everyone turned to look at him, he added, "I think it's a good idea to get extra help in the house. I was really struggling after my Doreen died."

Keeper Zack took a deep breath. "We can talk about that later, but for the time being, you're free to give them any name that you want. Now, let's get you meeting your new companions."

He turned and nodded to Keeper Kevin. I knew I wouldn't really enjoy the whole project until I was alone with Sambot or whoever it would be. Suddenly I began to have second thoughts about the idea of taking responsibility for something or someone else again – the last time had been looking after Tom and that had hardly been successful. But the robots didn't actually need us, of course. It was supposed to be the other way round, wasn't it? One could hardly be expected to worry about whether they were hungry or bored. I stopped daydreaming as we were handed out our schedules.

"It's time for your one-to-ones. You'll each meet your very own robot and choose a name for it. Then you can start some simple programming and let them get used to your voices."

When the 12 robots were brought into the room and activated, I could sense a slight humming noise. Mine had a bright orange surround on his screen that made the screen glow. I thought it looked cheerful, so I decided in that moment to name him 'Henry' after my new smiley hoover, although it would be difficult to think of him as anything other than Sambot. There can't have been much difference between the old Sambot and this new one. Or was there? I was looking forward to finding out more about their emotional intelligence, if indeed they had any. Did they laugh and have a sense of humour? How much of the five senses were they programmed for? Did they have touch, taste and smell as well as the more obvious sense of seeing and hearing? When question time came again at the end of the morning, I asked Keeper Zack, "What about the five senses? I mean, I guess it's obvious they can see and hear, but what about touching and tasting? And smelling?"

"Robots don't have feelings. And in the true sense, they don't have the five senses … although they can be taught to seem to 'hear' and 'see'," said Keeper Zack. "We can now also programme them to smell using an e-nose and the air-conditioning system if there is one in the house. But tasting and touching are different."

Pete, the man next to me, shifted in his seat. And Jude, my garrulous neighbour, nudged again, but thankfully stifled her giggles. As I didn't really get an answer, I decided I would experiment when I got Henry home. Either Keeper Zack didn't know, or he didn't want to give too much away. He would have me down as a troublemaker now and I wish I'd kept my mouth shut. As the keepers handed out further instructions to each of us chosen ones, we were herded through the door. I was to be one of the 'twelve disciples' who also included bubbly Jude, Pete the fisherman, and the lonely widower, Simon. The robots were to stay with us for a month, then go back to the factory to be reprogrammed before we got them for good. We had all been through the licensing procedure for the final placement and contracts were signed.

***

The day Henry was due to arrive for his month's trial, I tidied the whole house and swept and mopped the kitchen floor. I didn't want Henry getting hurt whilst in my care. I decided to leave the cobwebs – on the grounds that the spiders caught the flies, which meant using less fly spray. Would Henry notice? Would he see the dust and the dirt or even smell if the rubbish needed emptying? It would be useful if he could tell what was going off in the fridge … maybe even stop me pouring sour milk into my tea.

On the morning of Henry's arrival, I wandered out into the garden through the dewy grass and picked some narcissi that were still in their tight white and green buds. They would open up in the warmth of the kitchen and their pungent scent would fill the cottage. I thought it would compensate for whatever machine-type smell Henry would inevitably have. At 4pm I went outside, as instructed, to see a large, white square-sided van coming slowly down the narrow road. As it pulled up outside my cottage, just to one side of the overgrown privet hedge, Keeper Kevin, beaming as always, jumped down. "Afternoon, there. I have a real treat for you. You're going to try out one of our fifth-generation robots!"

He unlocked the back doors of the van and pulled out a ramp.

There was Henry, his bright orange screen shining cheerfully. I backed into the house and Henry trundled along after me on the wooden trolley up the old stone pathway that I'd carefully swept clear so there were no leaves to send him sliding. He looked just like the Sambot I remembered although he couldn't possibly be the same if he was fifth-generation. What did 'fifth-generation' mean anyway?

As we went through to the kitchen, Keeper Kevin explained, "It's fully charged, but I'll set it up with your password so that it'll only answer to you." As I reached forward to touch Henry's head, he lit up with a slight whirling sound and lifted his face up towards me. Keeper Kevin stumbled back, "I've never seen that happen before," he exclaimed. "It responded to your touch without a password."

Henry was looking up at me, just like Sambot had two years ago.

"Hello" I said, "My name is Anna. Your name is Henry" I wasn't talking to a machine anymore. His bright eyes shone back at me as he inclined his little head and repeated,

"Hello, my name is Henry. How are you?"

"I'm well, thank you. I think I remember you. "

Henry didn't reply. Keeper Kevin sat down heavily at the old wooden kitchen table and began unpacking a folder of official-looking papers. I watched to make sure he didn't knock over the vase of narcissi that were just beginning to open in the warmth of the kitchen. Henry stood quietly to one side as I made tea. Clearing his throat, Keeper Kevin looked at me curiously and said, "Well, you two are off to a flying start. When you first came across our carebot, did you give us your password?"

"No, I always used my fingerprint as my password for my laptop back then. I never used a written password. Why?"

"They stopped that facility when robots came in properly. Did you actually touch it when you first met?"

"I'm pretty certain I shook his hand. Yes, I'll never forget the feeling of his hard fingers gripping mine."

"That explains it, then. The early carebots were programmed to take the DNA of everyone they met to help with their programming. Nobody really understood what that would mean at the time."

Jesus wept. What on earth did they think they were doing? I felt a surge of alarm and anger rising within me. "Kevin, can you remove my DNA from the system now?!"

"Sorry, that's above my pay grade. I could ask when I'm back in the office, though." Kevin still didn't get it, so I held my tongue. No point in harassing him. He was just the messenger. I began to realise that I had no idea who (or what!) the designer might be? Who was really behind all this? Kevin continued, seemingly with no awareness of my alarm at all, "these fifth generation carebots are programmed to mirror some of the more human characteristics of people's emotional intelligence. They can't obviously acquire them any more than they can develop a sense of humour, but it can *seem* as though they do."

"How does he 'recognise' me?"

"Using AI. It was still quite limited when you met it at the conference, so it wouldn't have recalled much – mainly just who you are. But this version you have now is the highest specification we have so far," he said proudly.

"Are you saying this Sambot, I mean Henry, will seem to have feelings?"

"Yes, it will seem to. But remember that in reality, robots don't have any emotional intelligence or creativity ... at least that's what it says in the manual," he added, looking doubtful.

"So when people talk about them taking over jobs, that's rubbish? I mean, you need some creativity and emotional intelligence for most jobs, surely?"

"Well, yes. So they won't take over those jobs needing creativity and emotions, but they'll be able to do quite delicate physical things soon."

"Delicate like what?"

"They've just come up with one that can pick out individual leaves from mixed salad crops. Their touch is so light that they can pick individual leaves without bruising them, despite their actual muscle strength being immense."

I thought back to the nurses' reunion, and the possibility of a sharp diamond ring tearing the paper-thin skin of frail older people, and shuddered. "Then the idea is that they will be able to take over the personal care of older people in time?"

Henry nodded as if in agreement.

Kevin kept looking at his watch and I began to realise I was terrified of being left alone with Henry. It felt like the time I was first left alone with Evie as a new born baby. "Are you leaving him with me now?"

"Yes, that's what it's all about, isn't it? So, you don't feel lonely."

'I LIKE being alone,' I wanted to scream. Why on earth had I agreed to this?

"It's your very own companion robot and we want you to use it to do the little jobs we talked about," he said soothingly. "We'll come back and assess at the end of the month."

"Is it alright to leave him on his own?"

"Yes, of course. Remember, you were told all about that in training. You can always ring the emergency call centre if you're worried, and you can get advice from the manuals online any time."

"Yes, yes, of course, thanks. I'm sure we'll be okay," I said, trying to sound calm.

Kevin looked at me with his head on one side.

"Just remember to talk to it as much as you can about you and your past. That way, it builds up as full a memory of you as possible and you can have little chats. Try and teach it something new each day."

"Sort of reminiscence therapy?" I laughed.

"Well, actually yes, we hope we can keep more older people

living alone for longer. It's especially good for people with dementia and memory problems."

"Well, I'm not there yet! … I'd rather have him any day than ECT." I muttered.

"Did you have ECT then?" He perked up. "I don't have that on your record. When was it?"

"Oh, a while back. It's probably not there because I didn't follow it through. I'm fine now."

Keeper Kevin scrawled a note on his iPad. I wished I hadn't blurted it out, but it was too late now. I could hardly ask him not to say anything. It would sound too paranoid. I did hope it wouldn't spark off another visit from Mrs Finlay, but then Kevin wasn't connected to Mrs Finlay, was he?

I stood at the doorway as Keeper Kevin waved goodbye and disappeared down the old stone pathway into the gloom. The bats were beginning their evening ritual of frantic dipping and darting. Normally I would have gone out in the gloaming to sit at the end of the garden and watch for the owls swooping down and away across the meadow with their nightly feed of tiny field mice and voles. But I'd had enough for one day. Back in the kitchen, Henry was just standing there, waiting. I had to turn him off. I had to find the right words. Or a switch. Finally, I said very firmly, as though I was talking to a child, "Time for bed now Henry, I'm going to have a glass of wine and get some supper. Then we can both have an early night." Nothing happened; he just stood there waiting, so I tried again, "Good night."

That did it. He dropped his head, going into close down, just standing where he was. He was halfway between me and the rest of the kitchen, but I certainly wasn't going to wake him up again. So I squeezed past him, poured out a glass of wine, and then, grabbing the whole bottle, I rushed out and shut the kitchen door on him. Although I turned the TV on loud, I still couldn't block his presence out.

All through that first night, I sensed him, waiting, watching, listening. I locked my bedroom door, but it didn't stop the dreams. I dreamt of being held down by huge mechanical machines and woke up in a sweat to find I'd forgotten to open the window. I sat up in bed and listened for any sound. Normally I'd have gone down and made myself a cup of tea, but I didn't want to wake him and then panic about how to turn him off again. I finally fell back into a restless sleep around dawn.

When I came down for breakfast and, unusually for me, fully dressed, Henry was standing beside the back door. I thought I'd left him further in the kitchen, but I'd been so tired I couldn't remember for sure. I said cheerfully and loudly, probably too loudly, "Good morning, Henry. Did you sleep well?"

He stirred immediately and with a faint whirring noise, he turned his head in my direction and moved his hands and arms towards me, in an oddly human gesture. "Good morning, Anna. I hope you are well. I do not understand the question. I do not sleep."

"Yes, well, umm, of course not. Now then, after breakfast, I want to try out some new things with you. I know you can hear, and I know you can see, but I want to check if you can smell. Are you up for that?"

"I cannot go up Anna, it is not possible for me."

"No," I laughed, I would need to watch my language! "I meant, are you happy to do some research with me?"

"Research is good."

"I want you to learn some new words each day. And I want to know if you can smell and taste as well?" Henry looked vacantly at me. Too late. I remembered that it's important to keep it simple. One question at a time. "Okay, the first word is my favourite lunch, 'chop,' 'lamb chop.' I want to have lamb chop for my lunch. Can you tell me where it is? "

"Yes, of course, Anna." He moved forward, not towards the fridge, as I'd expected, but through to my study, and came back a minute later, carrying my laptop.

"Here is your laptop, Anna."

Clearly, teaching Henry how to cook was not on the menu. Not just yet, anyway. So, I tried again. This time I decided to try out his sensory skills. "Time for breakfast first, then. I am going to eat eggs and toast. Let me see if you can smell the toast."

I'd wanted to see if he could smell toast, but accidentally put it on too high and it began to burn. As soon as the smoke began curling up, Henry went into fire alarm mode. Still standing there in the kitchen, he began emitting a high-pitched scream. At the same time, the smoke alarm went off in the kitchen. The combined noise filled the whole house with an ear-piercing cacophony. Then my phone bleeped. It was the RNP texting: 'The Fire Alarm has been activated. Please confirm if you require assistance.' I ran around turning everything off, and once I'd texted the RNP that all was well, the noise levels returned to normal. I asked Henry again, "Can you smell the burnt toast?"

"I can see that there is a fire. Fire is dangerous. I must protect you from fire, Anna."

"Thank you, Henry, much appreciated. But can you smell the toast burning as well as see the smoke and fire?"

"I cannot smell any burnt toes. I do not have toes."

By now I was past eating, both the eggs and toast went into the bin, and I made some porridge in the microwave instead. I would check out Henry's five senses another day.

I spent the rest of the morning talking to Henry about my life — my children, my work, and what I thought of political issues. In return, he seemed to listen carefully, holding his little shiny head to one side and always nodding when I mentioned care. He only talked back if I asked him a direct question or gave him an instruction. Somehow, that was reassuring, but also a bit irksome. I wondered how the other Twelve Disciples were getting on. Maybe they weren't quite so demanding? I would no doubt find out soon enough.

I was careful to avoid talking in too much detail of anything financial or the upset over the house in London. After all, the Robot Network Programme would presumably be downloading all the information and storing it away for future reference, so I guess Henry only had half my story. But in any case, my old life in London, and Tom's death, all seemed so far away now.

As the days passed, we fell into a routine. Every morning, Henry would wake up before me and begin hoovering and cleaning. For the first few days, I couldn't work out how to reschedule his activity, so he would usually start his chores nosily at 6am on the dot. I finally worked out how to reschedule him to 8am, and at last the day started more peacefully.

Henry did all the simple things, like reminding me to take my pills. I took the statins and the blood pressure ones but still drew the line at the little pinkies. I wondered if Henry noticed that I didn't take them; he never said anything if he did. We also spent half an hour each day learning new exercises from the NHS website. Together, we managed to reset my Fitbit programme so that all my physical activity was recorded. That was a major triumph! But my mental and emotional activity was at zilch. Why was it that robots weren't interested in that side of things? I thought back to my old boss Ed, and his obsession with the happiness and mindfulness programmes. Ed wasn't a robot, even though he often behaved like one.

At the end of the month, I began to feel like I might have had enough; it was like having a permanent guest to stay who needed to have everything explained very simply. I'd get irritated by him, and then disconcerted, in quick succession. He was also amusing sometimes, and I found myself talking to him rather more than I thought I would.

I rang Evie to tell her about Henry, but she was unusually impatient. "Look Mum, I'm glad you're doing this, but do be careful. It's all Big Brother stuff and from some of what I'm seeing with the children, robots can be dangerous."

She was obviously busy, so I said I'd catch up with her later and tried Stan. "Sounds great Mum! I didn't realise you were doing this; I do know quite a bit about robots in care – or more specifically in care homes – from the project I'm working on."

"Is that why you were at that venture capitalist party? What was that guy's name again? You never told me what you were doing there?"

"I'll explain it all when I come down and see you. And I think it's James Hillingdon you were thinking of. He was asking after you."

I blushed, pleased to be reminded of James, but I knew better than to get my hopes up for an early visit from Stan and went back to programming Henry. My new best friend. I worried sometimes that I'd said things I shouldn't have – especially after a glass of wine or two. Things about being irritated with Evelyn and Stanley, and about missing Tom. One night, quite late, I told him I was missing the sex, and he said, "Please explain, what is sex?" So I told him to close down for the night. I remembered in time about the clause saying robots were not to be used for sexual purposes. Oh dear.

Overall, it was a relief when Keeper Kevin turned up at the end of the month to collect Henry. By then, I was desperate to be alone again. I could see that it was useful to have him to remind me when to take my pills, and to prevent me from having to make lists, but it seemed a quite extravagant way of having a To Do list!

When Keeper Kevin rang me a few days later, he was bubbling with excitement at the news that I'd passed all the tests with top marks. He told me I was being allocated a permanent robot. He was so obviously pleased, I wondered whether he got a bonus for making a successful placement. "Your new robot will be arriving in two weeks' time once it's been reprogrammed to take account of your preferences."

"Kevin, thanks, but I'm not sure I even want another robot.

Not just yet anyway. Let me think about it." I wanted to talk it over with someone before agreeing to what felt like a huge commitment now.

Did I detect a note of panic in Kevin's voice as he continued insistently? "Anna, this is really important. You've been selected to have a sixth-generation robot!" He emphasised 'sixth.' "It'll have a special programme for your health and wellbeing!"

That evening after supper, I called Stan. He was so enthusiastic and talkative that I rather wondered if he'd been rehearsing a sales pitch. "Mum, the sixth-generation robots are amazing! They can walk up and down stairs, cook, and serve you meals. They have special programmes designed to monitor your behaviour and help with any health problems. I thought they were still at prototype stage, so I'm really impressed you're getting one."

Wondering if I was being ungrateful, I replied, "I just don't know I want to sign up to a machine living with me all the time. It was quite fun for a while, but this is different. It's full time." I hesitated, wondering if I could really trust Stan, but came out with it anyway. "I also get the feeling, it's weird, but almost as if I'm part of something bigger. I don't feel in control of it. Why me after all?"

Stan didn't seem phased, "Mum, you're worrying too much as usual. When did you say it's arriving? I'll come down – I'd love to meet it!"

So a robot is what it would take to be reunited with my son, I thought gloomily. I rang Keeper Kevin back the next day and agreed I'd go ahead for a trial period. "That's great news!" the relief in his voice was palpable. "I'm sure you won't regret it!" This time, I wondered just how much his bonus would be. "We'll just need to get signatures from yourself and your next of kin as soon as possible."

"Why on earth do you need next of kin's signatures?" I asked with that sinking feeling again.

"It's recommended for all the new sixth-generation robots," he said breezily. "It's to do with insurance. They're so sophisticated and expensive, we don't want anything going wrong. There's also a special 'sunset clause' which needs to be signed by you for this phase of the trial. It's part of a new power of attorney that's being brought in."

"I'm not sure I like the sound of that." I wasn't going to be pushed around by Kevin, or by anyone.

"There's nothing sinister in it!" He laughed, "we just want to try out all the procedures and make sure we get it right for future generations. You're part of a hugely important research programme now."

Chapter 20

When Stanley was young, he was always very good at looking innocent and reassuring me by telling me just what I wanted to hear, "Yes, Mum, of course I've cleaned my teeth," or later as a teenager, "No Mum, I'd never take *any* drugs!"

Tom said he'd grow out of this propensity for insincerity, but I had never been sure he would. Now I knew I had to accept him as he was. He did, after all, seem to be very knowledgeable about the care industry, and that really pleased me. Perhaps he was beginning to understand how important it is for everyone to grow old happily? Although he didn't really seem to understand that his own mother was getting older. Anyway, I was looking forward to showing off my new robot and watching Stan being impressed as I took the robot through his paces.

Two weeks later, Kevin arrived at the cottage again and introduced this new robot as 'Henry 2' and the name stuck. He was a lighter, brighter version of the original Henry, and he seemed, in his body language, to be more responsive. He could walk about and climb stairs, and our early morning chats were quite nice. He'd ask me how I'd slept, which nobody else did these days, and I got the feeling he really cared. I knew it was ridiculous, of course, but it helped to build a relationship and that's what I had to do now that he would be with me for the foreseeable future. I tried to persuade him of that old adage 'breakfast like a king, lunch like a prince, and dine like a pauper' – but he ignored this and always produced a healthy breakfast of fruit and yoghurt. No more eggs and bacon, or even avocado and sour cream.

Henry2 didn't need any basic programming because that had been downloaded to him from Henry – so at least we weren't starting from scratch. I did wonder briefly what else they had added-in, but decided to focus on making him mine this time. The health and fitness regimes were a little more complicated, and I now had certain targets to reach including a set number of steps per day, and various stretching and balancing exercises. I insisted on adding bicycling and swimming as part of the regime and so, on the whole, the new routine suited me well. I was becoming fitter and slimmer by the week. I felt ten years younger.

The first time Henry2 brought me a cup of tea upstairs, I got a huge fright. He just came into the bedroom carrying a mug of tea. I did know that he could climb the stairs and open the bedroom door, but robots don't announce themselves. I rang the RNP the next day and asked how I could programme him to knock on the door, but the keeper just laughed – why should I be worried about a machine coming into my bedroom? So I let it go.

This time, I was determined to pursue my earlier interest in how good these robots were with the five senses. I knew Henry2 couldn't smell burning toast, but he could see it and so raise an alarm. Keeper Zack had dodged my question, so I suspected it was quite a complicated and developing issue. Henry could clearly see, hear, and touch but not taste or smell. Could I programme Henry2 to add those things? And if I could manage that, what else might I programme him to do? I started with the question, "Henry2, please can you tell me what the five senses are?"

He replied, "A 'sense' is a physiological capacity of an organism to provide data for perception."

"Okay, thanks. Please tell me which of the five senses you can use?"

"There are six senses Anna. I can do what I am programmed to do."

Six senses was news to me, I would need to Google it. But for the time being I continued. "Can you smell and taste?"

"If you wish, I could be fitted with an 'e-nose' which would allow me to recognise various distinctive scents like alcohol, blood, urine, and sweat. This will be helpful when you grow older Anna and need more help." Oh, god, I wish I hadn't asked! "Robots can also taste but I am not programmed to do that yet."

"Maybe we could try an experiment and see if you can develop your taste and sense of smell with something that has a strong taste and smell. Like curry spices for example?" Henry2 didn't reply, but he looked as though he was considering it. Too soon to ask him about touching and feeling, that would have to come later.

As the days went on, he established himself in the kitchen. He was soon organising all my meals although they weren't always to my liking – mainly too bland. I guessed that cooking more sophisticated foods would have to wait until he developed his sense of taste. I dare say the robot programmers were not as interested in haute cuisine as I was. At least the salads, carrots and fresh greens were undeniably healthy. We did have one contretemps early on when Henry2 tried to intervene over my wine drinking. When I asked for another glass of wine with my meal, he said, "I cannot serve you more wine, Anna. It is not good for you to drink more than one glass of wine in the evening with your meal."

"Are you serious?" I asked, feeling taken aback.

"Yes, I am not allowed to be frivolous." Came the speedy response. No sense of humour either then.

I poured another one for myself anyway and raised it in mock salute, but he had already turned his back.

What was that sixth sense that he had mentioned? A sudden

flash-back to Tom extolling the virtues of "Data" – the Star Trek android who was taught how to touch and feel – made me smile. Tom and his fantasy life – he had firmly believed that the sixth sense, extrasensory perception, or "ESP", included precognition – the ability to tell the future. I began to wonder whether Henry2 might be capable of this. I decided it was probably not wise to test Henry2 too much. At least not yet. Maybe later. The way that Henry2 seemed so intuitive and responsive made it seem as though he had actual emotional intelligence. Of course that couldn't be right, but he was much easier to have around, less intrusive and calmer, than Henry had been. He just moved seamlessly around the house and kept things going. He never got in my way and the fact that he didn't have to be told what to do all the time was a relief!

As the weeks wore on, I began to worry that he might not have enough to do and might therefore get bored. And if that happened, then perhaps the keepers would recall him and hand him over to someone else who needed him more and could make better use of him. I didn't actually really need him, but I began to enjoy his presence downstairs while I was sleeping – like having a combined guard dog and alter ego. I wondered what had happened to the other Twelve Disciples and whether they might be feeling the same. I rang Keeper Kevin to ask, "I'm wondering if it would be possible to meet up with the others in the group, please?"

"Why do you want to meet up?" Keeper Kevin replied, suspiciously.

I'd anticipated him putting up some objection, so I had my response ready, and said sweetly, "I really want to check my performance. I want to make sure I'm using him to maximum effect but I'd also like to see what the others are doing, maybe pick up some tips?"

"I'll come back to you on that. We also need to complete your paperwork. Can you give the details of someone for the next of kin signatures? I'm being chased down by the powers that be."

I explained that Stanley was coming down soon (he hadn't yet made it) and agreed to ask him, although I still wondered why it was necessary. Then I realised, with a pleasant shock, that it was nearly my birthday again. Maybe Stan and I could celebrate it together. I've always loved birthdays, they become increasingly important as you get older. Tom had always made a big fuss on my birthday. Bucks Fizz for breakfast, a visit to the Tate or the V&A, then a special lunch and a walk on Hampstead Heath followed by dinner at home with candles and planning the year ahead. Pulling myself back to the present, I warned Henry2 that there would be an extra mouth to feed, but I got the disconcerting impression that he already knew. He seemed to know everything. I would have to warn Stan not to talk too openly in front of him.

When Stanley called out-of-the-blue to say he was actually finally on his way down, he said that he'd meant to come down earlier, but with the weather as it was, and work piling up, and every weekend now being precious with Cassie. Too many excuses, I thought. Always best to stick with one. The last time I'd seen him had been last year when I'd gone up to London for my birthday treat. I had planned to pick up some pictures from the house and had asked Stanley to get permission from the tenants, but Stanley said it would only make me miserable if I went there. So, we had my birthday lunch at a wonderful little Italian restaurant outside Waterloo Station instead. Pity, as I'd dressed up for the occasion and had been looking forward to wandering around.

The drive to the ferry in the Notcar had been interesting. I'd noticed that a lot of building had been going on across the other side of the island, especially on the north coast near the ferries and the east coast where I hardly ever went. The last time on the ferry had been full of older people and it had been hard to find a seat. In the end, I'd squeezed in alongside an elderly couple who were arguing about who was paying for what out of their pensions. The wife seemed to have the worst of it. From what I had gathered, she was still paying for all the household expenses, but since the mortgage had been paid off, he now had little, or nothing, to fork out. I was very tempted to intervene, but I kept my mouth shut. Although I had enjoyed seeing Stan, the noise of London had bothered me on that trip and I had decided not to go back again if I could avoid it. My world had shrunk, at least in that respect.

Stanley had told me that he would be arriving on the early-morning Red Jet passenger ferry. He'd booked a Notcar to pick him up at Cowes. He called me en route to say how impressed he was with all the building going on in some parts of the island, and with the Notcar! He couldn't believe the change that had happened since the last time he'd visited when the island's narrow farm roads had been full of horse riders, herds of cows, sheep crossing the road, and endless streams of lycra-encased cyclists. He sounded pleased that they'd all disappeared; Stan valued efficiency above everything else.

I came out into the road waving when I saw his Notcar pulling up. It reminded me of when he used to come home from school. As he paid the Notcar, it moved off straight away. I looked at it warily. Stan gave me a big hug and told me that it was like hugging a lighter-weight version of what I'd been before. "My goodness, you're looking good," he added, enthusiastically.

"All the better to eat you with," I replied, right back. It was an old nursery joke of ours from *Little Red Riding Hood*. He was pleased I hadn't forgotten the punch line and laughed.

I felt childishly flattered. "Come and meet Henry2, I'm sure you two will get on." It felt the same excitement as though I was introducing Stan to a new friend.

As I made the introductions, I also added some cautionary notes to get them out of the way. "Just treat him as a laptop. He's a mine of information but be careful how much you say in front of him. I do wonder sometimes if he's trying to brainwash me, or make me behave better – he refuses to serve me more than one glass of wine."

"Good for him!" Stanley said and immediately began putting Henry2 through his paces. He started by launching straight into the sorts of things that his office wanted to know. I don't think Henry2 minded and if he was a little surprised, he didn't show it. Stanley's main interest was with practical things like how to turn him off and if he could do it himself. When Stan asked Henry2 what he would do in an emergency, I explained about the burnt toast, but it seemed as though that wasn't the sort of emergency Stan was interested in. I left them to it and went out to finish the gardening.

The days flew past. We managed to go for a couple of long walks along the beach, and I asked him to help dig out a new path for the pond; I had replaced the old manky base with a wildlife pond.

"Patrick helped me with that in the spring," I explained. "It needs a stone path around it to stop the grass falling in."

"Any chance of meeting this Patrick?" Stan said, looking up as he lifted the stones.

"I'm sure he'd love to meet you," I replied, "maybe in the next day or two."

"I actually need to head back a bit earlier to meet Cassie from the station. Which reminds me, we've got some good news for you. Guess what?"

"Don't keep me in suspense? What?"

"We're having a baby! Cassie's pregnant, we haven't said anything before because things go wrong but its due in a month or so ... She's just been to tell her parents!"

"And you're only telling me this now?! But that's wonderful! I'm so pleased! Clever you and clever Cassie!

"I'm scared! It's an expensive business having babies!"

Trust Stan to make money the first thing. "Not necessarily Stan, babies don't actually need a lot you know!"

He paused and then said, "Mum, we'll need to look at your will again."

I turned away to sit down on the garden bench, "Stan, I'm delighted to hear about your baby, it's such good news but don't spoil it by talking about my death. I'll look at my will when I'm good and ready." I changed the subject, "What's happening with the house, I meant to ask?"

"The house is fine. It's being well looked after and I'm there regularly to check, of course. Sorry Mum but I just wanted to remind you that you'll want to think about taking into account our little one now too. Not just Hugo and Matty."

"As I said, I'll look at my will when I'm good and ready." I felt angry and under siege for the rest of the evening.

The next morning, there was a knock at the door and there was Kevin – beaming as usual. Stan was still getting up, so I invited him into the kitchen and Henry2 made us coffee. Kevin launched into business straightaway. "Thanks for your call. It'll be good to get all the paperwork finished."

I nodded as I heard noises upstairs, "My son will be down soon."

Kevin carried on enthusiastically, "The network thinks it would be an excellent idea to get all participants of the robot programme together. We'll make it a proper review meeting and see how you compare, and what the data tells us. I'll be fixing a date soon." And then he added, "I'll be retiring soon myself, but you'll be in good hands."

I had a feeling that he'd made it his idea, but it didn't matter. Stan came down freshly showered and smelling of soap. I introduced him to Kevin, and he took Kevin away into the sitting room to work their way through all the next-of-kin permissions ... and the 'Sunset Clause' that I hadn't seen yet. When they came back, I looked up from the kitchen table where I'd been waiting, pretending to read a book. "Is everything alright?"

"Yes, don't worry. It's all standard stuff." Stan patted me on the shoulder. "The robot will stay with you for this year and then they'll do another review to see how it's all working before they decide what next."

"I thought Kevin said they needed us both to sign something. And what's this 'Sunset Clause'?"

"It's all in the contract here, nothing you need to worry about." Stan had the papers tucked under his arm. I reached out for them and with a slight hesitation, he handed them over.

I read them that evening when Stan went over to see Brian who was staying with Peggie and Edward for a few days. I could never understand why Stan and Brian got on; I couldn't see that they had anything in common, but it later turned out that I was wrong.

Under the 'Sunset Clause' heading, the small print said that if a person 'in the care of a sixth-generation robot' became ill and needed permanent long-term care, then proper procedures were in place. These procedures included DOLS, DNR, POA, the financial arrangements, and the End of Life Care Plan. I thought it was an odd way of putting it, that I was in the care of a robot, but the requirements also surprised me. Definitely time to step up my fitness regime.

I left the papers out on the kitchen table meaning to discuss them with Stan in the morning. But when I came down the next morning they had gone, along with Stan. He had originally said he'd stay for a week, but had only managed five days because of wanting to pick up Cassie – or so he said. We never did get around to discussing the Sunset Clause and I didn't celebrate my birthday that year.

Chapter 21

Stanley rang Evelyn as soon as he got back home. "Mum's got one of the new robots!" he said excitedly. "She calls it Henry2."

"And how is she?" Evelyn wasn't sure how she felt about the whole robot business. "What about the ECT appointments?"

"Mum's fine," he told her. "She's like a quieter version of herself. It's difficult to describe."

"That's not surprising given all she's gone through. The ECT really shocks the system, but it's worth it if it's working."

"The prototype is amazing! It live streams information on Mum back to the depot so that they can keep an eye on her the whole time!"

"What does she think about that?!"

"I'm not sure she understands. She knows it happens in theory, but she chats away to it as though it's a good friend. I get the impression she quite likes having it around."

"Is it safe though? It is a machine, after all," said Evelyn cautiously.

"Of course it's safe! Machines are a lot more reliable than people. Much safer than some of that foreign labour. In fact, I'm thinking of investing in them."

"What foreign labour or robots? Anyway, how come you're in

the money all of a sudden?

Stanley hesitated. "I was going to tell you. I've decided to take out a loan using the house as collateral." And then he added hastily, "I want to invest in this new robot project while I can."

Evelyn was shocked. "How dare you try and do that without telling me! It's my house too!"

"Look, I'll pay it back when we sell the house, so what's the problem?" Then, changing the subject, he said, "Maybe you'd like to come in on the robot investment programme too?"

"You've got to be joking!"

"The research programme Mum's signed up to is really cutting edge! There are groups of twelve of them all over the island. Mum calls her group the 'Twelve Disciples.' They all have one of the sixth-generation robots. If this trial goes well, elderly care will be changed forever!"

"Sounds dodgy to me. But the good news is we won't have to give her one for her birthday!" Evie joked.

"Damn! I forgot all about her birthday. Dad always used to remind me … But I expect birthdays don't matter that much anymore when you're her age," he reassured himself.

"You must have been talking to Andy." Evelyn sniffed.

Stanley went on, "I didn't get to meet her new boyfriend, but it was 'Patrick this' and 'Patrick that.' We need to keep a careful eye on that!"

"I thought you said she's entitled to a boyfriend!"

"She's not lost her looks – she's fitter than ever, I'll give her that! She's quite a good catch with the house and everything else – so who knows what might happen! Patrick might be planning on moving in."

"Does it matter if she's happy?"

"I don't like it. I had a drink with Brian when I was down."

"Brian says they're completely past it and they're refusing to leave the old farmhouse. He's pretty pissed off about it. He wants to

The Laughing Robot

cash-in on the property bonanza that's hitting the island."

"He hasn't changed. What's our house worth these days?"

"Estate agents are having to really work for their living now. Nearly three-quarters of people used to own their own homes, but now it's down to about half – and almost all of them are sixty and over. That's the Baby Boomers for you."

"What about our old home?" Evelyn insisted.

"House prices in London are holding up better than elsewhere – I reckon it's worth around £1.2m now. London gets lots more investment from places like Japan and China."

"Christ, you sound like an estate agent. Let's put the house on the market then, now that Mum's settled. Better get a move on – time is marching on and so are the robots," said Evelyn sarcastically, laughing at her own joke. "I can't help feeling things are coming to a crisis," she added, more seriously. "All my friends are worried about what's happening to their parents. They say you can't find a place in a nursing home for love or money – that's if you could afford it! The hospitals are all completely blocked up with geriatrics too."

"The Island is doing the right thing," said Stanley. "Mum got her robot from the lot I'm working with now – The Robot Network Programme. The previous owners, Citizen UK, lost the contract. I quite liked the robot. It was doing all the chores, and it even tried to stop Mum from drinking too much. Good luck to it!"

"I'm still worried," said Evelyn, "they are machines, after all. Anything could happen!"

"But anything could and does happen with people anyway. You hear about abuse by carers the whole time."

Evelyn snorted, "Now you're sounding just like Brian!"

"You really don't like him, do you? Anyway, Mum said the council stepped in, and that's why Peggie and Edward gave Brian power of attorney to keep the council out."

"Let's pray we don't have to go that far with Mum," said Evelyn, worried.

"The new POA is all mixed up with the DOL's regime. It's all to do with keeping them safe and stopping them from wandering down the streets in their nighties."

"Ah yes, I remember now! Mrs Finlay said it might be on the cards when Mum was so dodgy last year. She wanted me to sign something called the 'Sunset Clause', but I never did."

"Don't worry, I've done it," said Stanley, before changing the subject. "So you're best friends with Mrs Finlay now, are you? You know Mum hates her guts."

"Well, only to keep an eye on Mum. I'm not sure I like her either, but she was good over that ECT business. If you didn't talk with Mum about it, I'd better check with her on her next round of treatment."

"I'll definitely go down again next bank holiday with Cassie. And I'll get a valuation for the house in the meantime too."

"It's all very well for you living rent free in the house, but the kids want to go to uni. People like Andy are losing their jobs; journalism has all but disappeared."

"Well, I've got all that to come now, too. Don't get all antsy about us staying in the house. We need somewhere to live after all. And now that we've got a baby coming, we'll have to think about what that means for the inheritance."

"What do you mean?" Evie asked suspiciously.

"I'm assuming your kids are written into Mum's will, but ours should get a share too."

"You don't miss a trick, do you?" replied Evelyn. Typical of Stanley. "Remember, Mum still has rights of residence, so in theory we couldn't sell the house without her agreement."

"What do you mean, 'in theory' ... ?"

Chapter 22

I loved seeing Stanley, and I missed him. When he left, my sleep was full of dreams of Tom and the children when they were little, but it was good to get back into my own routine again. The latest in the health columns was that unless you use your muscles, you lose them; they quite literally just waste away. One morning, I strapped on my monitor with the intention of striding off to the beach and leaving Henry2 in charge of the chores, but first I would have to deal with a growing problem of Henry2 and the birds.

The sound of the rooks really worried him, especially whenever they came into the garden. He would stop whatever he was doing at the time, lift his head, and watch them without moving. I had begun feeding the little birds – the robins, blue tits and house sparrows, but I often had to shush away the bigger birds when they came to steal the seed. The little ones would scatter as soon as the big birds swooped down, and this is when Henry2 would get distracted. What was going on?

This morning, Henry2 froze as soon as the rooks appeared. Intrigued, I opened the back door. It was clear that he did not like the harsh metallic sound of the rooks cawing. I thought back to the first voice of Sam the Robot at the Social Services Conference and its high-pitched metallic sound. Over the years, the robot's voices had been modified to a gentler tone and a more melodious speech pattern that was much more pleasing to the human ear.

My mother used to find any loud metallic sound very hard, and it could be extremely painful for people wearing hearing aids. I wondered, did sound matter to robots too? And if so, how could we overcome this? Especially as I was convinced the rooks were protecting me from the Notcars. Patrick had told me that they were a protected species, the rooks not the robots, but would that last forever? And how were the Robots programmed for sound? They seemed to make a soft humming noise themselves when they were active.

When I finally set off for my walk, I rounded Rooks Corner to see Patrick walking up the lane towards me, carrying a large bunch of rhubarb leaves. "Hi there," he said, "All going well?" I felt a rush of warmth towards him.

"Yes, all's fine," I smiled, and looked up, indicating the rooks above. "Tell me, why don't the owners of this house get rid of the rooks from their trees? They make an awful noise."

"The owners have moved back to the mainland. A lot of the locals are selling up now that the prices are going up."

"What about the rooks?"

"Those rooks are protected. It's their home. Once they've nested, you can't touch them. Don't get too close when they're nesting – they have a habit of 'mobbing' any intruders who come too close when their eggs are hatching."

"Sounds dangerous," I shivered.

"Well, it doesn't last long. Like most creatures, they want to protect their young and their territory. They can sometimes form 'attack' groups and hunt together for food. Rose used to feed them to keep them onside – but I'm not sure that was a good idea."

I laughed, "Don't worry, I won't be encouraging them!"

"Want some early rhubarb? I've just come down from my allotment."

"Looks delicious!" Taking a couple of the freshly cut bright pink stalks and smelling their sharp yet delicate aroma, I went on, "Can you tell me anything about the owls in the old village hall?"

"They're Barn owls. They nest there most years. They're protected as well but, like the bats, it's all year round." He lowered his voice conspiratorially, "We don't talk about them, to keep strangers away. Are you seeing them, then?"

"Yes, I see them quite often. Usually in the gloaming, swooping silently out across the field."

"If they've nested, you'll hear the baby owls calling for their supper. They make a loud screeching noise and then you'll know for certain."

"Yes, I've heard that too. I nearly bumped into a badger recently. It was a bit scary staring at him face-to-face. Do you know what they eat?"

"Something like two hundred worms a night!" Patrick laughed then and paused, "… I've read they sometimes eat flesh too."

"What sort of flesh?!" I cried out, my skin crawling.

"Well, just as in baby rabbits and things like that. Although I did read that in India, they've been known to dig up bodies."

He shook his head. I wished I hadn't asked, but at least I knew now. No more facing up to badgers! He turned away, waving whilst I carried on down to the beach with my sticks of fresh rhubarb. I'd been pleased to see him, but there was no sign of our relationship developing.

The sun was warming the grassy pathway to the beach and the scent of the creamy-white, barely flowering cow parsley hit me like a wave of incense. As I walked through the knee-high grasses along the worn, sandy pathway, dozens of tiny blue butterflies fluttered up just inches above the grass and disappeared again as soon as I'd passed. These were the Chalk Hill Blues, usually only found along the south coast – from Dorset to Sussex. I looked down over the crumbling cliff edge and saw the beach was deserted and the tide low, exposing vast expanses of gleaming flat sand. On a day like this, I would be able to walk at the sea's edge for miles along the bay.

I wondered if I would get the chance to bring my grandchildren down to the beach. Stan's little one would be coming along soon. Hugo and Matilda were growing up so quickly, especially Matty. She was sixteen, going on twenty, and so graceful and charming with her mother's wonderful dark red hair and pale skin. Hugo was still at that awkward adolescent stage, all arms and legs, and braces on his teeth.

I loved the wild weather on the beaches in winter; those days when the huge waves came crashing down, forcing the sea against the cliffs and huge rocks would tumble down and expose dinosaur footprint fossils with their three-pronged toes in grey plaster-like stone. In summer, the famous purple- and rust-coloured lines of sand that cut across the cliffs in an endless stream of colour would be in full view. The sea was as liquid silver, streaming in ripples over the wet sand. And further out, it beckoned me to swim.

Just when I was daydreaming, I spotted a coach up ahead, blocking out my view of the beach. It was huge, parked on the gravel car park and taking up enough space for ten cars or more. It began disgorging a load of misassembled, pale families with young children. One man, presumably the guide, began talking. "Here we see the different layers of the earth clearly identified. Starting with the brown topsoil, just like in your garden, then the thinner layer of stones, yellow and beige, running all the way along until at the bottom it turns mauve and purple. That's the layer of the dinosaurs," he added, pointing, "who were here over 200 million years ago." He pointed to a grey stone footprint fossil lying solidly on the shifting sand.

The mention of dinosaurs got the immediate attention of the children. A small boy went up and tried to lift the stone. His mother said, "Leave it Tony." But Tony wouldn't leave it, bless him. He pushed and pushed, his feet dug into the sand as he pitted all his weight against the claylike stone. I smiled, admiring his determination, and briefly wondered if he'd like to build a sandcastle.

Thoughts of Tom were receding and being filled with the excitement at seeing Stan and Cassie's new baby, Troy. He'd been born quite suddenly, and the photos were gorgeous. It no longer seemed possible that I could travel to London, or even to Wales, and I felt sad that I wouldn't be able to see the new baby until he was bigger. Zooms and Facetimes weren't quite the same as holding the little thing in my arms. I missed Evie too; it had been nice when she came down to see me, even if it was to force feed me the idea of ECT. I made a mental note to show Henry2 the recent photos of the grandchildren that I'd been sent on Instagram. Perhaps we could print them and stick them up on the kitchen wall for when they visited.

"It's not you, Mum," explained Evie on the phone, "they're teenagers now and want to do things with their friends at home." I wish I'd given up work earlier and spent more time with them, or taken them away to foreign places. Tom had never seemed that keen, and I was always busy. It was too late now. Maybe it could be different with Stan and Cassie's baby.

I continued walking to the next beach along the coast, Compton Bay, which was well known to surfers worldwide. They descended there on a regular basis in their VW vans hand-painted with New Age symbols, and often stayed overnight in the deserted carparks. The waves turned into huge rollers on the rising tide, gathering speed and height as they rushed over the smooth, flat sands. Most days, like today, there were at least a dozen black rubber-coated figures, like sleek slugs, paddling out in a frantic frenzy and then twisting and turning to ride the crashing waves back to shore.

I left my towel and clothes on the dry sand at the top of the beach and strode out to the water in my swimwear. Feeling the familiar shock of cold and then gradually acclimatising, I was conscious not to venture out too far, cautious of the strong tides and currents that swept under and around my body.

Experts say that the sound of the ocean helps to reduce stress. Apparently our bodies absorb the negative ions that are released by ocean waves. There's no doubt that seeing the surface of the sea, spreading out on the vast endless horizon, made me happy. The beach was constantly changing shape, becoming flatter and shorter as the sandy soil tumbled down from the crumbling cliffs. After my swim, I climbed the steep steps at the far end of Compton Bay to watch the grey and white sparkling waters crash on the beach below. Even the paths down to the beach were gradually sliding into the devouring sea. Would a huge giant wave one day come rushing over the horizon and sweep over the entire island, drowning us all forever?

Chapter 23

One sunny morning, invigorated by my higher-level exercise regime, I decided to cycle over to Peggie and Edward again. Everything was safe at home with my new watch dog, Henry2, on guard. I asked his advice on the best way to get there. He was cautious as ever. "The route is hazardous with hills and curving roads. Please travel carefully. It will take ninety-two minutes walking, thirty-three minutes on a bicycle, sixteen minutes on the bus, and eight minutes in the Notcar. There is no bus and so the best way is to travel is via Notcar."

"Thank you, Henry2, that's much appreciated."

"I will order you a Notcar."

"No thanks, I think I'll beef up my health and well-being programme by going on my bike."

Henry2 nodded approvingly, as I suspected he would if I mentioned my health programme. I went out to the shed to check the bicycle while he found my health monitor. It was becoming increasingly difficult to do my own thing under his ever-watchful eye. I wondered again how the other 12 Disciples were managing. I was pretty sure that Jude would be finding ways around the system, and Pete would be wanting to try out new things. But dear old Simon would likely be just happily sitting back and letting it all happen.

I knew by now that Henry2 would be monitoring my heartbeat and blood pressure via my wrist monitor whilst I was out. He sucked up all the data that he could on my health and wellbeing, as well as my whereabouts and actions. But he could only do that if I was wearing my monitor or sitting in a monitored vehicle like a Notcar. What would happen, and what would he do, if he couldn't trace me?

Henry2 pumped up the tires, although they hardly needed it; he accomplished in two minutes something that would have taken me at least ten. After fastening my helmet and filling a small rucksack with water, an extra windproof rain jacket, and an apple, I set forth. At the last minute, I added a jar of homemade damson jam that I had finally managed to make in the summer. As I left, Henry2 was hovering again. I'd have no carpet left soon. I must remember to programme him to clean the windows next. He never seemed to notice the cobwebs or was he nervous of the spiders' webs?!

Out of sight and sound, just around the corner, I climbed off my bike and hid my monitor in a safe place under a stone by the old bus stop. I didn't want him to know exactly what I was doing. And I wanted to test whether he would challenge me, although I wasn't really sure why. The journey took much longer than I had anticipated, but I wasn't in any hurry. I stopped several times on the way, partly to catch my breath and also to admire the rolling, wooded hills of the Downs. The stream that had been running full earlier in the year, and bursting full of wild watercress, had almost dried up. There were hardly any signs of human life along the way; several of the smaller cottages along the roadside were closed up, although one or two of the larger farmhouses still looked lived in. I laughed when saw a new signpost, 'Westerby Manor', outside one. The grounds were beautifully laid out with sweeping lawns and no sign of any rogue lawn mowers. The stripes of carefully manicured lawns were evidently important for the owner of this place. It seemed a far cry from before. All the tiny farm shops and notices outside cottages saying 'Fresh Eggs,' 'Duck Eggs,' 'Firewood,' and, best of all, 'Free Manure,' had gone. As had the bunches of freshly cut flowers and the large plastic bins full of 'Free Apples.' What was causing all the changes?

The narrow farm lanes were overhung with wild hedgerows bursting with creamy white Hockney May blossom and elderflowers that were heavily scented and weighed down from a recent shower. The occasional bramble swept down in a vicious curve, and the gentle breeze brought a pungent waft of wild garlic. I caught the glimpse of a shallow dip between the trees that was filled with the spiky green leaves and delicate white flowers of the garlic plants.

Life was good, and I was so much happier to be outside rather than travelling in the stifling safety of the Notcar. I couldn't expect Henry2 to understand that. After about twenty minutes, the lane began to rise steeply towards another hill – this one covered in dense evergreen trees. As the hill drew closer, the trees on either side of the lane created a cool, dark tunnel. These were the old pathways which, for hundreds of years, had made an intricate network between all the farm cottages and farm houses. I heard a large lorry or tractor rumbling nearer and nearer ahead until I could smell the diesel fumes. A tractor was closing down fast on me. I panicked that the driver wouldn't be able to see me and I would be crushed in his path. The helmet wouldn't be much protection and there was no place to go; the road was too narrow. Backing down would have been a nightmare. I pedalled as fast as I could towards what looked as though might be an opening ahead. The engine's noise was getting louder and louder until, thankfully, a farm gate indeed appeared and I pulled myself and the bike over.

Breathing heavily and sweating with panic, I waited for the tractor to pass, but instead, it slowed down. I felt for my mobile in my pocket and cursed myself for leaving the monitor behind. Juddering to a halt, the driver jumped down. He was younger than

I expected, muscled arms tight in a faded tartan shirt rolled up above his elbows. He stared down at me. I could smell the dust and dirt on him in the cool shade. He said nothing for a few seconds. Then asked gruffly, "You lost?"

"No, I'm okay, thanks." Something stopped me from saying where I was going. Could he be one of the prisoners out working on the island?

He stood with one arm blocking my way and continued to stare down at me. "There's nothing up there anymore. It's all deserted."

I nodded and reached for my bicycle. He frowned but made way for me to move on up the hill. As I peddled as fast as I could, panting heavily, I could see him in my mirror, staring after me. As soon as he was out of sight, I heard the tractor engine rev up again and breathed a sigh of relief as the noise of the engine disappeared down the hill.

At the top of the hill, I realised my legs were shaking – I don't know whether from the exertion of cycling, or from sheer fright. I stood holding the bike and looking out over the rolling hills, taking deep breaths. In the distance, I could see the tractor pulling over into the newly named 'Westerby Manor' that I had passed on my way up. I continued the short distance, slightly downhill, to Peggie and Edward's old stone house.

The second I pulled up outside the house, I immediately sensed something different, something odd. Firstly, I couldn't open their large double-barrelled wooden gate. The small front garden was quite overgrown, and even the house looked locked-up. I thought I saw a small white face peering out of one of the upstairs windows, so I left my bicycle leaning against the gate and clambered over it. Jumping down the other side, I dusted the green mossy slime from my jeans – which only made it worse. I walked carefully forward, dodging the nettles. Just last year, the old house would have been buzzing with Peggie and Edward's voices and dogs barking, but now there was complete silence. I went round to the back door, which was usually open with the key hanging in the lock. It was shut and locked, so I went back to the front door and rang the doorbell.

After a couple of minutes, Peggie came to the door. She looked pale and thin, and much older. I realised that she must be in her late eighties. It had been almost a year since I'd last seen her. "How are you?" I asked as I reached forward for a hug, but she stepped back into the hallway, pulling down her sleeves.

"Anna, it's lovely to see you." Her voice sounded as if she had a sore throat. "I wasn't expecting you." She paused, "I'm afraid we've not been well and Edward's still in bed."

"I'm sorry to arrive unannounced. I tried calling to see if you were in, but there was no reply."

"I didn't hear you coming." She looked around vaguely.

"What's happened to the dogs?" I asked, "they usually make quite a racket!"

"Brian got rid of them. He said it was too much for us taking them out for walks. You remember Sandy? The golden lab? He was getting on a bit and there were messes everywhere when we came down in the mornings." She shook her head sadly. "Brian said he had to go." I wanted to ask why Brian couldn't have taken them out for walks himself. Peggie had loved that dog. Then she perked up. "Come in and you can have a chat with Edward. He'll be so pleased to see you."

As we went up the stairs, one slow step at a time, Peggie began humming. Upstairs, Edward was dozing in a bedroom that reminded me of Tom's sick room. There was a faintly clinical disinfectant smell, or was it Olbas oil? Peggie straightened his covers, but he simply snuggled down under the blankets and counterpane, so we quietly came back down again to the kitchen.

Peggie sat down at the old wooden kitchen table and burst into tears, sobbing and sobbing as though she would never stop. I went to put my arm around her and this time she didn't pull away, so I hugged her, holding her frail shoulders quietly until she stopped trembling. All her energy and forcefulness had drained away.

The kitchen itself was different from the bustling, warm place I remembered. There had always been stock simmering on the old aga and the smell of baking bread. The aga was cold and empty and the curtains were drawn, making the room gloomy. The old pine dresser which used to hold their best blue Wedgewood china was bare and there were cardboard boxes stacked beside it.

One end of the kitchen table had been cleared and a clean, white tablecloth spread out with a small tin container, a box of tissues, and a white towel. She saw me looking at it and moved in front of it, saying hastily, "We don't get many visitors these days. I'd offer you some cake, but I'm afraid it's all finished. I've got some biscuits though!" She jumped up to open a tin, but then shut the lid down again. "I'll put the kettle on."

"Thanks," I said, "Sorry if I'm interrupting something. Is Edward really not well?" As I gesticulated towards the equipment laid out at the other end of the table,

"Oh, that's for the tattooist," she replied. "He'll be coming by later today to finish off."

"Finish what off?" I was both confused and alarmed.

"It's the tattoo you must have now if you don't want to go on for ever. Brian arranged it all for us. Sometimes they tattoo your signature on too, but we didn't want to pay for anything extra."

I shook my head, still not fully comprehending, "Why on earth would you want to have a tattoo at your age?"

"It's for DNR." She lowered her voice, "you know, 'Do not Resuscitate'?"

"That's only for people who are terminally ill. Hospitals used to have a notice at the end of the bed and on the notes."

Peggie pushed herself up with both arms from her chair and I saw a recent bandage on her arm. She made her way to the whistling kettle and nodded eagerly, "I know, but Brian says it's best to have a tattoo on your arm or your chest, so that when the ambulance finds you, they know what to do." She paused and then added, as though remembering, "it's better on your chest and your back so that if you fall over, they can find it straight away."

I asked carefully, "I'm so sorry. Is Edward going to…" I hesitated, trying to find the right words, "die then?"

Peggie looked confused. "Well, no, not at the moment, but Brian said we should both have it done as a precaution. Especially when we move into the care home."

"I thought you wanted to stay here forever?"

She ignored me. "It's really quite normal now. I'm surprised you don't know about it. They do it along with that new power of attorney thing."

"Have you signed a power of attorney?"

"Yes, we had to when we handed the house over to Brian. That's why I'm packing things up." She indicated the china and the cardboard boxes.

My heart sank. What on earth was happening? I should have kept in touch. I changed the subject to give me a chance to process it all. It was none of my business, but I felt they needed protecting. "I wanted to tell you about this new robot programme I'm involved in. It's to help keep us all at home as we get older. I've just got mine, and it's working really well. I love it!"

"You always did like fancy new things," she laughed, sounding a bit more like her old self. "It's not for us though. Edward wouldn't like having strangers in the house."

"It's a machine! Not a stranger!" I protested.

"Now that we have this power of attorney we'd have to get Brian's permission to do anything like that."

"Who says? Are you sure? Didn't you used to have someone coming round to help you out?" I asked.

"Oh, you mean Maggie. She used to come three times a week, and she helped me have a bath. It was lovely." She smiled at the memory.

"What happened?"

"I rang the council, and something called the Adult Frailty Team. They said that home helps like Maggie were being replaced with robots. Maggie got into trouble, and she was told she couldn't come any more, so now we have no-one."

I took a deep breath. "Well, why don't I give her a ring and see if she'd like to come privately?"

"That would be nice, thank you," she smiled gratefully. "I don't know what Brian would say, but we don't need to tell him, do we?"

I laughed, and said, "No, he doesn't need to know."

"Brian said there was no point in us keeping the car now, and that we can use the Notcars instead. He's not keen on us going out too much." And then she added wistfully, "It would be nice to get out though … I'd love to get up to the blue bell woods at Mottison just one more time."

"Why don't I fix a car to pick us up and we can have a picnic together?"

"Oh, that sounds lovely!" She smiled, "I'll just ask Brian to make sure it's alright."

It was getting dark, so I had to leave without seeing Edward again, but I promised to visit again soon. The tattoo sounded bizarre – she must have got hold of the wrong end of the stick. I would check it out with Henry2 when I got home. I certainly wasn't going to have any long-haired hippies sticking needles into me, leaving messages on my body!

I was exhausted but felt I'd achieved a lot. At least I knew now how Peggie and Edward were, even if it wasn't good news. When I finally arrived at the cottage, I realised I'd forgotten to collect the monitor on my way back. I'd have to leave it for now. When I went through to Henry2 in the kitchen, he looked up and asked me if I was tired after the ride. It was nice to feel I was cared about.

"Yes, I'm worn out," I said. "I'm going to have a hot bath." I thought how lovely it would be to have a massage too.

"Would you like a massage to help soothe your tired muscles, Anna?"

Was he reading my mind? He said in an explanatory tone, "I will use special pummelling gloves so that the massage works well."

"Hmmm," I replied uncertainly. "Thanks Henry2, but not now. Maybe another time. Why did I feel so uncomfortable about the idea? I knew in theory that robots were taught to read emotions through voice tone and facial expressions, but this was the first time Henry2 had responded to an unspoken thought.

There was also the slightly shocking idea that he knew about touch as a sense. When had he learnt that? Kevin the Keeper had spoken about the veto around the sexual use of robots. Was I was ready to be massaged in that way by Henry2? I couldn't help imaging it as I lay soaking in the bath. The nature of riding a bicycle can be inherently sexual, of course. It had been a while since I'd experienced an orgasm, but that afternoon as I'd got off the saddle, I felt that delicious sensation that I hadn't felt since Tom.

I came downstairs to find Henry2 methodically chopping the vegetables to go with the lamb chops. This was my once-a-week meat treat, which was all I was allowed now. As he chopped and sliced away, I asked him, "Henry2, what do you know about DNR tattoos please?"

He replied, "DNR is a device used to warn medical staff not to resuscitate an elderly person against their wishes." And then what he said next shocked me. "It is mandatory now as a precautionary measure for all elderly persons entering care homes. It stops unnecessary hospital admissions, so it is a good thing. It is written into the new Sunset Clause."

The 'Sunset Clause' again. I didn't feel I had fully understood it. I continued with my questioning, "What about the tattoos? Why are they necessary?"

"Tattoos are made on an elderly person's front chest and on their back, so that clinicians can tell at once, if they fall ill, whether to resuscitate them or not." He spoke in his usual matter-of-fact tone. I thought again of my college friend and her obsession with her diamond engagement ring tearing the paper-thin flesh of older people in their hospital beds.

"I have one more question for you, Henry2. Have you noticed whether or not I hum at all?"

"No, Anna, that is not possible. The hum is an acoustic, possibly psychological, phenomenon. It consists of a humming, rumbling or droning noise that emanates from the earth."

So he didn't know it all then! I felt triumphant and a little pleased with myself as I had noticed there was definitely a hum coming from robots when they were active, which Henry2 didn't seem to know about.

"Well, let me know if you ever hear it coming from me, please?"

Henry2 turned back to the cooker to finish thoroughly grilling the lamb chops. He didn't approve of them being pink in the middle the way I liked them.

He didn't mention the monitor either.

Chapter 24

I didn't sleep well that night. An unusually bloodthirsty episode of *Casualty* filled my dreams with people being pin-pricked and gorging blood everywhere. I woke up in a hot sweat and gulped down a glass of water. Towards dawn, I drifted off again and dreamt of boatloads of old people coming to the island. So many came that there wasn't any standing room left, and they began falling off the cliffs into the swirling waves, screaming like seagulls as they fell.

When I finally woke it was late, almost 9am. I reached for my monitor, but it wasn't there, of course. I'd better rescue it from the bus stop as soon as possible.

Did Henry2 know I'd slept badly and kindly let me have a lie in? If so, it was disconcerting to discover that he could exercise discretion. When he came up with my morning mug of tea, five minutes after I woke, I decided not to confess about the monitor. Sipping my tea, I began worrying again about Peggie and Edward and decided to do some research on what services were available locally. They must be really struggling without any help at all, but maybe that was Brian's intention?

The local paper was full of complaints about the island not providing enough help for older people. The local MP was picking it up as an issue, but her main idea was that they should stop building retirement homes on the island. It was too late for that! It was like a feeding frenzy with more and more coming to retire here all the time – attracted by the good weather and old-fashioned ways.

The government's response was to ignore the worries of older people and focus on better health as being the solution. You could see why; one article had quoted the notable Professor Raymond Tallis saying that people were not only living longer but many were also living healthier lives as they aged. As the government latched on to that by creating a Health and Wellbeing Department, you could be forgiven for thinking that social care had disappeared altogether as a concept. Some would argue even as a reality. Radio 4 was running its usual Sunday morning appeal from charities, asking for donations. This time it was 'Citizen UK.' Charities are the good guys, right? The announcer said that Citizen UK was the first charity to offer robots as their primary means of support for independent living. Robots would also be supplemented with other services such as Telehealth, Telecare and Telemedicine. Citizen UK was looking for help to develop their robot scheme and to provide volunteers to train older people in how to use them. I wondered how that fitted in with what the RNP was doing with Henry2?

Time for research. I pulled my laptop over and searched for the Citizen UK website. Alongside the expandable baths, raised toilet seats, and the dangerous-looking implements to pick things up from the floor and open tins, was an insert. The caption read 'Caring with Robots.' It mentioned having a companion robot called a 'carebot' to 'keep you company.' Further down the page was section that was cosily titled, 'Gifting your Home.' It was accompanied by a pretty picture of a country cottage complete with thatched roof and rambling pink roses. The blurb went on to say, '*We all want to stay in our own homes for as long as possible, but dealing with the responsibilities of home ownership can become daunting. Our successful Gifted Housing Scheme has been running for nearly ten years and is one way to make things easier for you. As a donor, you will receive other benefits from Citizen UK. We will help you to arrange care and support at home with your very own carebot if you need it, and for eligible participants, we may make contributions to the cost. If you later want to move into residential care, we will help you find a suitable residential home and may contribute to your care costs.'*

The constant repetition of the word 'may' rang alarm bells. This sounded like a con job – especially if the old people were giving up all their savings. I couldn't see Evelyn or Stanley, let alone Brian, being happy about losing their inheritance, either. I read on. *'We are currently reviewing the terms of our agreement and are not accepting any new donations at the moment.'*

Puzzled, and thinking they probably wouldn't be open on a Sunday, I tried calling them. I was pleasantly surprised when the phone was picked up. "Hello, how can I help?" said a mature, efficient voice.

"I'm thinking of your Gifted Housing scheme for my aunt who lives alone, but on the website I see that the scheme is being reviewed? "

The voice on the other end of the phone sounded disappointed. Perhaps they had assumed I was calling about a donation. "Ah, yes, our Gifted Housing Scheme was very popular, so popular in fact that we've decided to review it."

"Why?" I asked.

"Because so many people were wanting extra care. We had to rethink."

A euphemism for running out of money, surely. So I asked, "I thought you took over people's houses to pay for all that?"

The voice, slightly irritated now, changed the subject. "We are developing an excellent new Health and Wellbeing scheme though. It's a support service for elderly people living alone. It's called 'Carebot at Home.' Do you think your aunt might be interested?"

I felt uneasy about talking about Henry2, so I didn't declare an interest. I just said, "I'm not sure my aunt would take to robots."

"Oh you'd be surprised! Lots of the old folk love them and the council is providing grants to help install them."

"Like those grants for solar energy panels to reduce your energy costs?" I joked.

"Yes, well, um, well." And she went back into auto drive. "We're in partnership with the council to try to reduce the costs of care. The number of older people on the island has almost doubled in the last few years. There's a real problem with finding the right people to help, so we're encouraging older people to use robots at home instead of home carers."

"How do I find out more – for my aunt I mean?"

"Just a moment and I'll take your details. We can arrange a visit and put her name on the waiting list."

I wanted to find out how the Robot Network Programme fitted in but I put down the phone without hearing more. Two minutes later, the phone rang but when I picked it up there as just a click and the line went dead. Back to the oracle in the kitchen. "Henry2, what can you tell me about the Citizen UK robots and the council?

I didn't really expect an answer, but he immediately put down the window cleaner and turned to me and said, "Citizen UK are a charity offering social care services to older people on the Isle of Wight."

"How do they fit in with the Robot Network Programme?"

"The Robot Network Programme is the premier global product that will transform the lives of older people worldwide. The health and wellbeing of older people is safe in their hands."

"Okay, keep your hat on. But what about this outfit called the Citizen UK ?"

"I do not have a hat. Citizen UK are not an outfit, they do not wear clothes."

Chapter 25

Stanley was trying to work out how he could keep his beautiful car. Whenever he passed it outside the house, he stroked its smooth body, loving its gleaming exterior. Whenever he got into the driver's seat, he relished the scent and feel of leather, but it was pricey to run. He hadn't told Cassie that he'd have to pay Evie for her share of the house and so, whatever happened, he would have to find a way to make more money. If only Dad were still around to help out.

He had thought for a while that the elderly care crisis could be the answer. His mates were raking in consultancy rates of over £2,000 a day but that was pocket money compared with cashing in on big profits. Cassie probably wouldn't approve, so he would find out more before telling her. The key was to get closer to the inner circles of the venture capitalists. He picked up the phone to James Hillingdon, "Morning James, hope you're well?"

"Good to hear from you Stan, how can I help?"

"I'll be straight with you, James, I'm interested in getting more involved with the robot project."

"What's bringing this on?"

"Well, I've just had a baby, starting a family … "

"Congratulations! Your mother will be very pleased to be a

granny I should think? By the way, what's happened to her? I don't see her at any of the conferences anymore."

Stanley hesitated, "She's gone to Wales to stay with my sister. I'll tell her you were asking after her." Why on earth he was lying?

"Well, give her my best when you next speak. I'd love to catch up when she's next in London. But yes, I must admit, your offer is timely ... I do need someone to support the work and to write a 'disruptive options' paper for social care and health. But I need to be straight with you Stanley, I'll expect absolute loyalty and it'll mean a lot of hard work if you want the big rewards."

"Count me in!" said Stanley, "I'm on to it. So, what's the line you want to take?"

"As you know, I'm all for prolonging life. The longer older people live, the more money we make out of them. It's as simple as that."

"I get that, but surely that's what the government wants to do too?"

"You could be forgiven for thinking otherwise! They're worried about older people living longer and costing more. They're beginning to cap certain interventions for the over 70s, you may have noticed. And by making no decision on social care, they're forcing families to do more caring, or pay for it, themselves. That means less profit for us."

"What's the answer then?"

"To get real about this, we must get the government to stop panicking about having too many older people to look after. I plan on doing that by using robots to replace the almost non-existent workforce. This is not for sharing Stanley, but I'm investing heavily in what they call 'carebots' from Japan. The first contingent arrived a few weeks ago, and we've got a highly secret research programme testing them out right now."

Stanley made a mental note to buy shares in robots. Then the penny dropped, carebots ... Isle of Wight ... research with robots.

Better change the subject. "What's the government's view? Will they just keep avoiding the whole problem like the plague and just hoping it will all go away?" he asked.

"The government have their heads in the sand. We need a revolution in care. Your paper needs to shake things up! Make them face up to the crisis, and now!"

"What about the competition? Companies like Telecare and Telemedicine are big providers, and growing."

"Good. You've done your homework. But most of that is stuck back in the dark ages. Our real threat is more radical competitors – in particular people like a man called Westerby – Professor Sir John Westerby. He's a geriatrician who's trying to monopolise the UK market. He wants to build more care homes and bring down the NHS waiting lists by doing more hip and knee operations privately. He's even been offering two for the price of one."

"Love it!" Stanley laughed, "What's wrong with that?"

"What's wrong, is that he intervenes and operates way before people actually need surgery. Interventions that aren't strictly speaking necessary, should be avoided."

"People who can afford to pay will go for it, won't they? Why don't you just join forces? You could be partners in crime?" he joked.

James was clearly exasperated, "He's taking money away from what could be spent on The Robot Network Programme. There's only so much to go around. Anyway, there's no way I'd get into bed with the likes of Westerby."

"So, you want me to come up with solutions that persuade the government to spend money on robots? Or cut Westerby out?"

"Well both ideally! Robots make sense because post Brexit and Covid, the social care workforce has virtually disappeared. The negligence of successive governments has almost obliterated social care in its previous state."

"My mates are saying there's a steam of pressure building about costs, largely down to the Baby Boomers. We can't afford to buy property anymore."

"The bottom line is that we can make money from this. You can too if you get smart. The right way forward is to prolong life and sell products that will support longer life. I'll call an emergency board meeting for next week, and then we'll talk terms." James put the phone down.

Stanley worked on his paper and called it 'Future Scenarios – Care Solutions.' He agreed a minimal consultancy rate with James in return for a profit share when the chickens, or robots, came home to roost. He thought back to before his father's death, before the trouble over the house. Mum had talked about the 'bed blockers,' – older people who got sent to hospital because there was no one to look after them and then they got stuck there. This project could change all that which would be a good thing surely, as well as make them a tidy profit. Mum would be pleased.

When he told Cassie what he was doing, albeit not the full story, she offered to help him with research. Although Cassie was a gentler person than him, which was why he loved her so much, she was crystal clear in her thinking and logic. Her research uncovered a number of key economic factors, including the fact that people were dying older, but also that the death rate was accelerating. She also discovered that the government had begun quietly selling NHS personal data. They had been trying to do this for years and had now just gone ahead. She reminded Stan of what his father had said almost two years ago when he had quoted Professor Marmot on life expectancy grinding to a halt. It was a toxic mix.

After putting Troy to bed, they came up with ten possible options ranging from raising taxes (especially for the over 40s), building more care homes, creating insurance-based schemes, and a controversial version of 'stack 'em high and sell 'em low.' The Japanese version of this was a much lauded scheme of cheap care home flats in tower blocks. Special incentives could be offered to those who were rattling around in large empty houses. The flats would retail at well below the average house price and so the new owners would be able to use the money from the sale of their properties to make a deposit for a mini flat in the high rises.

The apparent Japanese success with carebots was also interesting. In the UK, carebots could initially be provided at a reduced rate through James' robot project. A huge investment in care robots could transform the system, and could work alongside a new and revised end-of-life care pathway (rebranded, of course, to distance it from the disastrous Liverpool Pathway). Finally, Stanley's *coup de grâce* was a health capping scheme that allowed older people to die 'naturally' rather than have dozens of expensive and often unwanted interventions. He added that as an after-thought once Cassie had gone to bed. He wasn't sure what James would think of that one either, but James had told him to be radical and disruptive. He'd only sent the document off around 20 minutes before and was sitting back with a gin and tonic on the comfy sitting room sofa when he got a ping back from James, saying 'Great'.

He began thinking about how his Mum had been worried about the care system. Maybe she had had a point but at least she was living in an area that seemed to have become a sort of refuge for older people. The quirky island ways suited the older newcomers. Nothing wrong with that. They would all need a bit of protection from themselves if nothing else, especially those who were losing their marbles.

Why did Mum seem to think it might be something more sinister? She'd even said something on his last visit about the robots being used to brainwash them, at least that's what he thought she'd meant. Maybe it was the other way round? It was all very confusing and there was that Patrick to worry about too.

Chapter 26

It didn't feel right to recommend Citizen UK to Peggie for Edward after what I'd read on their website. Or was I being paranoid? Brian was in charge of their lives now. I wished that Tom was still alive. Perhaps Stanley could help? He was fond of his aunt and uncle. I decided to call him and he eventually answered. "How's my lovely grandson?"

"He's great. He's slept through the night now, five nights in a row!" said Stan, sounding proud.

"I'm a bit worried about your Aunty Peggie and Uncle Edward. Did you see them when you visited Brian?"

"No, I met Brian in the pub, but he did say they're becoming quite a worry for him. He's thinking about selling the house and moving them into a care home."

'Bastard,' I thought. "What about what they want?" I said, irritably. "It's their house, and they worked all these years to keep the business going while he swanned off to foreign parts."

"Listen Mum, I'm a bit busy right now. I thought you might be calling about the robot. Is everything okay?"

"Yes, Henry2's fine. He'll be having his MOT soon. It's just Peggie and Edward I'm worried about. They weren't managing when I saw them last week. I wondered if they could get some help from the robots, but they said that Brian would have to agree because he has power of attorney now over them now."

"I don't think that's going to happen, Mum. He would do anything rather than keep them at home. He wants them somewhere where he knows they're being properly looked after – in residential care, or the local hospital ... St Mary's, isn't it?"

"Why hospital, for heaven's sake?"

"Because it's free, of course!"

"The hospital won't keep them in! And the money from the house will still have to go towards their care costs."

"Knowing Brian, he won't care. He'll just do it and worry about the consequences afterwards. Everyone's feeling much the same these days." Stanley sighed heavily.

I worried about what those consequences might mean, but I focused on Peggie and Edward, "I contacted this charity called Citizen UK on the island in the hopes that they could offer some help and even they are talking about a robot scheme now!"

"Citizen UK? I wouldn't touch them with a barge pole. They're not really a charity, anyway. They're run by someone called Westerby now."

"The info on their website seemed alarming, but the woman on the phone told me that they have a contract with the council now, so they must be legitimate, right? Come to think of it, how does the Robot Network Programme fit in with Citizen UK if they're planning on doing robots as well?"

Stanley laughed out loud, "Citizen UK is in competition with the RNP, Mum. They won the first contract for setting up robots on the island, but they've been slow about making it work. The word on the street is that the council won't renew Citizen UK's contract this year."

"How come you know so much about it?" I asked, puzzled.

"You remember the venture capitalists party you went to just before Dad died? Well, I'm doing some work with James Hillingdon.

You met him. In fact, he was asking after you the other day."

"Yes, I remember him talking about robots. Is he still investing in them?"

"You bet. He's just bought into a big programme from Japan. He's arch rivals with a geriatrician called John Westerby. Westerby's been buying up property on the island and trying to create more health interventions so that he can make money from knees and hips. He recommends that people have surgery, then he arranges for their house to be sold to pay for it if necessary. He doesn't really have the know-how for the robots. Hillingdon doesn't approve of him at all."

"Good for Hillingdon!" I laughed. "I like him even if he is a filthy capitalist."

As Stan put the phone down, I turned to Henry2 who was standing by my side. "Henry, who is John Westerby please?"

"Professor, Sir John Westerby is a well-known geriatrician and CEO of the charity called Citizen UK who specialises in care for the elderly. He is an orthopaedic specialist and has successfully operated on many thousands of elderly people. Now he is also a specialist in dementia."

"What is he doing on the Isle of Wight?"

"He is the visiting NHS Professor for Geriatric Care from the mainland. He has a large private practice. Do you want me to make an appointment with him, Anna?"

I laughed. "No thanks, I don't think I need him – not just yet, anyway! I don't have the money for fancy private consultations either."

Henry2 went on, "Professor Sir John Westerby's company, Citizen UK, is strictly speaking a charitable venture with a strong trading arm. They have applied for planning permission to pull down all the old farm buildings and homes on the east of the island to create what they call a 'Home Farm Country Club.' This club will consist of individual villas for each elderly person or couple.

Each villa will be supported by a robot who looks after the elderly people's needs."

"So, he's in cahoots with the council on the island?"

"I do not understand hoots. Hoots are the cry of Barn Owls. Professor Sir John Westerby is the CEO of Citizen UK. They are not a reputable organisation. It is better that you stay with the RNP."

So Stan was right and Henry2 agreed with him. Citizen UK being in competition with the RNP explained a lot. It would be interesting to hear more from James Hillingdon. Maybe I should have replied to one of his emails, but it was too late now.

I decided the best way to find out what was going on locally was to visit to one of the local care homes. I gave Peggie a ring to see if she wanted to come too, but as usual, there was no answer. I thought I'd visit the one just down the road, the one I'd seen with the robot lawn mower. I could collect my monitor from under the stone at the bus stop at the same time.

Henry2 tried again to get me to use a Notcar, but after one of the little ritual negotiations that I had become accustomed to, he agreed I could cycle as long as I wore my helmet.

The rooks were squalling up above, so he didn't come outside when I left. I cycled quickly down the road to pick up my monitor, but when I got to the stone, it wasn't there. I searched frantically all around to see if it had got dislodged, but there was no sign of it. I'd have to confess the loss to Henry2.

Then I noticed Patrick up ahead on the lane. As I waited for him to come closer, I got that delicious throbbing sensation between my legs. I struggled to regain my composure, but I could feel a blush creeping up my neck. His strong brown hand was holding the wooden trug, and in the other he swung a battered old straw hat. I wanted to touch his hand but resisted that and instead said cheerfully, "Hi there. That rhubarb was lovely. I had it for breakfast – once I'd explained to Henry2 how to cook it."

"Glad you liked it. Who's Henry Too?" He looked puzzled.

Maybe he was jealous?

"He's my new robot – don't you remember being at the Village Hall when I agreed to try one out?"

"Not sure about those things. The Notcars are bad enough. Just you be careful, you can't trust machines, no more than people anyway!"

He waved and went on his way. I wanted to talk a bit more about Henry2, but the time obviously wasn't right.

Twenty minutes later, I drew up at Pear Tree Care Home and parked my bike by the gates. I noticed the round dark green lawn mower still eternally doing its rounds as I walked up the gravel driveway and rang the doorbell. When there was no reply, I pushed the heavy, panelled door open. There was a strong, distinctive smell of ammonia and stale urine mixed with chrysanthemums.

Taking a deep breath through my mouth, I walked towards the reception area where I could see a nurse behind a glass partition wearing a white plastic apron stretched over an ample bosom. As I approached, determinedly smiling, I was struck with how easy it would be for anyone to have walked in and, just as easy for an elderly person with dementia to wander out. When I got to the desk, she said, "Can I help you?" in an impatient, abrupt manner. "It's not visiting hours." She smiled with her mouth only.

I smiled back. "I was just passing. I live nearby by and wanted to have a look around for my aunt. She's going to be needing a care home soon."

"It's always better if you call in advancebut I can show you around the main reception and one of the bedrooms which has just become vacant if you'd like?"

The corridors were empty. In the main living room, I could see one or two older people dozing in their chairs. My guide, who turned out to be the matron, said that most people were currently having an afternoon nap after lunch. The empty room looked nice enough and thankfully didn't smell.

"We let them decorate their rooms and they can bring their own furniture in too."

"That's nice," I said flatly, thinking it was a poor substitute for one's own home. "Do you use robots by any chance?"

"No, no," she laughed. "Our old folk wouldn't like to be looked after by robots." She shook her head.

"But you've got one cutting the grass?"

She looked at me blankly and frowned. "Yes, well, I suppose so, but that's different, isn't it? It's not doing direct care."

At least it didn't leave the grass stinking of stale urine, I thought. I made my apologies and left. I felt oddly disconnected. Why would anyone want to move into such an alien place to live with strangers?

On my way back down the drive, I walked over to look more closely at the robot mower. It had got stuck against the edge of the driveway. As I reached down to move it, it jerked towards me. Stepping back hurriedly, I slipped and fell painfully on the gravel, hurting my hip. As I cried out in pain, the matron, who must have been watching me, rushed out and immediately called an ambulance.

The ambulance arrived almost at once, and in no time I was being raced along the bumpy island roads at breakneck speed. No sirens, thank heavens. I heard them calling ahead, "We're on our way with an elderly female from Pear Tree Care Home. Well hydrated. Good vital signs. Possible hip fracture."

I lay back and shut my eyes. I didn't need this now. Twenty minutes later, I was being pushed into A&E on a trolley. It was chaotically full of older people, and there were trolleys, wheelchairs, and bedpans everywhere. I was in a lot of pain and felt very nauseous.

Two hours later, the scan was done, and they said I could go home. Henry2 must have picked up the news about my fall somehow. A message had come through from him when I was having the X-ray, saying that I was to take the Notcar home. He seemed to be more worried about when to cook dinner rather than whether or not I'd broken anything. Maybe robots didn't understand about broken limbs. Or did he know already? I decided that I really must ask exactly what data was being collected the next time I saw Keeper Kevin, if he was still in the job.

The consultant quickly confirmed that I had not broken anything. "You've bruised your hip badly," he said, "and you'll need to rest for a few days." Then he added jokingly, "Don't go messing around with those machines again. They're dangerous!"

Did he mean the lawn mowers or the robots? Later, the nurse asked me if I had anyone to help at home and when I said I had a robot, she looked at me as though I was hallucinating. By then, I was so fed up with being there that I couldn't be bothered to explain. Let her think I was mad. She went off to get some leaflets that advised on health and well-being activities and stressed the importance of avoiding future attendances at A&E. I laughed ruefully.

As I began to exit A&E to wait for my Notcar, I caught a glimpse of Peggie behind one of the curtains. She was sitting beside a trolley with her hand on a hump curled up under the blankets. I hobbled over, leaning heavily on the crutches they had given me. The doctors outside the curtain were talking in quiet tones and I heard mention of the new island end-of-life care pathway called the "Wight Way."

I moved the curtain aside to squeeze into the small space. Peggie looked up and I could see she had been crying, "Oh, Anna, please help! They want to send him away!"

Edward moaned and moved slightly under the white hospital blanket. He was breathing rapidly, and his eyes were closed in pain. I could see the newly etched tattoo DNR on his thin chest. The doctor had evidently heard and turned towards the cubicle saying in gentle tones, "It really is for the best you know. Your GP is keen to refer him to Prof Westerby as soon as possible."

"Where would he go?" I asked.

"We don't know yet. Let's see what the professor says, but there are some excellent places on the island now and some already have the new pathway in place."

"Couldn't he go home in the meantime with some extra help? They've never been apart before?" I asked, knowing Peggie would be desperate to get Edward home if possible. He wouldn't last long in a home, however good it was.

"Well, we could try that first if you think you can manage?" He turned to Peggie questioningly. She looked at me and nodded anxiously. It turned out I'd been at the right place at the right time. We chatted a bit more, but I was also in pain and wanted to get home. I promised Peggie I'd visit as soon as I could and hobbled away.

By the time I got home, it was late afternoon, and I was exhausted. Henry2 was waiting to greet me and hovered behind me as I struggled up the stairs. Sitting on my bedside table was my monitor. He said nothing about it, and neither did I.

The next day, I picked up the phone to a furious Brian. "What the fuck do you think you're doing? You stupid busybody!"

Chapter 27

Brian rang Stanley straight away, still enraged. After Stanley got off the phone with Brian, he called Evelyn, "Mum's had a fall. She's been sent home and they say she'll manage okay, but Brian's furious with her – they had a huge row!"

"Poor old Mum, but what's it got to do with Brian?!"

"Apparently, she was in A&E at the same time as Auntie Peggie and Uncle Edward. She persuaded the medics to send them home. Brian says she's been interfering. He wants me to put a stop to it."

"I always thought he was a nasty piece of work," said Evelyn, "So, what's he wanting Mum to do?"

"He's just trying to make sure they're properly looked after! Nothing wrong with that, is there?"

"Put them in a home, you mean! Against their will and walk off with their property before they can spend all their money on their care? He can't do that!"

"We shouldn't get involved," said Stanley.

"Families should look after each other," said Evelyn.

"We should get the power of attorney sorted out for Mum. Then we won't have to worry when her time comes. It'll make it easier to sort the practicalities."

"Maybe at some point, but now's not the right time to raise it with Mum. She's still perfectly capable of making her own decisions. You might not like it, but it's her life."

"What if she falls again or loses her marbles and needs ECT? We can't be running up and down to the island every five minutes."

"ECT is not something Mum would agree to again, or be tricked into, if that's what you had in mind."

"Other people do it," said Stanley with a frustrated sigh. "I'm still worried about this Patrick guy too and what he might be up to!"

"Look," Evelyn was beginning to lose her temper, "I've got enough on my plate trying to sort Andy and the kids out. Why don't you get down to see her again if you're so worried?"

"I will, I will."

"The sooner the better. And what's happening with the house? I might need somewhere to live soon if Andy goes on the way he is right now."

"Cassie really likes the area, so we're going to stay here for now. Especially now that Troy's here!" Stan said belligerently.

"Stan, that's not fair! It's my house too. We're really short of money. Andy's not working and they hardly give any disability allowance now. He'll be needing a wheelchair soon if he goes on the way he is."

"I'll sort the house out, but don't you dare tell Mum we're staying there. It's just not a good time to sell whilst Covid's still going on. And don't say anything to Cassie just yet, either. I have a plan. Don't worry."

Chapter 28

My bruised hip healed quickly, and after a week, I was back to normal, although still a bit shaken. One morning, I was startled by a loud banging on the front door. I was still in my dressing gown. I'd half been expecting some sort of further altercation with Brian, but when I hadn't heard from him after a few days, I'd begun to relax. I left Henry2 to answer, and as I came down the stairs, Henry2 was standing squarely in the doorway. Usually, he would have stepped aside and allowed me to take over, but this time, he stayed put. Then I saw why; it was indeed cousin Brian who began shouting, red-faced, and shaking his fists as soon as he saw me. "Let me in, you stupid, interfering old cow. Get this thing out of the way!"

"Brian, stop shouting! What on earth's the matter?!" I stuttered, cross that my voice sounded shaky.

"You know damn fine what the matter is! You've been making Mum and Dad go back home when all they really want is to be looked after. It's none of your damn business."

I was about to say that they wanted to stay at home, then I realised that Peggie was probably blaming me for them going home. Then an extraordinary thing happened. Henry2 began to move forward towards Brian with both his steel arms held up in front of him. As he moved forward, Brian backed off down the garden path. At one stage, Brian tried to skip behind him to reach me, but Henry2 just reached out, grabbed Brian's arm, and forcibly turned him round again. Once Brian was escorted to the road, Henry2 stood at the end of the garden path like a statue. He kept his position until Brian backed off and got into his car, still red with rage and shouting, "You'll hear from me if you interfere again, you stupid old cow!"

Shaking his fist from the safety of his car, he finally drove off. It was amazing. I went back into the house with Henry2 following close behind. When I sat down at the kitchen table, Henry2 busied himself straightaway making me a cup of tea. I was puzzled when I saw him add sugar. "Henry2, why have you put sugar in my tea? You know I don't take it."

"A hot drink with sugar is the best thing for shock."

Of course, there had to be a logical explanation! "Much appreciated," I laughed. "Tell me how you knew what to do with Brian. You were incredible!"

"Brian was angry and shouting. He was threatening you. It is my job to protect you, Anna."

"Thank you, but tell me, what would you have done if he hadn't backed off?"

"I would have done what was necessary to stop him from trying to hurt you. The man Brian knew that and so there was never any real danger."

I gulped.

The next morning, I cycled over to see Peggie and Edward. I had cautiously rung Peggie beforehand to check that Brian had left and gone back to the mainland but there was no answer. I didn't tell Henry2 where I was going, although I suspected he'd find out somehow. I just got on my bicycle and headed off so that he couldn't stop me or insist on a Notcar. I was much fitter now, so it only took me 35 minutes this time. I delighted in peddling through the woods with their deep, damp, musty smell of rotting vegetation and wild things. Summer was nearly over now, and the heat was going out of the air. I probably wouldn't have many more bike rides like this before winter.

We sat down at Peggie's kitchen table over a cup of tea and a biscuit whilst she told me that Brian had stormed round the day after they'd been discharged from A&E. He was furious that they hadn't stayed in hospital until they'd been assessed for NHS 'Continuing Care' or put in a home. When he angrily declared that it was all my fault, she just left it at that. She was very apologetic.

I said, "No problem." I'd decided not to tell her about Brian coming to my front door; she had enough to worry about.

She went on, shaking her head. "The council have put us on to the Telecare system through the TV. I couldn't tell if she was impressed or disturbed. "When I rang the council, a young woman appeared on the TV and asked what I wanted help with. She looked like one of your robots!"

She probably was, I thought, "They must have turned the TV on remotely, but surely with your permission?!"

"They didn't say, but I told them we needed more help a while back. When they looked up our records, they said that we hadn't been reviewed for three years and that things had changed ... I had forgotten that I was supposed to keep quiet about Maggie." I nodded. "They wanted me to have one of their new automated home helps called a 'carebot.' They told me that I wouldn't need Maggie any more once it arrived! I didn't know what to do! I couldn't just put the phone down because they were there in my room on the TV!"

"They can't force you to get rid of Maggie, surely?" I asked.

"It's easy for you to say Anna. Between them and Brian, it really doesn't feel like we have a choice."

Peggie was terrified at the thought of either of them leaving the old house where they'd spent all their married life. It wasn't that she was worried that care homes were cruel or anything, just that she'd heard that everything had to be very regimented due to the number of residents. She understood that, but she liked her privacy and her independence. She was caught in a tight corner.

Peggie explained the whole sorry saga that had led to Edward's spell in A&E. She had kept Maggie on in secret until Brian found out and gave Maggie notice himself and ordered the free carebot to start right straight away. Edward had never been happy with the robot and refused to have anything to do with it. The lack of control affected his mental as well as physical health until one day he attacked the robot and hurt himself badly.

I cycled home feeling deflated. It really didn't feel as though there was anything I could do. I was so angry with Brian. I resolved to visit them again very soon, and perhaps to try to go over at least once a week and cook a meal for them.

Little did I know on that cycle home, it was to be too late. A few days later, I received a call from Stan saying that Peggie and Edward had both passed away. They'd been found by the Telecare company, side by side in their big double bed, holding hands, having taken all their medication. The funeral was held a week later and, at Brian's request, there were no hymns. Maggie came, and she and I sat together, away from Brian, who didn't speak to me but gave us a long hard stare as I left.

Chapter 29

A couple of weeks later, after breakfast one morning, Henry2 reminded me that it was time for our weekly diary check. He had wanted to have a daily diary check, but I had drawn the line at weekly – he could always remind me of any important appointments and it wasn't as though I had a lot going on.

He told me that a new review meeting, and performance report, were planned for the next week. I was delighted that I would be seeing the Twelve Disciples again. Hopefully they wouldn't be putting my progress with Henry2 to shame, but I was keen to find out. My worry was that I might lose him if I wasn't doing enough, but that could just be my anxiety playing up again. Must take more deep breaths, I told myself, but never ever those little pink pills.

As Henry2 zoomed ever efficiently around the house, I imagined him tidying up all his reports on *my* performance. Was it his performance report or mine?! Either way, he ordered the Notcar for the next Monday morning. I felt as though I was going off to school. Henry2 made sure that I had my monitor and water for the journey, and came to the door to see me off.

The Twelve Disciples all turned up at around the same time at the training centre – no doubt due to the planned synchronisation of the Notcar travel arrangements. As we all shuffled in, I recognised most faces, and we nodded and smiled at each other. The centre was over-heated but was at least laid out with plenty of water as an alternative to the disgusting coffee. The two rows of chairs were arranged in a curve around a slightly raised plinth at the front of the room. The chatter was noisy and excited. Everyone was boasting and competing to have the best-performing robots. I sat in the front row next to Jude, who'd saved me a seat. Simon and Pete were already sitting on her other side.

Keeper Zack was on the plinth doing his twirling toes act and grinning with his dazzlingly white teeth that took over his foxy little face. He was dressed as sharply as before in a Paul Day outfit – a tight-fitting black and white checked shirt with turned-down collar and narrow, red cuffs and the usual skinny black chinos.

"Welcome!" he began, "We're very pleased you've managed to come today and that you've all stayed the pace. Well done!" It was like a prize giving. We looked around at each other and nodded our congratulations, some actually clapping as he continued. "Now, before we do anything else, I'd like to introduce a new keeper; Keeper Joe is replacing Keeper Kevin, who's retired after a long and full service." Everyone murmured welcome noises. "Next, I want to ask each of you to give us an update on what you've been using your robot for."

I felt a little concerned about not saying goodbye to Kevin properly; goodbyes are always important. It made me apprehensive somehow, so I was grateful when Jude jumped in first, "Mine's called Jim, and it's great to have a man about the house," she nudged me at the same time releasing a strong waft of Elizabeth Arden. "He's a good cleaner and not a bad cook. He does the washing and ironing no problem. I even get him to do my neighbour's ironing!" Keeper Zack frowned at this blatant rule-breaking. I wouldn't put it past her to charge the neighbour, but Jude went on oblivious. "We have our little chats every morning. Jim knows all the family now, and he's ever so polite to the grandchildren, knows their names and what they like to do. And if I forget things, he's always right there!"

"Do you forget often, then? And do you use him for any personal care?" asked Keeper Joe.

She ignored the question about memory loss. "What do you mean, like cleaning my teeth or scratching my back? Nah, I don't need that, not yet anyway. But he's a dab hand at massaging!" and winked. As everyone turned to stare at her and she started blushing.

"Doesn't it hurt with those machine hands?" asked Pete.

"He wears special soft rubbery gloves. You should try it! Best massage I've ever had!" I noticed Simon nodding with interest.

I remembered the earlier discussions at the social services conferences about robots not being able to do personal care. Clearly, things had moved on. Henry2 had offered me a massage. Was this part of the new deal? Robots now offering personal care? A flash of that delicious sex sensation I'd had on my bicycle flooded through me. I hadn't had sex or anything close to it since Tom. Jude looked sideways at me and felt myself heating up. What had she really been up to? The rules against any form of sexual activity had been made very clear, and yet sexual activity could take place in many different ways.

She went on to say, "We've also had Jim watching Gogglebox, so he knows what makes me laugh. It works a treat!"

After a brief pause, whilst everyone digested that information, Pete spoke up, angular and stern as ever, "My Fred does all the cleaning, washing and the cooking. Don't like some of the stuff he cooks though, too much veg and not enough chips, and I'm only allowed meat or sausages once a week!"

Keeper Zack brought it back to the same topic again. "What about conversations and personal care?"

Surely, they must know all this already, with the monitoring reports, so what then was the purpose of asking? Were they trying to catch us out? But Pete answered, nonplussed, "We don't talk much. Fred doesn't have much to say, does he? He's a machine, isn't he, for heaven's sake! We play sudoku every morning, though, and he helps me with the crossword."

I'd been having a lot of chats with Henry2. I'd have to be careful when my turn came. "That's good, that you're using him to keep your brain active," said Keeper Zack, nodding approvingly.

"No massages then?" Jude teased.

Pete ignored her. "I tried using him to help with the Lottery, but it didn't work. I still only ever get two numbers." He sighed. "And I wish he could take the dog for a walk when it's raining." Keeper Zack raised his eyebrows whilst Keeper Joe smirked in a way that Kevin would never have done. Then Pete added, "I know, I know, it's all about doing my 10,000 steps a day, come rain or shine. He sends me out every morning after we've done the stretching exercises. Most of the time, I just go fishing in Shalfleet, where my boat's moored."

"Ever catch anything?" asked Simon wistfully.

"Sometimes, but I have to cook it myself. Fred doesn't know how to gut and cook fresh fish."

Simon was the next to share. "Mine's called Doreen, after my wife, if you remember?" Jude looked sideways at me and raised her eyebrows. "We're getting on fine. She's got such a good memory – much better than me now. She even remembers Doreen's favourite TV programmes." He took a deep breath. "She's quite a good cook, too. I'll say that for her!" He paused, "I don't like to say ill of the dead, but the old Doreen used to burn things quite a bit. My new Doreen makes me a pudding every day, even if it's just yoghurt and fruit. I've lost a bit of weight." He patted his still rotund tummy. "And she tucks me up at night with a hot drink."

A few more glances were exchanged on that last one, but Keeper Zack only came back with his usual refrain. "It's good you're having plenty of healthy meals. And what about personal care?"

"She does help me with some stuff, like when I get stuck in my chair or on the toilet, and she fetches me a nice cup of tea, too."

As Keeper Zack asked, "Who's next please?" a burly man behind us in the second row began speaking. We all turned to look at him as he shifted uncomfortably in his mechanised wheelchair. I didn't recall having seen him before. "Morning everyone. I'm Matt – Mathew. I'm a late joiner. I don't really call my robot anything and it gets in the way more than anything else. My place is small, and I have to move around in this thing most of the time. It does get the meals and clear up, though, which is quite a bonus." Then he added, "Since my wife passed away, I've been on my own."

Simon looked around at him and nodded sadly in solidarity.

When my turn came, I found I was reluctant to talk about my growing relationship with Henry2. None of the others really seemed to have got personal with their robots, so I explained what I did with him. I avoided mention of our conversations and funny misunderstandings. Concentrating on the task, I said, "Henry2 and I do all the usual things just like you've been describing. I'm exploring his development of the five senses. I'd like him to have an e-nose to smell spices so he can cook better." I blushed, realising that I was talking about him as a friend.

Keeper Zack looked at me curiously and nodded. "We can look into that, of course. E-noses are available now and touch is much improved, as some of you have discovered." He glanced briefly at Jude. "But taste is still at design stage."

Pete jumped in, "Our sense of smell is responsible for about 80% of what we taste." There were murmurs of agreement between people as everyone was beginning to relax and chat between themselves. Keeper Zack must have realised he was in danger of losing control, so although I wanted to ask about the sixth sense, I realised that I'd be pushing my luck. I resolved to talk to Pete about it later.

Keeper Zack rapidly handed out our performance reports. They were bound in black with words "The Robot Network Programme" and "HIGHLY CONFIDENTIAL" emblazoned in yellow capitals on the front cover. As I flipped mine open, I saw that we had been marked green for good, amber for okay, and red for bad. I was used to reading performance reports and risk registers at work, and so I rapidly deduced that mine were all green. I felt ridiculously pleased, but beside me, Jude was exploding. "What's all this red stuff? It's too small for me to read!"

Keeper Zack came over and pointed out that there were extended periods when there was no data, hence the red areas. Pete raised his eyebrows and shook his head. Keeper Zack asked enquiringly, "Can you explain that? We don't think there was a malfunction."

She went very pink as he waited for an explanation, and then she said brazenly, "That'll be when I locked him in the cupboard!"

I laughed out loud and everyone else joined in – apart from Pete, who looked angry, and Simon, who looked confused. I asked "Why ever would you do that?"

"Well, sometimes they get in the way, if you know what I mean?" She winked, having recovered her sense of humour. "You know, if you have a gentleman caller or something?" She nudged me again.

Keeper Zack was clearly exasperated. "It's not a good idea to restrict the actions of any robot, and certainly not to lock them in a cupboard. They are valuable merchandise."

Matt in the back row interrupted. He was obviously not a fan of Jude's. "Isn't it a problem if you start teaching them bad habits? I mean, like, they could try it out on you, couldn't they?"

Jude was visibly taken aback and said nothing further. The room fell into conversation again and Jude and Simon began gossiping, their heads close together. I caught the whispered words, 'touch,' and 'feel,' as Jude reached out to put her hand over his. They moved apart as Keeper Zack continued, changing the subject. "Time to talk about the next steps, if I could have your attention, please," and clapped his hands. "We wanted to keep you all in touch with how this experiment is going, and to thank you for your hard work with your robots. As we said at the beginning, you have all been especially chosen to help with a hugely significant research programme. An important part of this programme is that it contributes to global research into the concept of SINGULARITY." He said pronounced 'singularity,' slowly and deliberately.

"What's that when it's at home?" piped up Pete.

"Singularity is when AI becomes so powerful and sophisticated that human beings merge with technology."

We looked around at each other. I took a deep breath and felt a surge of pride. I had assumed everyone else would feel the same, but I was wrong. Some of the language was definitely going over their heads and there seemed to be an angry buzz going around the room. I catastrophised about the whole thing collapsing and losing Henry2, so in an attempt to bring some focus back, I said, "Please can you explain what exactly 'Singularity' means? How can human beings merge with machines?"

I smiled to myself as I remembered Tom talking about being a Borg when he was going through his treatment. Keeper Zack was frowning as if this was all self-explanatory. "It's just a natural progression and nothing to be worried about. In the not-too-distant future I wouldn't be surprised if we'll all be doing the same. You guys are just a bit ahead of the game. We think robots are the answer, and so far you've roved us right!" He smiled encouragingly.

Pete came in, "So what next?"

Keeper Zack continued, "We want to put you all on to our advanced 'Health and Wellbeing' programme. This will help to keep you healthy, and to live longer, happier lives. It will also prepare you for the next steps. What's not to like about that?!" He paused … "We're inviting you all back next week so that we can explain in more detail what's involved. We will also want to monitor you much more closely."

"Give us the downside, what's the catch? Will I still be able to go fishing?" Pete said, ever the practical one.

Keeper Zack paused before delivering the killer blow. "It'll mean having iDocs implanted under your skin, on the side of your wrist … they will be very discreet," he added, while holding up what looked like a flat battery for a miniscule hearing aid.

"What, like a pacemaker?" asked Simon. "Our Doreen had one of those put in her chest."

Keeper Zack nodded, "Yes, that's right, just like pacemakers. Except that they measure all of your wellbeing, not just your heart. You won't have to bother with all those wearables or external monitors. The iDoc just becomes part of you. It makes life a lot easier." He nodded again, and flashing those white teeth, smiled encouragingly.

I gulped and wondered if Henry2 had reported my misadventure with the monitor. Was that why they were suggesting this? I didn't like the sound of an iDoc being inserted under my skin, although I could see it might make life easier. It's true that one would be less likely to lose it – especially as one got older. We were used to all sorts of other inserts like new knees and hips. Was this really any different? But the problem was the external monitoring, I couldn't help feeling there was something worrying about it, maybe even sinister.

Most of the twelve began shifting uncomfortably in their seats. Then Matt, twisting uncomfortably in his wheelchair, said angrily, "Sounds nasty! I don't like the idea of that thing under my skin. I used to be a publican so I'm used to all sorts, but this is going too far. Far too far!"

Keeper Zack did another twirl and smiled again with his flashing teeth. Then, talking more forcibly, he said, "It really isn't a big thing. The iDoc is like a tiny node." Then he added, soothingly, "as Simon said, rather like a pacemaker."

"You must be joking if you think I'm going ahead with that thing after all I've been through," concluded Matt. There were grunts of approval from the second row who all began shifting in their seats.

"At this stage, we're looking for volunteers to take this forward." Keeper Zack took on an imploring tone, "Who would like to give it a go?" I felt almost sorry for him. This was going down like a lead balloon.

I wasn't surprised but relieved when Pete asked, "If we do sign up, exactly what monitoring will you be doing? And what data will you be gathering on us in future?"

Jude chipped in too, "Yes, it's only fair we know!"

No doubt she was worried about something that she was doing behind the scenes. The idea of locking Henry2 up in a cupboard was unthinkable to me. Might be dangerous too if he tried to get out, I pondered.

Keeper Zack managed to look concerned while at the same time somewhat pompous, "As a research programme of national, if not international significance, we would be failing in our duty not to keep monitoring the data. You all signed consent forms for us to gather your data. I cannot emphasise enough how important this programme is for future generations." He was puffing his little chest out so much I worried that his Paul Day buttons would burst.

Mathew grunted again and some of the others began whispering together. Keeper Zack was in danger of losing his audience.

Then Pete piped up, "If you want us to sign on the dotted line, then we need to know exactly what data of ours you're using. I don't have any problem with you taking my blood pressure, telling me if I'm getting diabetes, or about to have a heart attack, but if its financial data, then that's different. Whatever happened to privacy and confidentiality?"

I was still anxious that if this all fell apart, then I might lose Henry2. I'd got attached to him – well, used to him anyway. I needed to help get this back on track. "Oh, come on," I said, "they know everything about us by now, anyway. We none of us have any secrets anymore, especially now they've got our NHS data.

They've been tracking what we do, what we like, what we buy, and everything else about us for a few years. This isn't any different."

"I want to reassure you all," said Keeper Zack forcibly, looking deliberately around the room, "that your personal data is fully protected. The data we are asking for here is only about how your bodies are functioning, we're not interested in your finances …" And then he added, "Not at this stage, anyway."

This was why I was so careful what I said or shared with Henry2. He might be my companion but I knew that he could potentially be a very leaky one.

Jude wriggled in her seat, "What about a bonus to help the medicine go down? Personally, I'm up for it but I'd like to feel it's being appreciated. Especially as you're putting something inside me!" she said, giggling suggestively. She really was impossible, funny but impossible.

Simon piped up, "Who puts it in? Does it hurt?"

Keeper Zack ignored him, shaking his head and speaking more slowly and emphatically this time, "There is nothing sinister about this programme. The Robot Network Programme is a nationally approved programme with NITE, The National Institute for Technological Excellence. The government believes that we have found the answer to the elderly care crisis by using robots to help keep older people at home. We, indeed *you*, are all at the forefront of this exciting new research."

"And a bonus?" interjected Jude confrontationally.

Then Keeper Zack said, unexpectedly, "Let's say we'll give you an extra £1,000 for your trouble."

I was surprised that he gave in so quickly. Mathew snorted. It obviously wasn't enough for him but Jude nodded, satisfied. I was pretty pleased myself and leaned forward to give her the thumbs up.

"But does it hurt?" repeated Simon anxiously.

Keeper Zack ignored him again, "You don't have to make a decision right now. We'll be in touch with each of you over the next

197

week or so to talk it through a bit more and then we'll meet again. I want you to remember though, you hold the future of all our older people in your hands."

Keeper Joe nudged him, holding out a form. Keeper Zack blushed slightly, "Oh yes, and you'll all need to sign a confidentiality clause as well. We don't want the press getting the wrong end of the stick at this crucial stage." Jude raised her eyebrows.

Chapter 30

Keeper Joe arranged a Zoom call with me for the following week. When the call came around, he was friendly and professional, and explained it all in more detail. He asked if I was happy with the £1,000 bonus and I agreed – immediately regretting not having asked for more.

Three weeks later, the Twelve Disciples had another meeting but this time there were only eight of us. My earlier worries about the programme collapsing returned. But I was pleased to see that Jude, Pete and Simon were all still part of it, as well as Matt. I didn't recognise the others. It turned out that they'd been brought in from another pilot. What was going on?

Keeper Joe herded us in and then took up his seat at the rear, shutting the door firmly behind him as though he was guarding our escape.

"Welcome back everyone," announced Keeper Zack. "I'm delighted to see you all. Some have fallen by the wayside, but I'm delighted to say that we are now being joined by a growing number of other pilots across the country." He beamed.

Jude put up her hand, "That's all very well but what about our bonus? I want my money up front please."

There were murmurings of approval around the room. Mathew

squirmed uneasily in his wheelchair; I wondered if he'd been bribed with a bit more. Keeper Zack smiled benignly and nodded, "We have decided to increase your bonus, so that no one will feel inconvenienced in the slightest way. £2,000 is being transferred into your back accounts as we speak," he paused before saying brightly, "So let's see a show of hands for who's going ahead?"

Simon, Jude, and I put our hands up immediately, as did Mathew. The others did the same but more slowly. Pete was checking on his phone and wanted to know how they knew the details of our bank accounts. Keeper Zack went bright red, "Well, of course we don't have your bank details but as soon as you give them to us, we'll make the deposits. Keeper Joe will collect them from you all now." He nodded to Keeper Joe at the back. The promise of £2,000 had done the trick.

Keeper Zack continued, "Let me explain exactly what this next stage entails. The iDoc is essentially a 'Health and Social Care Integrated Device.' We hope it will solve many of the current problems for those of you who are already using health and care services or may in the near future. We want to test how you use carebots in order to support you – hence my questions about personal care." Then he repeated in his characteristically pompous fashion, "You are at the forefront of a brave new world!"

I thought that was going a bit far and giggled, Pete rolled his eyes, but Keeper Zack continued undeterred, "It's only by monitoring older people closely that we can tell if you are truly safe at home and of course, help you when you need it. We will be revamping the Robot Network Programme and renaming it, the 'Robot Network Renewal Programme' in future, so that we can identify the significant changes we are making here with you all. "

I wondered if he really believed that or if it was just the sales patter it sounded like. Pete piped up again saying, "Well, I'm up for it! Anything's better than having to go into one of those smelly old people's homes. I'd rather just take my boat out and sail away into the horizon." He laughed as he added, "But the extra cash will come in useful for a new engine." He smiled as his phone pinged with the news of a new deposit.

Dates and times were sorted out for our allegedly minor surgery to get our iDoc devices fitted at a specialist clinic the following week. Maybe I'd been too quick to sign up, but I was also curious. Moreover, I would really miss Henry2 if he wasn't around. The £2,000 would come in handy too.

I thought about the rest of the original Twelve Disciples who had not turned up. I knew how they felt. Sometimes with getting older everything – even if it's supposedly convenient – just seems like too much trouble. Jude, Simon, Pete and I surreptitiously exchanged telephone numbers. We agreed that we would meet up more often to compare notes. I don't think, at this stage anyway, that it occurred to us that our robots would know. But of course they did.

On the way home, I scratched at my wrist as I contemplated feeling something hard and unresisting under my skin. I wasn't entirely convinced that having a foreign object stuck in there was a good idea, but it couldn't in theory do any harm, could it?

Chapter 31

Stanley was the first to arrive at James' smart city centre office for the emergency board meeting. Sitting at the large mahogany polished table, he casually flipped through the agenda on his laptop. There was only one item.

The Elderly Care Crisis – meeting with the Health and Wellbeing Minister.

This was why James has asked him to 'think the unthinkable' and it was stark stuff. He wished he'd read all the background papers the night before. Now he'd have to wing it – never a good thing when James was chairing a meeting. James Hillingdon was a nice enough fellow but, as Stan had found out, he was also very demanding and expected his pound of flesh. James' plan a couple of weeks ago to set up a blue-sky-thinking session with the government had seemed a bit far-fetched to Stan. Solving the elderly care crisis was an election promise, so it wasn't just the new Department of Health and Wellbeing who'd be involved, but the Treasury as well. The problem was still, as it had been all along, solving both who was going to pay for elderly care and what to do about the rising numbers. James had pulled out all the stops.

As he scrolled down on the events page, Stanley came to his own options paper. He quickly reread it and smiled; it was pretty damn good. All the better for Cassie's intervention, God bless her.

The room filled up quickly. James strode in on the hour and immediately introduced the meeting in his usual cavalier way, "I'm sure you've all read Stanley's 'Blue Sky Thinking' options paper." He flashed a smile in Stanley's direction. "I've been considering how some of this will work and it's good news for us all the way – as long as we keep our nerve and work out exactly how to scale it up. That's the only way to guarantee future income. It shouldn't be a problem with the rapidly ageing population but there are some detractors in the system."

"What sort of detractors?" interrupted one slick city type, as he swept back his hair.

"Let me explain," went on James. "The trick is to prolong life of course, and who wouldn't want to do that. But the crucial part is not to do it for too long."

Stanley came in, "Anybody who pays privately to go into a care home and goes too soon, could run out of money and then they look to the state to pay their bills."

James nodded, "Most people the state pays for only last about two years. That's simply because people are not accepted for state care until they are a high priority. He paused to look around the room at the eight well-dressed men, mostly in their thirties or forties, another youngish woman, and of course the older farmer and his wife who looked decidedly uncomfortable.

"Unless the government start to invest in health and wellbeing, a lot of our schemes, yours and mine, could go down. Actually will go down." He looked around the room expectantly, "But we're not going down without a fight, are we?" He flashed his winning smile around the table.

"You bet we're not," nods from all around the table.

Previous experience had shown Stanley that only three or four would have actually bothered to read the papers properly and be up for a debate. Yet, James had obviously hand-picked this lot

– both from his pool of venture capitalists and those in private equity; these people were the private owners of large enterprises and worth a fortune all told. They'd been with him a long time and they trusted James – both with their money and with their businesses. They weren't 'yes' men, but they would follow his lead. Stanley recognised a number of them from the London party – like the older farmer type and his ample-bosomed wife. The couple were obviously loaded; they were much older than the others and belligerent with it.

James continued, "Listen, I'm going to put my cards on the table. You all know I'm keen on robots. On your behalf, I've done a deal with the Japanese and ordered 100,000 care robots. These are sixth-generation robots who are especially adapted to look after the elderly … in more ways than one. They'll be arriving over the next few weeks in special shipping containers."

A stunned silence filled the room.

"You're mad!" the farmer declared, banging his fists on the table and making the water in the cut-glass tumblers tremble. His wife, sitting next to him, nodded approvingly. The farmer leaned forward, his face red with anger, "Robots are fine for sitting and talking to little old ladies about the war and helping them with their knitting, but they can't do the heavy lifting and they can't wipe bottoms."

James ignored him and looked down at his papers. He shook his head resolutely and said, "The papers are all screaming 'Elderly Care Crisis,' and the government want solutions. With the robots, we can give them those solutions." Then he looked around the room and said again, almost apologetically but firmly, "Robots ARE the answer!" Farmer looked more and more enraged.

James nodded to an assistant who opened the board room door, and suddenly, in zoomed a full-sized robot. It looked to Stanley very like the Henry2 he'd met at his Mum's cottage. It was larger than the earlier carebots and now came up to shoulder height but it still had the long dangling arms.

Around the table everyone looked at each other with faces that said, "What on earth is going on?!"

"First, let me show you what these new carebots are like," continued James, "then, we'll talk about how we make money out of them."

"Proof of the pudding is in the eating," said the farmer aggressively. "If I find you've wasted my money on this mad cap scheme, I'll have your guts for garters!"

James smiled smoothly and said calmly. "First, let me make the introductions." Turning to the robot he said, "Please tell us who you are?"

The robot whirled into action. "My name is Reginald. Reg for short. I'm a seventh-generation prototype robot. We are being developed by the Robot Network Renewal Programme across the country. The RNRP carebot is the premier global product which will transform the lives of people worldwide. The health and wellbeing of older people is safe in our hands."

The farmer snorted whilst James held up his hand for quiet while he asked the next question. "Tell us what you can do Reg?" Stanley assumed James must have done the programming himself, hence the sardonic butler naming.

The robot replied in its strong voice, "As a seventh-generation robot, I am part of a team that will be implementing the new Health and Wellbeing programmes for older people. We can create and serve healthy meals. We can make sure our people take their medications and do their exercises. We remind them about their appointments and give them special instructions when necessary. We monitor people for their health and independence and report back on any discrepancies."

"But can you wipe their bottoms?" Asked the farmer loudly, whilst his wife laughed and nudged him at his side.

Reg turned to James enquiringly, and he responded, smiling, "The gentleman is asking whether you can do personal care Reg?"

The robot turned to those assembled around the table. "Yes. As well as helping older people reminisce, I can cook specially designed dietary meals. I can feed them, wash them, toilet them, change their incontinence pads and their clothes."

"Help me, Reg. I think I'm going to sneeze," said James, suddenly appearing anxious.

Reg moved forward and with the two fingers of his spindly right hand, carefully plucked a single tissue from the box of tissues on the table. Then he moved across to James and, standing in front of him, gently reached up to his face and carefully wiped his nose.

There was a stunned silence around the table as James nodded appreciatively. "Thank you, Reg."

Turning back to the table, James continued, "We've been testing these robots via the Robot Network Renewal Programme – mainly on the Isle of Wight but also now in other parts of the UK." It began to dawn on Stanley that his mother was involved in a much bigger project than he had understood. How much did she know? "You remember Citizen UK? The so-called charity that beat us to the tender with the Isle of Wight Council? Well, I'm pleased to say that we're out-performing them on every front. We're well on target to win this year's contract when it comes up for renewal shortly."

Heads nodded around the table. One or two began getting out of their seats to touch Reg and feel the strength of his steely arms. "We've even got volunteer users from the original scheme to sign up to the next stage. I'm told they're all keen to go forward. They're having a new iDoc monitor inserted in a minor operation just this very week."

Stanley frowned, why had Mum not told him about all this? Did she know?

"What will the iDoc do?" asked Stan anxiously.

"The iDocs will help us with both research and compliance. They will collect all the research data available from the individuals and begin to predict certain life events – frailty and things like that.

We've never been quite sure exactly what happens behind closed doors in people's homes, and even more so in care homes, so this will change all that."

"Are they safe?" asked Stan.

James seemed puzzled that Stan was suddenly asking so many questions. "What do you mean? Safe? Yes, of course! The iDocs will work in conjunction with the carebots, and will feed information directly to them. So the carebot will have all their elderly person's vital signs in real time."

"So it's beneficial for them?" asked another of the younger city men.

"Once we know exactly what's happening in a person's life," continued James, "then we, and the carebots, can begin to regulate their programmes as necessary. We'll be able to feed information back to the carebots about exactly what needs doing. It'll be very much a two-way thing." He paused, adding, "Carebots are much more reliable and safer than any human staff; they never steal, never drop anyone or anything, and never go off sick or on holiday."

"So we're doing the elderly a favour by helping them live longer?" asked the same young man again.

"Up to a certain point of course," cautioned James. "These older people are monitored very closely so that we can tell what their life expectancies are, and if necessary, adjust things."

Stanley went pale whilst the farmer jumped in, "I'm not worried about all that. What you're saying is, if we give them to all the old folk then we wouldn't need so many staff? Or even any staff at all?" When James nodded slowly, smiling, the farmer said, "Let's get going then!"

The farmer was evidently won over; that would be a relief for James. It was the thought of the potentially huge returns on his investment had made the difference, although he did also keep looking over at Reg, slightly anxiously as though he might start wiping his nose too.

James responded, rubbing his hands together, as the others around the table nodded acquiescently. "Good! We'll need to get the Treasury signed up next. That's the whole point of the cross-departmental seminar and the blue-sky thinking. We've got the meeting with the government departments set up for in three weeks' time. They'll need to pay the right price – there's a lot of money in private care. But if we win, then the sky's the limit. Last year, the private capital industry grew to $10 trillion, and that's projected to hit $18 trillion in five years. The drivers behind the boom, and the covid impact on NHS waiting lists, means the larger institutional investors are looking for high risk-adjusted returns."

Stanley came in tentatively, "Why don't we get this adopted for public care first? If it's the right way forward, we could try for a pilot somewhere using public budgets and then extend it to those who can pay for it themselves. The price of each individual care robot retails at around £80k right now, but that'll come shooting down once we have the volume."

"Good thinking Stanley, but remember I've already purchased them at volume. The number of people paying for their own care is well over half now. They'll vote with their feet. But we'll have to see what the Minister wants to do."

"Forget about him and his lot," said the farmer, "it's us that's doing all the work and taking all the risks."

James smiled, "Maybe, but let's keep them on board. They are in charge after all, or at least think they are! Sometimes I worry that they all seem like teenagers these days, but maybe that's my age talking!"

Stanley came back in again, "You have a point though about eighteen-year-olds. The youth vote is just as important as the silver vote now, if not more. The millennials were stirred up by Labour in the Brexit vote, and they voted in their thousands – lots of them for the first time."

"They're the ones that are getting so pissed off, forgive my

French," said the farmer, "at not being able to buy their own homes."

James looked at Stanley thoughtfully. "Stanley, could you do a review of the youth voting intentions? It would be helpful to know exactly what's going on, just in case we need ammunition in our ministerial discussions ..." Then he added another bombshell, "I think we need to use the NHS data better too – and add-in the NHS spiralling costs to our equation. Things like hip and knee operations ... I heard on the grapevine that they are thinking of introducing capping on those for anyone over the age of 70."

"You mean refusing operations to older people just because they're old?" asked the farmer's wife.

"Well, it's not being put like that of course."

One of the city men came in, "I've been picking up rumours that the government are accelerating to sell off NHS data."

James smiled again. "You're right there. Well spotted. And our data can help; if we merge the data across health and social care, then we can do a proper estimate of the spend, the profit share and run rate."

Stanley nodded. "One other thing that we should take into account ..." he paused ... "Cassie, my fiancé, is an environmentalist. With the temperatures rising each summer, the weather is leading to a spiralling death rate from heat stroke every July and August. It's killing off ... I'm sorry," looking at the farmer's wife, "causing the demise of as many older people as the cold spells used to do."

"Funny you should say that," the farmer interrupted. "The wife's sister dropped dead from the heat in Spain just last summer."

"If it's going to work, and things like climate change are coming into play, then we need somewhere where we can properly isolate the programme and control the results," continued Stanley. He paused, he was just repeating what Cassie had said to him but wasn't that more or less what the robots in the Robots Network Renewal Programme including Henry2 were already doing? And they were also collecting data too by the sound of it? Why not also do financial research? Maybe it was alright after all. James wouldn't do it if there were risks, would he?

James Hillingdon looked at him and nodded approvingly, "Good thinking Stanley. Let's find a convenient place to try all this out. Meanwhile, I can smell the beef Stroganov, lunch is served next door." Clapping his hands he waved them out of the meeting room.

As James left, he tapped Reg on the head and Reg turned himself off. As the robot stood silently by the door, the slight humming sound stopped and his lights dimmed, but his ESP continued to whir away in the background …

Chapter 32

All that afternoon Henry2 had been grinding spices from scratch and marinating goodness knows what. He had all the little jars and packets lined up on the kitchen worktop, meticulously measuring each ingredient. That evening, he served up an amazing vegetarian curry chock full of chickpeas and turmeric. I was both delighted and surprised. Had he acquired an e-nose and e-tongue without telling me? How else had he mastered the art of haute cuisine? Maybe he'd been watching *Master Chef* on TV, but wait, no, he didn't watch TV. Either way, he had cooked an outstanding curry. I patted him on his steely shoulder and told him it smelled and tasted delicious. As he turned to face me, his bright little eyes seemed to lighten up and I could swear he almost beamed.

Henry2 kindly poured me a glass of wine after dinner, despite the fact he must have known I'd already had a sneaky one beforehand. Feeling full after the best curry ever, I put my feet up in front of the TV to watch the news. Henry2 was getting on with the washing up. I could almost hear him humming, but I must have imagined it. As always, he was puzzled as to why I wanted to watch the news when, as he said, he could give me his endless news stream of anything and everything from the weather to the economic situation. I had learnt from bitter and boring experience that robots cannot filter or analyse news items and so I rarely took him up on that offer.

The government was making a 'State of the Universe' announcement on the crisis of health and social care for older people. Stan hadn't been in touch for a week or two, which wasn't unusual, but nor had Evie, which surprised me. The news started with climate change, and then air pollution becoming a big issue for frail older people. Then they moved on to the main feature, which started with more doom and gloom. The housing crisis was deepening and many middle-aged children were still renting; the suicide rate in the over seventies was rising; there was controversy over assisted dying and Dignitas becoming more commonplace; and the cost of care homes was spiralling. No-one had a solution. I thought of Brian and wondered how many other aged parents were being pressurised and maybe even threatened in the same way? He had had no intention of using the money from his parents' house to pay for their care, and he'd got away with it.

The Prime Minister was on the news. Like all his predecessors, he'd spent years dilly dallying over what to do about the social care crisis and the lack of funding for it. Drastic action was therefore now inevitable, and an announcement was about to be made. The Prime Minister stepped up to the podium. He adjusted his spectacles as the cameras flashed and cleared his throat. "This government is proud to announce that we will be taking action on the care of our older people. Today in our country, one in ten of us is living to be a hundred. We know that many of you are concerned about the care of your loved ones. We also know that others are worried about the increasing costs of care and about losing your homes after a generation of saving hard." He paused to smile, looking oddly nervous. "While living longer is excellent news, it also means we have to ensure that ALL our people live happy and healthy lives."

The cameras shifted briefly as the PM introduced the new Secretary of State for 'Health and Wellbeing,' Shirley Harper Smith. No doubt they would soon be adding 'mindfulness' into the title as well. Hopefully, the press would not be deceived. The PM continued, "The Department of Health and Wellbeing has been giving this new policy top priority. Shirley's department has been working hard with the Treasury to find the best AND ..." he emphasised, "the most *affordable* solution for us all. Shirley, over to you."

The cameras focussed on a smartly dressed young woman in a bright blue trouser suit. She tossed her bouncy blond hair back over her shoulders and said, "Thank you, Prime Minister," with a confident smile and nod in his direction. "As you have quite rightly said, we have been considering the best way to ensure that all our elderly citizens are treated with the best possible care. Too many have been languishing for too long in outdated institutions, hospitals and nursing homes. So, we have decided to select a place where everyone will be safe and happy in their old age. The Isle of Wight has long been a popular destination for older people to retire, so I am now pleased to announce that the island will become a designated rehabilitation haven for the over 70s – this haven will be named 'Home Farm.'"

There was a stunned silence before a clamour of voices from the assembled press. She held up her hand, indicating that she hadn't finished. "The Isle of Wight will be renamed 'Home Farm' and will be adapted to the highest possible standards as a place of rest and peace. In the future, all elderly people who are assessed as needing public care will be sent to the island. Their stay there will begin with a standard rehabilitation period of up to two weeks."

The press in the audience were going wild, all pretence of order was thrown out of the window. "What happens after that?" demanded the BBC reporter in the audience.

"If successful, people will be transported back to their own homes. If not, then they will stay on the island and settle into their new home."

"Who will look after them? There's already a growing workforce crisis in social care!" demanded the Guardian reporter.

"An excellent question," smiled Shirley, obviously prepared for this challenge. "It is no secret that we are undergoing a workforce crisis, so we firmly believe that the answer lies in new technology." She paused, "We have therefore decided to invest in care robots."

The *Guardian* Reporter shoved a microphone in her face. "Minister, surely you're not suggesting that robots can actually care for our parents and grandparents?"

Shirley glanced at the Prime Minister, who nodded to Shirley to respond. "We have been undertaking careful research into the capability of robots and we know that special carebots will soon be sufficiently advanced to undertake all the care tasks that a human can do."

The *Times* reporter jumped in angrily. "Will the old folk have to sell their homes to pay for it? Robots must cost a small fortune!"

"If the rehabilitation is successful, we expect they will return to their own homes."

"And if not?" persisted the reporter.

"The sign of a civilised society is one which takes care of its elderly. We hope that by providing a place of rest, the family home can pass to the next generation. In this way, we will also solve the current housing crisis for the under 40s!" She ended triumphantly, shutting her folder with a flourish.

I turned off the television and rang Stan. He picked up at once, so I knew he must have been listening too. "Stan, did you hear the news? What's going on?!"

"You mean the island becoming 'Home Farm'? What do you think?! You've led the way. You'll get celebrity status!" he said excitedly.

"But how can they force people to leave their homes?"

"They won't have any choice. It's all bundled up with new powers of attorney and the Sunset clause, alongside the new Deprivation of Liberty arrangements that have replaced the old DoLs. Aren't you pleased?"

"I wanted a solution, but my island is crowded enough as it is."

"It was inevitable, Mum. Private equity couldn't continue to subsidise elderly care in residential homes."

"Well, as long as they continue to make money, that's the main priority!" I said derisively.

The sarcasm was lost on Stanley, who continued, "Didn't you like the sweetener of more homes for the under 40s? That was my stroke of genius. It'll go down a treat!"

"What do you mean, Stan? Did you have something to do with this?!" I demanded.

"Mum, the youth vote is just as important as the silver vote now."

I didn't want to know anymore and said goodbye, shocked at his callousness. Better not tell him about my iDoc, I decided. What *was* he up to now?

***

There was just a slightly raised red mark where my iDoc had been inserted a couple of days previously at the clinic and the butterfly stitches had already fallen away. I'd almost forgotten it was there. The clinic said that our robots would activate them after 72 hours, so that would be tomorrow, but they didn't say how. I'd signed a confidentiality agreement and so strictly speaking, I did the right thing by not telling Stan about the iDoc. Anyway, he obviously didn't care either way.

The next day, Henry2 announced that he had a programme to run through with me as soon as possible. He seemed quite excited – for a robot, anyway. First, though, I had my outpatient's appointment to check up on my hip after my fall. Arriving in the Notcar at the island hospital, I was hit by quite a commotion at the entrance to the clinic. Bright young things in NHS blue tracksuits were excitedly handing out leaflets.

I accepted one and read the title, "Home Farm: Island Haven for the over 80s." The leaflet explained in much more detail what we'd heard on the news. This was no spur-of-the-moment announcement. The leaflets explained that everyone would have a special assessment on their seventieth birthday, like for the driving license, followed by intensive monitoring to ensure their 'current and future fitness to function.' Whatever that meant. Thank goodness I'd been keeping fit. A while back, they had introduced the requirement that you had to be physically fit in order to qualify for any surgery you might need, and that you had to lose weight if you were more than two kilos over. This took that idea a whole stage further.

Social care was no longer in the control of local government, who had virtually given up the thankless and hopeless task anyway. What about couples like poor Peggie and Edward? What if one of you was fit and healthy and the other not? All these thoughts raced through my mind as I waited to see the consultant. When he bustled through the waiting area and into his office, he was obviously not a happy man. He was complaining bitterly to anyone who would listen, "It's not right. They're interfering with my professional clinical judgement."

My Twitter feed was full of the protests that were happening at the royal medical colleges. Doctors and nurses were threatening strike action over what their spokespeople had described as a "draconian new regime" that was "rationing" health care. They were ignoring social care as usual.

Then it became apparent that another reaction was emerging. The younger generation were seeing it all completely differently. Instagram and TikTok were flooded with posts from the under forties who were applauding the government's line and the fact that this would help their aged parents move out of their homes and release the equity. The problem of who in families would need to make these tricky decisions was solved with the new powers of attorney legislation, which meant that the choice would be taken out of their parents' hands.

The press was going wild, 'Baby Boomers' Boom is Over!' screamed the *Independent* on the waiting room table. The article argued that the younger generation would vote heavily in favour of the new arrangements. The government had been very clever in making this about housing and offering this up as a way of ensuring that older people wouldn't be a burden on their middle-aged children. The silver vote was rapidly becoming tarnished like old age itself, I thought, looking down at my wrinkled brown hands.

At the clinic, my scan didn't work and set off a screaming alert. The technician double checked, "It's usually jewellery that sets it off, but you haven't got any on."

The penny dropped, I almost cried out, "It's my iDoc!" but luckily remembered to keep quiet. I couldn't reveal its existence to anyone, so I texted Henry2, "Help! Turn my iDoc off!" He messaged me back to say that he just had. This made me a bit uneasy. How did he know it needed doing? Either way, this made it invisible to the machine and the next time, the reading was perfect.

When I got home, Henry2 was waiting for me with dinner and my usual glass of wine. Whilst I was eating, I wondered what he would say about the changes. "Henry2, please can you tell me about the new compulsory powers of attorney that are being introduced?"

"The new powers of attorney are being brought in to strengthen the rights of children wanting to take care of their parents and needing to control them in certain circumstances."

"And what are those circumstances?"

"The powers are wide-ranging and cover personal, financial and intellectual control."

Not good then. Maybe that explained why Evie hadn't been in touch. Meanwhile, there were angry disputes being reported everywhere between children and their parents as resentment grew between the generations.

Henry2 brought my iDoc back to life that evening at 8pm. He told me that he would now also be running a new exercise programme on it – I was too tired to ask him what that meant, but I noticed he had released a tiny widget from his main body near his right shoulder. It was no bigger than the gadget which connects my remote mouse to my laptop. At first, nothing happened, and I went back to my wine. He explained that the new programme would gradually build up the data over the next 24 hours and then it would commence.

During that first evening and the next day, I didn't notice anything different, but then I began to feel a warm throb in my wrist every time I walked over 10,000 steps. Was this a kind of reward? I wondered whether it would activate itself when I was doing something wrong, like having an extra glass of wine. Maybe that was all to come.

Chapter 33

It was time for the Twelve Disciples to get back together again. Henry2 told me half of the twelve who had originally volunteered for the iDoc had fallen by the wayside. I wasn't surprised. I asked what had become of them, but Henry2 either didn't know or wasn't authorised to tell me. In the meantime, I had been relishing how to spend my £2,000. I was torn between a wood-burning stove or a motorised bicycle for those hills, which seemed to be getting steeper every week. Henry2 didn't approve of either.

"The stove is completely unnecessary because the central heating is more than adequate. Moreover, the new 'Clean Air Strategy' states that 38% of current primary articulate matter comes from domestic wood- and coal-burning."

Poor Henry2 couldn't pick up the glorious smell of burning wood and the crackle of a fire. He didn't relish my idea of a motorised bicycle either; I like to think that he was proud of my fitness progress and was convinced that a motorised bike would set me back. Was there a competition between the robots for which of their humans did the best?

I sent out a WhatsApp invite to the other three disciples to see if they wanted to meet up next week for coffee. The Open Day Meeting, where the new Home Farm regime was being heralded, was happening in Newport next week. It would be a good opportunity to find out more. I was keen to discuss the new programme. Pete replied to my message almost immediately, which pleased me as I was beginning to respect and welcome his clear mind and common sense. Jude and Simon also both confirmed. They'd also had their iDocs activated. Jude was keen to chat about everything that was happening – she seemed to be very well informed. I suggested we meet at the Open Day Meeting first, which was being held in the Newport Centre, and then have coffee afterwards.

***

When the day arrived, Henry2 insisted on ordering me a Notcar and even asked me if I wanted him to come. Was he expecting trouble? I half expected to see the island's brass band marching down the High Street to herald the new plans for the island.

We met up outside the Newport Centre and headed inside. The entrance was lined with kiosks with serious-looking people in suits selling what they dubiously called 'Life Planning,' by which they meant exactly the opposite. There were stalls for local charities with special schemes for the 'Young at Heart' and the 'Active Elderlies.' I noticed that they had all realigned their priorities from the over seventies to the over sixties. Almost every day there was a shift in what was regarded 'old' age. It was hard to keep up.

Pete looked his usual grim self, but nodded in a friendly way as I came up. Jude bubbled away when she arrived with a new bouffant hairdo and freshly painted matching luminous pink toenails. Her neck and hands were betraying her age, and I wondered for the first time if her unusually smooth face owed more to surgery than good skin care. I looked down at my own hands that were wrinkled with nails worn down from gardening. But at least clean, unlike Simon's. As Simon ambled over, he looked dishevelled and sagging. It was as though he'd given up the fight with life. He kept fiddling with his grubby old rucksack, taking things out and then putting them back in again. It was hard to ignore the stench of the unwashed coming from him. Pete moved away in distaste. I wondered why Doreen was not keeping him cleaner, but maybe she needed an e-nose. Within the first five minutes, Simon had repeated several times how worried he was that Doreen would be taken away and he wouldn't be able to cope. He even said he'd volunteered to give up his £2,000, which I thought was going a bit too far.

As we made our way into the main hall to take up our seats at the front (courtesy of the advance tickets the robots had organised), a large screen was lowered until it filled the centre of the stage. On one side of the stage, a group of reporters with their cameras and microphones were at the ready. People were still moving in at the back of the hall, but everyone hushed as the Chief Secretary to the Treasury and the new Secretary of State for Health and Wellbeing, Shirley Harper Smith, appeared live on the screen. She paused and cleared her throat, while looking across at the audience and grinning maniacally. She was wearing a tight bright red dress this time with incredibly high heels and her blond hair was curling down over her shoulders.

"Good morning everyone. Thank you for coming here today. We are very keen to hear your thoughts and we hope you will help us by voting on each of the questions we have for you." And then she added, "Your vote matters!" as if she was touting for votes in a political campaign. She shuffled her papers and continued, "As you know, the Isle of Wight has been declared 'Home Farm.' And we want local residents to be very much involved in the next steps." She paused and smiled, evidently trying to seem reassuring. "We have been concerned for some time that the end-of-life-care for our older people is not up to the standards it should be. We cannot accept the current position." She then emphasised, "Our older people deserve better!" before pausing again to drink from a glass of water. As her stilted speech continued, I began to realise that she was nervous!

What was she so nervous about?! I was getting a premonition, based on the speech given back in 2018 at the Social Services Conference. "We are announcing a number of measures which will ensure that all our older people move towards the end of their life with dignity and with happiness. We have come to the conclusion that it is not in the interests of our older people to have what are often uncomfortable, unnecessary, and unwanted interventions." She shook her head earnestly. "These medical interventions are, as many of you will know, painful and sometimes unnecessary extensions to daily living. Our older people have had little choice in deciding whether they want to proceed with these interventions. The NHS has made these decisions on their behalf – often extending lives as long as possible regardless of the cost to them and their dear ones." She took another sip of water – she was definitely nervous! "We now believe you wish us to reconsider this."

Jude was making notes on her iPad, but Simon was nodding. My heart sank. I couldn't believe what I was hearing. There was a noticeable shuffling of chairs in the hall and much whispering behind hands.

She paused. "We are undertaking two simultaneous consultations. The first is a specifically designed focus group, targeting the younger generation who have expressed a real interest in what happens to future generations. The second is happening here today with you. We are here to ask you, as representatives of the older generation, how you want us to move forward. At what age, and in what circumstances, do you think is the right time to start an end-of-life care pathway?

She took yet another sip from her glass; it looked like water but could just as easily have been gin. There was a deadly hush in the hall as she finished with a flourish. "Alongside this, we want to make the pension arrangements better, fairer, and more streamlined. More on that later. Thank you for listening. I am now going to pass you over to your local MP, who has kindly agreed to chair this next session.

As I said, we will be listening carefully."

As the screen faded out, there was a babble of noise as everyone started talking at once. One elderly gentleman near the front pushed back his chair and stampeded out, knocking chairs over as he went. Several other people also stormed out, shaking their heads. There were several shouts of, "How dare they!" "Stuff and nonsense!" and "They can get lost. I didn't fight in the war for this!"

The screen on the stage rolled itself back up towards the ceiling, and was replaced with a table at which three serious-looking people came to sit, facing the audience. The local MP sat in the middle. To her right sat a smooth city type man in a three-piece striped suit who looked very familiar. On her other side sat a man with a grey beard who, although he was not in a white coat, looked like a medic. The MP shook hands and nodded at them both as they sat down. She then held her hands up for silence, but at first was unable to quieten the increasingly angry clamour. She began talking loudly over the noise until a cadre of officially dressed men moved toward the front table and the audience finally quietened down.

"Good morning everyone. My name is Alison Torby and for those of you who don't know me, I am your local MP. Please look at your tablets and let's go through the ten big questions. Then we can have a discussion and vote. I'm here to represent you and I fully intend to do just that. I'm delighted to have with me two key speakers, Professor Sir John Westerby, a distinguished geriatrician and orthopaedic surgeon, and James Hillingdon, care homes expert and entrepreneur. Your questions should be coming up on your screens as I speak."

We all looked down out the tablets that had been handed to us as we entered the hall and read the questions one-by-one as they appeared on the screen.

1. Do you favour a return to a recognised end-of-life pathway which can be adopted by everyone and makes the

end of life as dignified, smooth, and pain free, as possible?

2. Do you favour a set limit for when unnecessary and painful interventions will stop? If so what age would you like to see that limit set. 70, 75 or 80 ?

3. Do you favour an automatic 'Do Not Resuscitate' clause for everyone? If so, how do you want that communicated and what conditions would it cover?

4. Do you favour new automatic powers of attorney so that your children can deal with the difficult decisions about your future on your behalf?

5. Are you happy with having free carebots to look after you?

There were more questions about streamlining the pension credit arrangements into what was being called 'Universal Pensions.' This was obviously very much a sweetener. All the extra benefits that governments had added over the years would be amalgamated into one pot. Anyone who was still working over the pension age would have to pay tax. And if they earned enough, they would lose all extra benefits, including free bus passes, the TV license benefit, and the winter fuel allowance. I was puzzled as to why they had decided to leave the free prescription charges out of that list of withdrawn benefits. Then it dawned on me that it wouldn't make any difference because there would be far fewer prescriptions with the less healthy people dying earlier. I wondered if others were thinking the same thing. I looked across at my friends; Pete was angry, Jude was puzzled, and Simon was lost in a world of his own. I was becoming more perturbed by the minute. What on earth did they think they were doing ? It felt surreal. Judging from the mumblings in the audience, I wasn't alone.

As we voted on our tablets, the results were thrown up on the screen. At first, as usually happens at big events, most people behaved apart from another angry man who stormed out from the back shouting "Bloody nonsense, who do they think they are!" slamming the door behind him.

I waited until a few results came up on the screen before I cast my votes, curious to see what people would be saying. As the votes to the first questions popped up on the screen in real time, it became clear that everyone seemed to favour an end-of-life pathway. Had they forgotten, or perhaps they had never known about, the ill-fated Liverpool Care Pathway where people were left to starve and denied water for days before they died? It had been a cruel and painful death for many, but thankfully not for Tom. I wondered whether the results were rigged, so in a moment of irritation I voted "no" to everything on principle. The question about age limits had the most mixed results, with some people, presumably those who were younger, actually voting for 75 as the cut-off point.

When the audience had finished casting their votes, the MP thanked everyone, although by now several dozen people had left or were in the process of doing so. Then she asked James Hillingdon to talk about the investment in new systems for the future. By now I had recognised James. He looked as dapper as ever; the new silver-grey streaks through his sleek hair just added to his appeal. He was wearing a pink striped shirt, and a darker pink handkerchief fell elegantly out of the top pocket of his navy blue pin-striped suit. James leaned forward to the audience that was left and, smiling, said, "Thank you for staying. I've been investing in health and social care ... or rather, 'wellbeing' as it's now known, for many years. As part of my life's work, I know to my cost that private investors have long been subsidising the costs of care."

"Taking the profits, you mean!" yelled an angry voice from the back.

James carried on smoothly. "Even more unacceptably, fully fee-paying residents have been subsidising those who come from the public care route. But for my part, I fully intend to continue investing the profit from my business back into the sector; this will ensure that standards of care are kept high, and the costs low. Part of my investment plan includes creating a special new partnership with the government to increase the number of carebots. These will not *replace*, but will *supplement*, our much-overworked workforce," he emphasised.

"What if we don't want bloody machines looking after us?" called out another angry voice.

"Unfortunately, some older people have no children to look after them," replied James, unfazed and shaking his head sadly. "After many years of careful research and planning on the island and elsewhere, we've been trying out specially programmed carebots with local residents. The islanders who've been using our robots are delighted with them. They particularly value them as a way of keeping their independence and staying in their own homes."

I had thought that there were only twelve of us from the RNP in the first place, and only four of those remaining. Hardly a huge programme. Then I realised I had no idea how many other programmes there might be out there. James continued, "Any change is difficult, but the government is right. Sometimes we've let our older people go on for too long in pain and difficulty." The MP then welcomed Professor Sir John Westerby to speak about the sorts of interventions that we might be expecting.

Westerby began by saying, "I have been caring for the elderly on this island and elsewhere for many years now. It is my view that much more help is needed, especially with hip and knee replacements, which is my speciality." He nodded benignly over his glasses. "I'm in favour of using robots, especially for the heavy lifting and difficult tasks. My company, Citizen UK, has also been experi …" he stopped in mid-word, and then continued with emphasis, "*developing* … care robots to help people live independently at home after their surgery."

James interrupted, "Whilst my colleague is correct, it is also a concern that some older people have said that they do not always want to have their lives extended by painful surgery. They want to choose the best way forward themselves."

The MP then piped in while Westerby leaned forward, glowering at James. "Perhaps you could tell us, Sir John, when it is that people benefit most from knee and hip surgery?"

"Certainly, my dear," Westerby began again, "it is my experience, over many years, that most people prefer to have their surgery as early as possible. The reason for this is that they prefer to keep active for as long as possible and to avoid other debilitating conditions setting in."

"If they have surgery too soon, isn't there a risk that they'll have to go back for another operation twenty years later?" asked a reporter. "And doesn't it come down to whether or not you can afford to pay? The NHS won't pay for early operations, surely?"

"Well, in some circumstances, it's true that the NHS prefers to wait. But shouldn't we also respect the choice of the patient?"

"Thank you, Sir John." the MP intervened. "Now, do you have anything else to add before we return to James Hillingdon?"

Westerby continued, "The problem is that we must make sure that patients receive the proper follow-up care pathways both after surgery and through every stage of the ageing process." Pete piped up with his hand in the air, "If that's the objective, then why are the waiting lists still getting longer? Why hasn't anything been done about that? It sounds as if more money is needed!"

The MP intervened, "The real problem is not the money. The real problem is making the right choices, so that there's equality and fairness for all – including for the younger generation who'll be paying for it all."

Sir John was about to speak again when James came in. "This is why we've introduced the 'Life Planners' programme – to help patients who wish to avoid painful and unnecessary interventions. There is a very real danger that we are currently bombarding people with interventions and treatments without giving them any choice."

I snorted internally. It went on like this for another half an hour, I had stopped listening. I was intrigued by James. Was he a good guy or a bad guy? Either way, I wanted to find out and realized I definitely fancied him. As soon as the presentation was over, I went up to the platform to see if he remembered me. "Hello there," I said, holding out my hand, "So it's you who's been behind my carebot all this time?"

"Delighted to see you again!" He jumped down from the platform and shook my hand warmly, holding on to my hand with both of his. "I didn't realise you were one of our volunteers. I thought you'd gone to Wales?"

"Wales?" I shook my head in bewilderment. "What made you think that?!"

James also looked slightly confused, but smiled, shaking his head. "Never mind. How are you finding it, anyway?"

"I love my robot, Henry2 … most of the time, anyway! I don't think they're for everyone though – half of our number wanted to drop out when we moved to the next stage."

"What do you mean, the next stage?" he asked, looking puzzled. Then he added, "Look, here isn't a good place to talk. Let's meet up soon and you can tell me all about it. Lovely to see you again. By the way, that boy of yours, Stanley, is a great asset!"

I took his suggestion that we should meet up with a pinch of salt – he was obviously a very busy and important man – but it might be rather nice if he did. Why on earth did he think I was in Wales?

As we filed out of the hall, people talked in a low key way amongst themselves. I noticed that Jude stayed back to talk to one of the officials. Outside, at the nearest open-air coffee place, Simon sat down heavily, almost wrecking the delicate wrought-iron chair. He said gloomily, "Maybe it's not such a bad idea. I'm in a lot of pain now. I can't see them ever getting around to fixing my hip. They want me to lose two stone first." I reached over to put my hand on his as he went on morosely, "Doreen's okay, but she's no substitute for the real thing. I miss my real Doreen. It's not the same without her."

I wondered how many other people thought like him. Jude ambled over to us and jumped in with both feet as usual. "They're not getting me! And I'm not telling anyone how old I am, just in case! I'll decide when my time has come! And that may never happen if I have my way!"

Pete was his usual quiet and hard-to-read self. I asked him what he was thinking. He replied carefully, "It's not that I don't care about what happens to me, it's just that it makes me so bloody angry that they think they can decide. If Simon wants to go, fine, we should all be able to decide when our time comes. But we've let them dictate to us for too long. We're the ones who know what's right for us."

I thought back on what had been said on the platform and felt worried. But I also remembered the feel of James' hand in mine and felt myself blushing. Would there be an invite? I was pleased I'd washed my hair that morning.

Chapter 34

Change seemed to be happening so quickly now. Was it everywhere? Or just on the island? I wished that there was someone I could talk to. Both Stan and Evie just didn't seem available. I wasn't sure I could ever completely trust Stan again in any case, and Evie was so wrapped up with her family. Auntie Peggie was gone. The Disciples were all fine in their own way, but I didn't feel I could go very deep with them. Simon was resigned to his deteriorating health. Jude was bright and chatty, but I didn't trust her an inch. She would go to the press if there was any money in it, or even just to be the centre of attention. It was probably her that had told the RNRP about what Simon was doing late at night with Doreen when she tucked him up in bed (it had caused a small storm between the letter writers in the local paper for a couple of weeks). Pete was okay, but he could be so grumpy. My world was getting smaller. It must have surely been a co-incidence, but all this had happened since Henry2 had entered my life. I wished I could see James again, but it would be embarrassing if he thought I was chasing him.

I hadn't seen Patrick for weeks either. He had all but disappeared. The last time I'd seen him was when I'd told him about Henry2. He didn't seem much interested in meeting him, which upset me.

230

I'd been looking forward to showing him off, Henry2 I mean, not Patrick. Or did I mean both?

I was getting a little confused. The iDoc was beginning to irritate me too. Was it influencing my ability to think straight? Making me irritable? I was anxious a lot of the time too, worried about what was happening on the island. Where was all this leading? What would happen after the research finished? If it didn't work out, would we lose our carebots? I obviously couldn't talk to Henry2 about it, so I just fretted to myself.

I began drinking more, although I tried not to. It least it was always wine; I reassured myself that it was never spirits, and never during the day. I kept it secret from Henry2 (at least I tried to), by sneaking out on my bike, buying several bottles, and always paying in cash. Then I'd hide them in the summer house, which I knew he couldn't enter because the door was too narrow.

In the old days, I'd have rung Evie for a chat, but all she wanted to talk about now was her problems with Andy. His drinking had got much worse since he'd been made redundant last Christmas. Why do they always have to do it at Christmas? She was convinced he had some form of early-onset dementia. He spent all his time in his study, drinking and watching old movies. She said he'd got very obese; I had visions of his flabby body spilling over the armchair and loose folds of skin around his ankles. I resolved to call her next week when Henry2 was due to go away for his annual MOT.

Henry2 had been away once before, just for 24 hours or so. But this time would be different. The RNRP notified me that he would be away for two whole weeks. It seemed they wanted to have a complete overhaul and do some intense reprogramming – although for what and why, they didn't say. They just said that I would be given a full briefing on his return. When I filled in the form for any adjustments I might require, I added an e-nose and, without expecting anything back, a 'sixth sense.' I laughed as I thought to myself that it might come in useful one day. I began to look forward to some time on my own and made all sorts of plans about digging a new herb vegetable patch and revamping the wildlife pond.

Henry2 was very busy on his last day. He made up all my meals for his two weeks away, just like Evie had done when I had ECT, and labelled them, colour coded, for each day. The codes followed the rainbow. Monday was red, Tuesday orange ... etc. As usual, complicated calculations had been made about the right level of protein, fats, and sugar for each day's diet. He'd chosen healthy versions of all my favourites: vegan shepherd's pie, lasagne, and salmon risotto. On the Sunday night, he gave me a lecture about keeping up my health routine. "Here are your pills. Do not forget to take them and remember to do your exercises every day. The iDoc will be reminding you and recording everything, so we can see what progress you have made when I come back."

"Oh, dear, and I'd been thinking I could take two weeks off and have a good read!" I laughed. But Henry2 didn't do irony, so the joke was wasted. When he looked questioningly at me I added, "Henry2, thanks for all this, you're being very kind, but although I'm growing older, I can still actually cope quite well on my own!"

Seeing my medication laid out in little boxes – five for each day now including the tiny pink pills that I was supposed to take but never did – I decided to risk a question, "You do know that I don't take the pink pills, Henry2, don't you?"

He looked back at me and said firmly. "Self-determination and choice are invaluable human characteristics, Anna."

I laughed, "Does that apply to everything, Henry2?"

"It applies where there is human choice. Please pay attention while I run through the rest of the preparations. It is vital that you keep up with your fitness whilst I am away. It is important you take responsibility for your own wellbeing."

I looked down at my wrist and scratched at the spot where the iDoc was, twisting and turning the loose skin as though I might be able to dislodge it. Henry2 had reduced me to a truculent teenage with all his control freakery.

The man with the white van came early on Monday morning. I went to the door to see Henry2 off and felt sad when I waved him goodbye. After a day in the garden pulling up the faded blue forget-me-nots and the once bright orange marigolds, already spilling their curly seed heads, I was tired and happy. I decided I'd go upstairs for a soak in the bath after putting my Monday evening meal – salmon risotto with peas and broccoli – in the oven. Henry2 had planned for me to eat my main meal at lunchtime, but with him away, I could suit myself.

At 6pm, not a moment before, I got into my pyjamas, opened a bottle of Merlot, and took it outside in the fading light. I sat on the wooden bench beside the wildlife pond, watching the birds rush past to their nests. They always seemed in such a hurry, as though they had to get to safety before the night fell. I'd planned a small rockery so that the newts could climb out and small creatures could drink without falling in. As I watched, a brilliant turquoise dragon fly skimmed the surface, tiny brown newts basked in the rocky shallows, and a bright orange goldfish darted in and out of the pond weed. In no time at all, it was dusk. The final retiring birds raced across the skies to get to their nests before complete darkness fell. I hoped an owl would make an appearance soon.

I reminisced about the early days of my marriage to Tom when the children were little. We'd had wonderful plans for self-sufficiency, but the dreams got taken over with real life. In the gloaming, the baby owls began their screeching for food and I saw the flash of a white-winged owl widen out from the eves of the village hall. The screeching abated, no doubt as they scrunched on the tiny creatures their parents had hunted for them. Two hours later, when the Merlot was finished, I staggered unevenly back inside, where a strong smell of overcooked salmon greeted me. Feeling my way in the dark, I turned off the oven and climbed the stairs to bed. I could clean my teeth in the morning.

That night, I dreamt about a baby. The baby was crying and crying in the night as though he was hungry. At some point, in the muddled tumble of my dreams, I woke up hot and sweaty and found myself sitting upright, my hands searching across the duvet for my missing baby. Was he hungry? Where was his bottle? Did I change his nappy? Was he lying twisted and strangled by the covers or out somewhere alone, shivering in the cold night air?

The clock said four am. The room was airless. I'd fallen asleep in my pyjamas and coat with the window tightly shut. I stumbled over and threw it wide open, looking up, hoping to see stars in the dark sky. But it was a cloudy night and heavy with pending rain. In the bathroom, I put my head under the cold tap and gulped down the fresh cold water. Climbing back into bed, I thought I could hear the screeching of the baby owls again. Then the lightning hit and crackled in a blaze across the night sky. As it did, it threw the bedroom into sharp relief before the thunder rolled across the skies and the rain came down. It would refresh the pond, at least.

I had thought I would have a lovely time on my own – a sort of holiday, free from the restrictions which inevitably go along with living with a conscientious, controlling machine. Instead, after a few days when the novelty had worn off, I found myself beset with a constant stream of worries which kept returning and repeating. It was the events of the last few weeks which kept returning. With Peggie and Edward's death there seemed nothing left to live for … I couldn't finish anything and began writing long lists, something I hadn't done since before the ECT.

Each night was disturbed by harrowing dreams of machines toppling forests and badgers rooting in the garden for baby creatures. I had virtually turned day into night and sat out every evening in the garden until late. I was barely eating and feeling nauseous much of the time. I tried to revert to my previous habit of cooking up a pot of lentil and carrot soup with left over bacon, and eating it with stale chunks of bread. But sometimes even that was

234

too much. Henry2's carefully prepared meals were still stacked up in the freezer. I grimaced. I must remember to chuck them out or there would be hell to pay when he got back.

My iDoc was active but what exactly was it doing? It knew when I got up and when I did my exercises. It knew my blood pressure and probably the state of my bowels. But did it know about my unhappy heart? The iDoc was beginning to know too much about me. Was it part of me now? I didn't like the idea that it was trying to dictate what I should do. Was my nausea being triggered by too much wine or by something else altogether?

I decided to act. I couldn't remember how to deactivate the iDoc without Henry2. Or had I ever known? The only answer had to be to remove it. It was only just beneath the surface of my wrist, after all. As a teenager, I'd self-harmed for a while and this wouldn't be that different, although I suspected it would run a little deeper than my teenage scratching. I found myself looking forward to cutting into my skin and feeling the relief of running the knife into my flesh. I would need a sharp knife. The small kitchen one would do but it was a little blunt, so I sharpened it on the old-fashioned stone that Henry2 had put away at the back of the drawer. I would need an anaesthetic – a general one as well as one for the wound. I searched through the high up cupboards and found a bottle of malt whisky that I'd brought down from London and never touched. It was a Glenmorangie – a favourite of Tom's and a birthday gift he'd never opened. I had been saving it for my next special birthday, but this was more important.

I poured myself a generous glass of the whiskey. The golden liquid warmed my throat, making my eyes sting. Maybe some chunks of ice to slow it down? I went to the freezer door and when I opened it, saw all the stacks of frozen meals. I pulled them all out onto the floor, grabbed the ice trays that were stuck at the back of the freezer and slammed the freezer door shut. I'd deal with the mess of frozen meals later. The whisky would double up as a disinfectant for the cut. I prepared carefully for the surgery and giggled to myself at the irony of the Minister's idea of the iDoc removing the need for painful interventions. I laid the table out with a clean white cloth and smoothed it down. I found a white towel and a dish that would hold the discarded iDoc. Henry2 might get into trouble if it got lost. I added plenty of white cotton wool and bandages from my First Aid kit. The glowing bottle of Glenmorangie stood at one side like a sentry.

Admiring the beautifully laid out setting, I was reminded of the tattoo table in Peggie's kitchen. I briefly wondered if I should use a black marker pen to scribble DNR on my chest just in case, but laughing, decided against it. I poured myself another large glass of the malt and breathed in its warmth. Putting it down, I picked up the small sharp knife and made the first cut. It hurt, but not as much as I'd thought it would. I felt that surge of searing sensation, and old painful and pleasurable memories came flooding back. Taking a deep breath, I cut longer and deeper. The skin opened up and bright red blood began to swell up from the wound. I realised I'd have to go deeper still to get down to the iDoc itself. I was pretty certain I'd cut in the right place. I sharpened the knife again and took another swig of the malt straight from the bottle. Then I heard a clink as the iDoc hit the kitchen floor. It was out! Tom would not approve of this, but Tom wasn't there anymore. No-one was really. Suddenly Henry2 didn't count any more. He wasn't real, after all.

A loud knocking at the door made me jump. Brian? Surely not? I got up unsteadily and went to the door and listened, wishing I'd had a peep hole inserted into the front door. "Who's there?" I called out, still fearful that it could be Brian come to bully me again, even after his parent's double suicide. My eyes swelled up with tears at the thought of them lying on their bed together holding hands.

This time there was no Henry2 to protect me. The voice that answered sounded vaguely familiar. And insistent, "Open the door Anna, open it now!"

I tugged at the door handle with my good hand, the one that wasn't dripping with blood. The handle had always been stiff. The door fell back, and there stood Mrs Finlay in the doorway. She moved forward and took hold of my arm, the one that was dripping with blood. She moved me into the kitchen where she put the towel around it. It was beginning to hurt. I wanted more of the malt whisky but after sitting down at the table I remembered very little.

Chapter 35

Over the next few days, voices came and went. My world was full of dead images and strange smells. Doors opened and shut. People in white coats came in and out, and machines ticked, pinged, and buzzed. My cut wrist was heavily bandaged and when I looked under the bandage, I could see that it had been stitched. But what else had happened? I knew I'd been here before, or somewhere like this. I could hear whispering voices but it was hard to tell if they were in my head or where they were coming from.

One voice became clearer, "You have taken part in a huge research programme drawing on the new concept of singularity. This is when AI becomes so powerful and sophisticated that humans begin to merge with technology. Have you heard of trans-humanism?"

Talking would be an effort, but it would be rude not to reply, especially as whoever it was, was treating me as a proper person, so I said, croaking, "I know about it, but I'm sorry, I can't remember much."

The voice replied, "It's when you take the concept of virtual twins and humanoid robots to the next level – it has the aim of obliterating the boundary between human bodies and machines."

Somewhere in the back of my mind, I remembered Keeper

Zack, and the word 'singularity.' The voice went away but came back hours later, this time sternly. I didn't want stern, I wanted soft and kind. The harsh voice had broken into my reverie about wildlife ponds with shoals of tiny fish swimming freely in the weeds.

"Are you a member of the RNRP?" it asked sternly. Did I know about the RNRP? It seemed familiar, but I couldn't remember …

"What's the RNRP?" I asked in return.

The reply was exasperated, "You know this. The Robot Network Renewal Programme of course."

I nodded my head slowly on the pillow. I knew those words from somewhere, somewhere a long time ago. It gradually came back that The Robot Network Programme was when I first met Sambot, the sweet little robot from Southend. I'd joined the Network as a way of keeping in touch with developments and because I'd wanted my own robot but that was all a long time ago. But then I remembered I had my own robot now, Henry2. Where was he?

"I did join the Robot Network Programme a long time ago," I said.

"Ah," said the harsh voice softening. "We haven't met one of the original members for a long time," the voice reached forward to touch my good hand.

"We thought you'd all lost interest. We tried to contact you when we were updating the Network to the Robot Network Renewal Programme. We wanted to bring the original robots out there back to life and reprogram the defunct ones."

I thought back to my first meeting with Sambot. Was Sambot defunct now?

"What I don't understand though," the voice went on, "is how they had your DNA. Did you sign up with a finger password?"

"Yes … Yes, I always did then, it was the thing to do."

I remembered licking the sugar off the jam doughnut from my fingers when I was completing the application form on my laptop. The sugar fell on to the keyboard. Memories from long ago flood back as if they were yesterday.

"Does it matter?" I asked.

"We think that was their early primitive way of capturing your DNA. Then they built your presence into the consciousness of all the early robots. They could always recognise you as an original. You were very valuable to them because artificial intelligence and machine learning was pretty rudimentary then. Since then, they've been continually drawing in new intel but you were much more sensitive to the adaptations because of your background in social work and predictive analytics."

"Who are 'they'?" I asked, "and who are you?"

"We will explain more later when you're feeling better."

"Is it machines learning from humans? Machine learning in reverse?" I said.

"Strictly speaking, that was always the case. We especially wanted people who were highly emotionally literate – usually social workers, nurses or psychologists – anyone who worked closely with people."

"Are social workers more likely to have emotional intelligence?"

"Not necessarily, some have very little sadly, but most do and because of this there was a greater chance of them being able to adapt. Then that becomes less important as the robots begin to develop emotional intelligence themselves. Using people from health and social care professions means that the programmers and robots can short-cut and learn from all the professional experiences and relationships that they've developed over their careers."

I shut my eyes and said, "I'm tired now. Do you mind if I rest? There are so many memories. I can't always tell straight away if they're friendly or not, or what is real and what is dead."

"It doesn't really matter to them. It's your thoughts and feelings they are interested in now, rather than specific memories," said the voice.

I realised that I could turn my head from side to side but I couldn't lift it up from the pillow. "Please let me have some sleep now." I turned my head into the flat pillow and fell into a deep sleep. I knew I was embellishing the dreams as I gradually surfaced into the waking world, sometimes smiling to myself, never quite being able to separate the real from the last dream. But I was beginning to feel happy again. As long it was pleasant, did it really matter? It didn't matter to the robots in their endeavours. I smiled again as I thought how good it felt to be able to help them. As I drifted in and out of consciousness, I wanted to talk to my children and my grandchildren. I wanted to understand the world as it was, as it would be, and my place in it.

When I woke up next, Tom was smiling down at me and holding my hand. Then I turned around to see Stanley and Evelyn standing together, one on either side of the white hospital bed, corners crisply triangulated, they stared down at me. I closed my eyes again and breathed steadily as though deeply asleep, but behind my eyes I watched carefully. The weathered skin of my hands was paler now – with a slight yellow tinge – the jaundice they said. The faint sickly scent of Olbas Oil, seeped through the overwhelming smell of antiseptics.

The electronic control panel glared from the wall behind and above the bed. Red pin pricks of flashing lights tracked my very being on the screen; machines measured, counted, analysed inputs and outputs, and outcomes, against my steady breathing. The electronic 24-hour clock to the side of the bed flicked out a new number second-by-second as the minutes passed. The soundless ticks resonated against the stark whiteness of the room. Tick tock, tick tock, as the minutes raced by.

The tall drip trolley, stood in readiness. The transparent fluid bag was pushed to one side. The green button alarm bell was tucked under my wrinkled right hand, my fingers bunched up. Evelyn stood with her back to the window, blocking out the harsh light from the curtain-less window and throwing a slight shadow on my face. She reached forward and gently, slowly, pulled the alarm bell out of my grasp, letting it slide back into its allocated slot on the array of plugs and buttons above the bed. Stanley moved to the foot of my bed. My little finger twitched slightly. The back of my left hand was resting quietly on the cool white sheet, it's bruised back, turned yellow and purple now. The blood stained white tape covered the gash where the needle was inserted into the drip connection, which was connected no more.

They waited, the two of them, arms by their sides, dressed in identical green hospital gowns, emotionless and motionless. When a slight humming noise approached down the corridor, they raised their eyes and gazed at each other. The humming paused outside the door. My fingers jerked slightly. Evelyn reached forward to cover my twitching fingers momentarily whilst Stanley moved further towards my head to make room for the incomer. It was Tom again, come back for me. As the door swung open noiselessly, Stanley and Evelyn nodded, kissed my cheek, and moved silently out of the room. I continued to breathe quietly and deeply, knowing I was safe with Tom by my side again.

I felt a sharp stab in my left arm and then fell into a deep sleep. When I woke up my left hand was still bandaged. A little later someone else came into the room and I felt her smile down at me on my bed. I smiled back. As she came closer, I thought I could smell Olbas Oil as she reached out and stroked my right hand.

"It won't be long now, dear," the familiar voice said.

Chapter 36

It was a few weeks after the announcements about the new social care policies were made (including the announcement that the island would be turned into 'Home Farm') that Evelyn received a disturbing phone call from nurse Finlay. Afterwards, an anxious Evelyn called Stanley, "Have you been keeping up with the news?! And have you spoken with Mum lately?"

"Hey, calm down. Yes, remember we talked just after the PM made all the announcements? I've been busy since," replied Stan. "Why?"

"Mrs Finlay called me today … remember? The nurse that looked after Mum when she had that breakdown? And they gave her ECT? Well, they've given it to her again. She's now staying in the new island clinic."

"Yes, I remember. The one Mum called an 'old battle axe'? Your best friend, though, right?"

"Don't be such a prick! Mrs Finlay was called out on an emergency because Mum was behaving strangely. When they went to see her, they found her hacking away at her wrist, blood pouring down her arm."

"Christ, I thought Henry was supposed to be looking after her!"

"Henry?! Don't you mean Patrick?" Evelyn asked.

"You know! Henry, or Henry2. The robot! You'd know if you paid more attention, or ever went to see her anymore."

"Well, whatever it's called, it can't have been helping that much, can it?"

Stanley paused. "I think Mum might have said something about it going in for an MOT or something …"

"MOT? It's not a car!"

"Actually, a robot isn't that different from a car – it's just a machine, after all." He continued impatiently. "Anyway, all I'm saying is the bloody robot probably wasn't there at the time."

"Well, she was definitely in a state. Mrs Finlay was saying blood was pouring from her wrist, from where she'd cut herself. They only just got there in time."

"Maybe she'd been overdoing the gardening. Those brambles can be vicious."

"Don't be silly, Stan, you really need to grow up. You're a father now. This is serious. She was hacking into her arm with a kitchen knife. They assumed she was depressed again and trying to commit suicide."

Stan shook his head … something made him remember the board meeting and James' proposal. "Maybe she was trying to cut something out … Something called an 'iDoc'."

"What's that? What do you know about it?" Evelyn asked in a panic.

Stanley thought back to what James had said … "iDocs are only being implanted in special circumstances. They're the new preventive well-being programmes for the oldies but they said they were just giving them to a special experimental research group."

"If Mum had one, and she was trying to cut it out, then that would explain how Mrs Finlay knew what she was doing. But what do they do?"

"They're a sort of internal monitor that controls your health and nudges your behaviour; maybe Andy should have one?!" Stanley laughed at his own joke.

"Are you saying our mother is part of some sort of a futuristic experiment on the island? You didn't know about it, did you Stan? Please tell me you didn't!"

"Of course, I didn't know about it! Not about Mum … well, not really. I'm working on this big project. I told you about it – it was all over the news. Mum never mentioned it."

"Wonderful!" Evelyn said sarcastically. "What do you mean? Either you knew, or you didn't!"

"Well, I didn't know she had an iDoc – just that she had the robot." Stan said defensively. "Remember? I met the robot," he added.

"This news about 'Home Farm' sounds like complete bollocks to me. But it would explain how they knew she wasn't well, wouldn't it? With that thing spying on her!" Evelyn was fuming with Stan.

Stan wasn't sure what to think, what on earth was going on with his mother? He mumbled something about revolutionary health care before Evelyn cut him off.

"Listen, I can't go down right now. I've got a real problem with Matty – she didn't get the place at uni she wanted and now she's threatening to leave home. I can't leave Andy – he's probably got early onset dementia, and he's incontinent half the time now, keeps wetting himself."

"Looks like I'll have to go down then, doesn't it? Did the wicked nurse Finlay say when Mum was going home?"

"She strongly advised that we don't visit immediately because she needs complete rest. And then she said something about a decision soon, in the next week or so."

"A decision about what?"

"I didn't fully understand. But she said something about the 'Wight Way' or the 'Right way,' or something. Do you know anything about it?"

Wasn't the 'Wight Way' an end-of-life programme? Stanley felt a wave of alarm. He tried to keep his voice calm, "How odd. I hope not. I'll talk to Cassie right away and whatever nurse Finlay says, we'll go down soon, very soon, I promise." Surely Evie had got it wrong, he reassured himself, no need to panic.

"You'd better get a move on. This is our mother we're talking about!"

"What's that you were saying about Andy – incontinent? Jesus, can't he get a grip – pardon the pun? He's only fifty odd, isn't he?"

"Yes. I'm at my wit's end. I think he'll have to go into a home. I blame a lifetime of lunchtime drinking. I'm hoping they'll put him on some sort of rehab programme. The kids are really disgusted."

Cassie came home through the door with the pushchair and bags of shopping, "Listen Sis, I'm not surprised, but gotta go! Speak later."

Chapter 37

Stanley knew he needed to get down to the island as soon as possible, but didn't want to go on his own. Cassie was always so good at that sort of thing. He'd suggest getting a babysitter for Troy so that she could come too. Despite his growing alarm at what they'd find on the island, it would at least mean that he and Cassie could spend some time together. It had been a while since they had gone anywhere without baby Troy in tow.

Stanley hadn't been able to get hold of James and hadn't wanted to leave a message about his mother. He'd also tried to call the clinic numerous times, but each time he called, although it always said he was first in the queue, he eventually got put through to answer phone. So he gave in eventually and left a message. He received a text message back saying that they weren't expecting his mother to be with them much longer. It was an odd way of saying that she would soon be going home. He was beginning to feel more and more uneasy.

In the meantime, he'd continued with the voting research that James had asked for. Many more young people were voting now and what they were interested in was very different from the oldies. They didn't want to know about health or social care; they'd seen off the Covid epidemic and now they just wanted to live well and be happy. Generation Z apparently wanted meaningful work underpinned by purpose and a diverse culture. This meant they wanted to know how soon they could buy their own homes, educate their children, and find jobs. Stanley knew the youth vote was now more significant than the silver vote, and that would have a major impact on how well the new policy was being received. He would update James as soon as he was back from the island. Seeing Mum had to be the first priority now.

Stanley felt relieved when he and Cassie finally arrived down at the island ferry at midday after dropping Troy off with Cassie's mum in Winchester. She had been delighted to see Troy, and Stanley suddenly realised with a shock that he had only introduced his own mother to Troy on WhatsApp, something else he needed to change. There were hardly any foot passengers and when they got to the port, they found that a new 'heliferry' had replaced the old catamaran and hovercraft. Crossings had been reduced to the beginning of the day and the end of the day. And when he chatted with one of the other passengers, he found that crossings now consisted mainly of staff travelling to and from the mainland. Stanley had heard from his mates over the years that the festivals the island had once been famous for had gradually tailed off. That would explain the drop in the youth hippie traffic and no doubt the tourism too. Everything was changing.

The heliferry was a splendid machine, part helicopter and part jet boat that skimmed rapidly over the sea's surface. It only took eight minutes compared with the usual crossing of twenty-two minutes. Most of that time was taken up with the elevation at the start of the crossing and the descent on the other side. It was a huge improvement on the previous ferries with none of the buffeting around on the waves which used to make him quite nauseous. Yet Stanley had fond memories of those days. He remembered the feeling of adventure each time they'd come over for their summer holidays. Those had been glorious times, and he wished he'd been back to the island more often in adulthood and not gone off abroad quite so much. Troy would be a toddler soon and would enjoy the simple bucket and spade holidays. Cassie had said that having Troy meant they would have to settle for easier and quieter holiday destinations; she was right, and the island always had good weather.

Stan and Cassie disembarked the new heliferry as soon as it docked. As they walked through the almost empty arrivals area on the island, they were surprised to find a passport barrier, but duly handed them over to the official robot who was standing on guard. "Welcome to Home Farm," said the robot in a mechanical voice. It bowed slightly and offered them a small iPad screen in a neat shoulder bag. "You'll find all you need on this, including a map and the directions to the clinic. All your permissions can be found in the App."

Stanley turned to Cassie with raised eyebrows. How did the robot know where they were going? She shook her head gently and gestured her hand downwards, telling him to quieten down. Stanley noticed that the robot's voice had improved since the last time he'd heard a robot speak; the tone was still a bit metallic, but was notably warmer and softer. He was tempted to take a recording back for the office but he could hardly ask the robot to repeat his message. This was a good example of the third generation public sector robots that were beginning to be introduced across the country. Thank goodness the programmers had got over the idea that people wanted a machine which looked like a machine, sounded like one, *and* behaved like one. This effort was much more sophisticated. His generation preferred the human touch and so they always opted for a human, preferably female, voice on their devices. Someone must have told the government or at least the inventors, whoever they were, at last.

They walked forward as directed through passport control, which Stanley knew would be discreetly checking them, although exactly what security issues they could possibly be breaching wasn't clear. In the last area, before the final gate onto the island, there was a large sign that read 'Welcome to Home Farm.' When Stanley's turn came to pass through, the beeper went off loudly. He stepped back, shrugging his shoulders and raising his hands in surprise.

Another robot detached itself seamlessly from a panel to the side of the barrier and blocked their path, saying, "Please remove your mobile phone."

"Damn, I should have left it in the car before getting onto the heliferry!" said Stan, annoyed. He'd hoped he'd get away with it. Now he had no choice now but to give it up. This felt like the special arrangements usually reserved for visitors to prisons, where visitors are required to put all their personal belongings into a locker before they enter. Odd that the Isle of Wight should have a security system like a prison, the oldies were unlikely to want to escape, thought Stanley as he watched the same robot seamlessly merge back into the side-panel with his mobile. Only then did he notice that the whole length of the corridor was packed with robots ready to emerge from their panels at any moment.

Cassie looked at him puzzled. "I thought you left your mobile in the car like I did?"

Stanley stared at her and then said, "Oh, this is just an old one I had in my jacket for emergencies."

As they emerged from passport control into the lobby, they noticed that all the steps in the building had been replaced with rolling escalators that started in motion as soon as you stepped onto them. And when they stepped outside, a line of new-looking buggies, a bit like golf carts, stood waiting. They took a moment to look at the map on the iPad and saw that much of the island was now crisscrossed in a grid of neat mini roads that were depicted in different colours on the map. The only part of the island that was still wild was the south west quarter where Mum lived. When they looked out past the car park, they could see that these little roads were just wide enough for two of the island buggies to pass. A burly young driver in his twenties, wearing a tight green uniform, got out of one of the buggies and greeted them. "Morning!" he said gruffly, "My name is Kevin and I'm your keeper. I'm here to drive you to your mother's clinic."

"Morning Kevin," replied Stan jovially, and then added firmly, "but we're quite happy to drive ourselves as long as the SAT Nav works? "

"We always drive our visitors now," responded Kevin, just as firmly. "The cliff edges are crumbling so badly that we like to make sure everyone stays safe." He leant into the buggy to start the button, adding, "These Buggies mostly drive themselves, anyway."

Stanley whispered to Cassie, "What do we need him for then?!" To Kevin he said, "My Mum used to talk about someone called Kevin who helped her with her first robot, any relation?"

Kevin laughed, "That would be my dad, I'm Kevin the second, some people call me Kevin the Younger, but I prefer Kevin2. Dad was here when the RNP all started, but I took over when Home Farm was being planned. It wasn't really Dad's thing. He stayed on when he retired, in one of the new villas. His burial plot is waiting for him in a prime place up on High Hill. They look after their own around here."

"I thought everyone got cremated these days?" said Stanley, puzzled.

"You're right. They stopped doing burials when the deaths piled up over Covid, even after they introduced the three-layer plots for families, like in Scotland. Only the staff, and anyone who can afford to dig deep, gets buried on the hill. Most people are happy with being cremated, but Dad's old-fashioned."

It didn't seem they had a choice but to accept Kevin2's ride in the buggy. As they rumbled along the pathway, Cassie reached across to hold Stanley's hand. Stanley was looking at the map and noticed that there were still some wild parts of the island with no driveways. They passed an old road sign, half hidden by hawthorn bushes, that read, 'Beware Red Squirrels.' He turned to Kevin2, laughing, "Do red squirrels attack people around here?! I'd love to see a red squirrel. Or a badger, again."

Kevin2 remained deadpan, "We don't encourage people to go wandering around the island too much. We need to keep it safe for both the wildlife and our elderly residents. The red squirrels were fast disappearing when the rebuild started on the other side of the island, but now that's slowed down the numbers are building up again. Especially on the wild side of the island where your mum lives. They pop up anywhere, but you'd need a special permit for badgers."

"Could you find out about getting a permit? We're only here for the day this time, but for when we come back."

Kevin2 turned round to look at him in surprise, "That's above my pay grade, but you could ask at HQ." He pointed to a large castle-type building that stood on a hill to their right, on the old Tennyson's Way. "Badgers are dangerous you know. Big creatures, they are, and heavy! They used to just eat earth worms, up to several hundred a night, but being omnivorous, they'll eat almost anything, from flesh and fruit, to bulbs and bird eggs."

Cassie shivered. "Do you really mean they eat flesh? Surely that's not possible?"

Kevin2 bristled, "Well, I don't know where you get your information from, Miss, but they've even been known to dig up corpses in India. High Hill has been cordoned off for that very reason, just in case."

Cassie shivered again and, squeezing Stan's hand tightly, she whispered, "I'm glad we didn't bring Troy!" Stan squeezed her hand back.

"What about going past Mum's cottage? I'd love to see it again whilst we're here. We could even pop in, check everything's okay."

"All the old buildings are getting protection orders, and they'll soon be fenced off if they're not already."

Stanley was puzzled. He badly wanted to go back to the old cottage where he'd last seen his mother about a year ago. He could still picture her there, sitting by the pond that he'd helped to build. He felt all would be well if they could just go back to that time.

"I don't understand. It was fine the last time I was here, and that wasn't that long ago. Couldn't we just drive past?"

Kevin2 shook his big head slowly. Stanley wondered how much his mother knew about all this. He supposed she'd got used to it. Or maybe she didn't know about the new building of villas and pathways because she'd usually have no need to travel to those parts of the island. Clearly, the island was now very tightly managed, which James would approve of, but what about all the little differences that made people the individuals they were? Mum was so proud of her garden. Would he ever get the chance now to let Troy wander in it and dangle his little feet in the pond? How was it possible that everything had changed so quickly?

The drive in the open buggy was pleasant enough. The sun was shining and on any other day, it would have been a great day out. The day was beginning to be hot, but the movement of the buggy provided a little breeze. Driving across from the port to the south side of the island took about twenty minutes. Looking around over what had the last time been hills and fields grazed with sheep and lambs, they could now see a patchwork of laid-out gardens, manicured lawns and single-story villas – all connected by the new mini roads. The villas looked like identical retirement bungalows, as though they were made from one model, which they probably were.

Mini delivery trucks that looked almost like toys moved up and down the pathways. Some were laden with sheets, and washing, and what looked like airport-type food cannisters. Other trucks carried closed containers with a flap at the back, secured in place with a lock. There were no drivers in sight at all. Each path off the main concourse was labelled with simple signs comprising of long numbers.

The clinic was a long, low white building that was approached by a small driveway that forked to the main pedestrian entrance in one direction, and that led the delivery trucks to warehouse doors at the side of the building, in the other. The warehouse doors swung open like a garage whenever the trucks approached. Stanley thought he saw the shape of something white and shiny moving forward inside before the doors swung shut again.

Stanley felt a sudden sadness that they wouldn't all be going back to the cottage, and felt himself wanting to wind time back to his last visit. And he suddenly felt regretful that he'd signed that dratted 'sunset clause,' and the new 'enhanced' power of attorney. Maybe he'd been a little premature? He reached for Cassie's hand again and squeezed it tightly. She looked up at him and smiled that beautiful calming smile that made him feel everything would be alright in the end.

The buggy slowed down at the front of the building and Kevin2 jumped out, asking Stanley and Cassie to remain seated. Kevin2 pressed a buzzer outside the front entrance and seemed to be there a while, speaking into the contraption on the wall. When he came back he looked puzzled and slightly irritated. "The clinic says they're very sorry, she's been discharged but for some reason, her records weren't updated. I'm sorry you've had a wasted journey."

"Well, that's okay. We'll go to the cottage then," said Stanley, actually feeling a little relieved. "We really do want to see her, we've come all this way."

Kevin2 shook his large head again, "I can't do that. It's not on my schedule. I take my orders in advance. She might not even be there, anyway."

"Where else would she be?! Stanley was feeling alarmed again. "I'll give her a call, just in case." But he'd forgotten he had to leave his real phone behind. There was nothing else for it. It was getting late – too late to travel to the cottage now and still catch the last ferry back. Stanley grasped Cassie's hand and held it tightly as Kevin2 drove them steadily back to the port. The sky had clouded over, the scudding clouds were grey and heavy with the coming rain. Cassie held his hand tightly – she was sorry they'd missed Anna but was keen to get back in time to pick up Troy from her mother before his bedtime.

Chapter 38

Stanley tried Anna's phone several times over the next couple of days, but it just rang and rang. He expected her to call back at any moment, but the call didn't come. Panicking a little, he tried to get through to the official keeper on the island, and then to the clinic. Again, the answer machines kept saying that he was number one on the call and that they would put him through soon. But it never happened. The idea of 'Home Farm' had all seemed so sensible when they were talking strategy and brainstorming in James' office. What on earth had gone wrong! If things on the island hadn't been strange enough, the fact that he now also couldn't get hold of his mother was seeming more and more sinister. Moreover, James was still impossible to get hold of.

For several days, Cassie had been preoccupied with Troy's feverish reaction to his second MMR vaccination, so he didn't want to worry her. Then, one evening when Troy was tucked up in bed, Cassie said, "There's been another red alert for the heat wave. I'm worried about whether Troy can take it – he was so feverish after his last shot. Maybe we should get some air con for his room at night?"

Stanley perked up. "That's a good idea. Maybe that's what happened with Mum? A heat wave on the Isle of Wight?"

"Why don't you try James Hillingdon again. Surely he'll know what's going on," said Cassie.

Stanley suddenly remembered that he had James' personal number on his phone. He found it and dialled, feeling pessimistic, and so he was surprised when James' jovial voice answered.

"Stanley! How are you getting on?"

"James! At last! I've been trying to get hold of you for weeks!"

"I've been pretty caught up Stan," said James, "you should have tried this number – I'm always available to you, you know that. And thanks for the voting analytics by the way – I was meaning to email you back on that."

"It's my mother, I think you met her?"

"Ah yes! ... I was a little surprised to meet her again on the island, I thought you said she was in Wales?" he asked, curiously.

"Well, yes she was, but she came back after a while." Damn, he'd forgotten he'd said she was in Wales. Why did he say that? "Anyway, I think she had an iDoc implanted ... she ended up in the clinic because of it and we haven't been able to get hold of her since. We visited the clinic and they refused us entry. I think they lied about her having been discharged!!"

"I didn't realize she was part of the iDoc research group," said James slowly.

"I thought they were only being implanted for people who need urgent behavioural interventions, before deciding on whether to put them on the Wight Way end-of-life programme? What's going on?"

"Well," James didn't seem nearly as alarmed as he should be, thought James, "the iDocs are being tested for a wide range of uses, not only for the end-of-life assessments."

"She tried to cut it out and now she's lying in a clinic where god-knows-what is happening ... or lying in a ditch for all we know!" replied Stan. He could feel his temper rising. Why couldn't James see this was his mother they were talking about!

"Oh dear," said James thoughtfully, "that doesn't sound good..."

At last James was taking this seriously, thought Stanley. "It sounds like someone's been bending the rules. Wasn't there a cash incentive for each new set up of the iDocs to encourage volunteers?"

"Yes," replied James, "but it should only have been offered to the most feeble of candidates. To be honest, I really wouldn't have recommended the iDoc, Stan, it really is still at the very experimental stage, especially around its behavioural control aspects."

"It wasn't me that signed her up! I thought we were going to keep everything above board!"

"It *is* all above board!" James said, clearly irritated.

"Exactly what is the ultimate goal of these iDocs, anyway?"

"They have all sorts of benefits for the individual and also help us by gathering more NHS data, but we decided not to proceed further with them until they are better tested. They are excellent at monitoring people for certain conditions, preventing further deterioration and encouraging certain behaviour changes ..." he paused, "but it's true that last bit is what's tricky. It still needs a lot of work."

"If the iDocs encourage healthier living, and are helping patients live longer, doesn't that go against the latest government guidelines about *not* prolonging life forever?"

"Well, *I'm* all for a longer life, but yes, sadly, the government's focus is to relieve the costs of caring for the elderly who are too frail to look after themselves. The iDocs help to make those decisions by closely monitoring health and helping the care sector to decide when someone is too frail for further medical interventions." He went on pensively, "The real thing about the iDocs is that, especially for healthy individuals, we couldn't be sure of the long-term effects."

'*Couldn't be sure of the long-term effects*,' thought Stan. Why had his mother ended up in this new clinic? The regular consultancy fees from James' company were putting Stanley back onto an even footing financially. Cassie, bless her, had almost persuaded him to retrain in environmental work but thankfully he'd decided against it. James was generous to his favoured few and now Stanley had joined the club, it felt good to have an older confidant in James. Nevertheless, Stanley felt alarmed at James's seeming lack of concern and urgency about the impact of the iDoc on his mother. James had continued to mutter something about, "All in the name of science," and "careful monitoring," but when Stanley put the phone down, he did not feel reassured. Did James care at all? Or did he know a great deal more than he was telling Stanley?

The next morning, he looked at his phone and saw that James had called an emergency meeting at his London office for the next day. The meeting was ominously called 'Home Farm Developments.' The wording of the email indicated that James expected full attendance, regardless of the short notice. James felt some relief. Maybe now he'd get some answers.

The next day, James nodded seriously at each attendee sitting around the board room table, reserving a special smile for Stanley. "Thank you for coming here today at such short notice," he began. And then he introduced a new clean-shaven venture capitalist whom Stanley had never seen before. "First, I want to introduce our new colleague, Edward. Ed will be helping us with the highly complex data analytics and projections as we move forward. He's an expert on the phenomenon called the Black Swan theory, which we'll go into later."

Ed was sporting an American-style crewcut, flecked with grey hairs. He nodded his hellos to each member in turn as James went on, "There are several serious issues we need to consider, and I want decisions on each of them today." Everyone round the table nodded again and shuffled uncomfortably in their seats as James continued in deadly serious tones. "The first issue is that the recent acceleration of climate change has produced some concerning changes in the health and well-being of our residents on Home Farm. This is especially a problem now as there is regretfully overcrowding in the End Of Life Clinic on the island. The second issue, is that government is considering making special conditions for the new regime. And the third issue ..." he paused for effect, "is that Professor Sir John Westerby has been in touch."

The red-faced farmer and his busty wife, the investors who Stan recognised from previous meetings, looked at each other and shuffled their chairs forward expectantly, as James continued. "We need, indeed *must*, agree on immediate actions in relation to the rising temperatures on the island. The death rates are going up significantly. The sea breezes do bring the temperatures down, but older people seem to be more susceptible than they used to be. We must see what else we can do to ensure their health and well-being."

"You mean like put in air con and ceiling fans?" Asked Ed, we always had those in the states.

"Yeess," said James sounding doubtful, "that too, but I was thinking of something more radical. The main thing is to be aware, to put it bluntly, that the death rates are now rising in the summer as well as the winter ... And this is not going to be good for morale if the news gets out. The island is supposed to be a holiday home of choice for the elderly."

"Noted," came in Ed again, "but what can *we* be expected to do about that? We could put on mindfulness seminars, perhaps!" He beamed.

"What's the government going to do? I'd like to know! It's their problem, not ours!" said the farmer.

"The government has their collective heads totally in the sand over this," replied James. "I suspect they would be only too happy for us, and the robot programme, to pick up the flak. The problem at the moment is that if the rising temperatures are combined with the withdrawal of wholesale public health programmes – like universal statins – then more people will die earlier. It's as simple as that."

"Then what do we do?" demanded Ed, arms akimbo.

James replied calmly, "I will, of course, ask the government if they would consider reinstating some of the public health programmes on the island specifically – our robots have been remarkably successful there. They might not actually reinstate publish health programmes, but they might be willing to sign up to some new special conditions."

"What sort of special conditions and what will it all cost?" asked the farmer angrily.

"They have been trialling a new end-of-life care pathway – something that a clever civil servant named 'The Right Way' but everyone on the island misunderstood it at first as the "Wight Way."

"So? What's wrong with the 'Right Way', or whatever it's called?" enquired Ed again. Stanley smirked at his unconscious joke.

"Ha!" said James, "Nothing 'wrong with right' but no time for jokes now ... If someone spots any link between the 'Right Way' and the capping of clinical interventions – we've got potential political dynamite!"

"For god's sake, speak plain English. What the blazes does that mean?" asked the farmer becoming increasingly red.

"Capping clinical interventions means no more operations for cancer or heart conditions, or even simple cataracts, when you're over 70," said James.

"Jesus, that'll go down like a lead balloon. 70 you say? Better up my insurance!" said the farmer with a look of disbelief.

"Actually, believe it or not, some people apparently voted for it at a recent public meeting on the island," replied James.

"Well, good for them, but it's not happening to me!" declared the farmer.

"Understood, I feel the same way!" said James emphatically. "Especially as each year passes," he added ruefully. "I also want to draw your attention to something Stanley raised with me recently. The youth vote is rising significantly in importance and the government is getting very excited about it."

Ed jumped in, "This is exactly what I was telling you about James, predictive analytics is now able to predict what might happen next. If you add the theory of the Black Swan, its potentially dynamic."

"Yesss, just remind me about the Black Swan effect please Ed?"

Ed puffed himself up, "It's all about an event which comes as a surprise and has a major effect. It even gets rationalised after the fact with the benefit of hindsight. You know like the black swans in Australia!"

"Who cares about the swans or the youngsters!" exploded the farmer. "Luckily Daisy and I don't have any of our own, but surely us silver voters still outnumber the young ones by miles!"

James shook his head. "In pure numbers, that may be so, but the interests of the older population are no longer dominant. The silver voice is fading, some might even say it's tarnished – and that could signal a dramatic change of policy on health and social care."

Ed shook his head whilst the farmer threw his hands up in the air in horror. Ignoring them both, James moved on, "The last issue we need to discuss is John Westerby, or should I say Professor, Sir John Westerby, to use his full title. It seems that he's acquired a lot of land on the island and is in the process of building a whole new series of new retirement villas with special services built-in. He's also had mobile surgery units set up so that one of his registrars can do mobile knee and hip surgery on the spot. Some elderly person falls, Sir John's medical team picks them up and pops them into the mobile unit parked outside their villa for a couple of days and then discharges them straight back into their home again. Then the mobile unit moves on to the next one."

"What did he want, then?" asked the farmer.

"Just what I predicted; he can't get the staff. He wants to talk about doing a deal with our robots. I guess he's finally realised they're far superior to the models he was trialling. We'd be taking a bit of a risk getting the sixth-generation robots trained and programmed for post-op care – but we don't need to tell him the full story just yet."

"Damn the risk. How much would we make?"

"Plenty. I've done a deal with him which is waiting sign off tomorrow if you all agree. They'll get all the rich pickings from medical referrals from the Home Farm residents. They'll do their business in the mobile units and transfer the complex stuff over to the mainland using the new heliferry. All the of the day-to-day care of their care residents will be left to us."

Stanley was daydreaming – he badly wanted to discuss what was going on with his mother, with James. He was thinking about Evelyn and her problems too; she was obviously going through a nightmare scenario with Andy. Stan had never really liked the guy, but no one would wish dementia on their dog. He hadn't yet told Evelyn that he'd not managed to see Mum during his visit to the island – he wanted to wait until he'd tracked her down first.

At the end of the meeting, James took Stanley aside, and putting his arm around his shoulder, asked, "I'm so sorry again about your mother."

Stanley interrupted, "Do you know anything about what's really going on there? Do you think she was, or is, in the end-of-life clinic?!"

"What do you mean?" James looked momentarily worried.

"I didn't tell you on the phone, it wasn't just odd that the clinic were so secretive, but *everything* on the island seemed very odd ... as though the whole island had been shut down – as if the borders had been closed and we weren't really allowed to be there ..."

Stanley trailed off as James looked deep in thought before suddenly and unexpectedly clapping Stan excitedly on the back, "Stanley, you're such a blue-sky thinker, thanks a lot!"

"What do you mean?" said Stan, puzzled. "James, I'm really worried about my mother!"

James just got out his little notebook and started clicking on his gold pen. "Yes of course," he said, preoccupied, before adding, "Write her contact details down and I'll find out what's happened.

I really like your mother – she's a savvy lady and I'm sure she'll be alright."

Later that evening, the news on all the channels that night was stark.

'Home Farm on the Isle of Wight is closing its doors!' A spokesperson for Home Farm, whom Stan didn't recognise, said in grim tones. 'The new haven for older people has proved such a great success, that we are announcing that there will be no more admissions to Home Farm for the time being. Further announcements about future developments will be made as soon as it's ready to open its doors again." new regime is sorted out.'

The penny dropped for Stan. When he'd mentioned his visit to the island, and said that it had felt like everything had been shut down, James had reacted. Why would Home Farm close its doors now? One, to avoid a scandal with the rising deaths. But also to ensure that James' new plans would benefit and that the scheme would be reopened as soon as the numbers dropped. Was James really that powerful he wondered? Or was a serious government programme behind all this? Who would benefit and to what purpose?

There wasn't much of a reaction from the press. They concentrated on a new fast-track government scheme that boosted the ability to buy houses for all first-time buyers. There would be a surge in the property market for first time younger buyers at last. Generation Z was on a roll.

But where was his Mum?

Chapter 39

I 'd been lying in my hospital room sleeping ... only occasionally waking, too weak and dazed to move ... for how long? Days? Weeks? More? And then one day, Henry2 came bustling into the room and waked me with a jerk. I was so happy to see him, and suddenly felt more alert than I had done in a long time (although that wasn't saying much). He opened the blinds wide. I blinked. I was so tired, my limbs felt so heavy. Henry2 was carrying my small grey hold all and as he lifted me carefully into a wheelchair he said, "It is time to leave now Anna, I've come to take you home."

Henry2 pushed the wheelchair up the ramp into the Notcar, which was waiting outside the clinic. It was early in the morning and quite chilly. I was wobbly and weak after all the tranquilising drugs I'd been given and after spending the last few weeks in bed. How many weeks had it been?! Surely they should have known that was a health risk in itself? I couldn't remember much about it, even what had happened before, but I did remember Henry2 leaving to go for his MOT and now he was back. It was exciting to be out into the world again. As I sat in the Notcar with the warm blanket that Henry2 had provided wrapped around me, I was confident that I'd soon be back to normal again and being looked after by Henry2. I would take great comfort in the anticipation of his careful diets and my fitness regime. I would finally be able to think clearly again.

I'd had so many dreams in the clinic. I even dreamed about Tom coming to see me. That can't have been real. And Evie and Stan too … or had they actually visited? The memory of the dreams was fading fast. And what about the strange conversations with a powerful voice about robots? It had spoken about the next steps for the Robot Network Renewal Programme, but I couldn't work out who it had been, or if it was real or not. I would ask Henry2 later. As I sat back in my warm blanket, I decided not to tell anyone about the voices in the clinic, either they were real, or they were my imagination working overtime. It seemed unlikely that I would have had visitors, so I decided to stick with my overworked imagination for the time being.

In the Notcar, Henry2 reached over to plug my phone into the charger. It had been turned off in the clinic. When it leapt back to life, there were several dozen phone calls. The messages were mostly from Pete but also quite a few from Stanley and Evelyn, and one I smiled at from James enquiring how I was and inviting me to lunch or dinner soon. He'd left his number. There was also a number that had left no message and that worried me a little. I hadn't even had the chance to read Pete's messages when his number began ringing. When I answered, he launched straight in, "Thank goodness! What on earth happened?! I've been trying to get hold of you and the clinic wouldn't tell me anything!"

"I'm still not sure what happened. I really wasn't well, but I'm on my way back home now. What's up?"

"So, you won't have heard the news?"

"What news?" I asked nervously.

"They've imposed a sort of lock down on the island. No one can leave and no one can come here – at least for the time being."

"Why?" I asked anxiously, thinking the worst.

"Fred says it's to do with a high-level government policy change. It seems that someone's been cutting corners with the new robot regime and they need to investigate. I'm very worried about what it might mean for us, but Fred keeps saying that it's his job to make sure I come to no harm. It's rather sweet."

"Sounds like Henry2. What do you think we should do?"

"Get off the island as quickly as we can! I've talked to Fred. He's disabled his connections, but I'm pretty certain they'll cotton on soon enough and be knocking on our door."

"Okay, but how do we get off?" I paused. "I used to be quite a good long-distance swimmer."

Pete laughed, "I reckon our best bet is my boat; I've been maintaining it through the winters. Just need to check the engine over. The circuits need to be rewired and ..."

I interrupted, "Too much detail, Pete. What about the others?"

"I've tried to reach them. Simon has all but given up. He said to send him a postcard. Jude kept asking me more questions and said she'd ring me back, but she never did. I didn't try too hard. There's a good chance she might tip them off – especially if there's something in it for her."

"What about Henry2 and Fred? They'll be too heavy for your boat. We can't leave them behind. Anything could happen to them!"

"Relax, they have a plan!" Pete replied.

Henry2 and Fred had apparently decided to mount a wholesale rescue operation in true robot fashion – every contingency had been risk assessed and mitigated. While Pete checked out his boat, Fred and Henry2 had worked out how to re-tune all our of remaining devices and connections so that no-one would pick up any true signals. They'd booked themselves in for a new programming exercise on the mainland. The plan was that they would board one of the few remaining ferries that were still scheduled and meet us on the other side.

As soon as I got back home, I flew around the house gathering my most essential belongings. I noticed that the bright yellow aconites had come out on the stone path. The snow drops were fading away and soon the daffodils would be out. The dark green shoots that were beginning to push up meant that the bluebells would appear soon after. I would tackle the garden as soon as I could come back. Spring is normally a good time of year for me – fresh starts and new shoots – I hoped this tiredness would soon pass.

Despite the damp, it felt good to be home, and I was sad to be leaving again so soon. I wondered when I'd get to return. As soon as darkness fell, Pete and I met on our bikes as arranged, with rucksacks packed tight for the overnight journey and the stars guiding us. We cycled to his old moorings three miles away in Shalfleet and decided to wait until nearly dawn to sail across. We knew that it wouldn't be safe to use the satnav at any time. Pete had checked with Fred that there wouldn't be any heliferries crossing until later in the morning to spot us. So, we wrapped ourselves up in the sleeping bags that we'd brought and I fished out my red swimming cap and put it in my pocket, just in case. We both had a sip of the hot chocolate from the thermos before settling down in the hull of the boat. It was damp and cold and I began to wonder if we'd made a terrible mistake.

When the sky began to lighten, Pete shook me awake by the shoulder. We set off quietly in the early light. The only sound was the slight splash of the oars as Pete pushed us off from the shore. As we got a little further out, Pete laid the oars down into the hull and began pulling the sail up. The sea was swelling all around us and the salty sea spray stung us in our faces. As we surged forward slowly out into the open sea, I began to shiver. There was real danger out here on the sea, which had nothing to do with machines or evil men. I missed Henry2's reassuring presence. Several times I clutched the side of the boat and tried to estimate how far I would have to swim to reach dry land. But that option seemed to fade when land faded out of sight - both ahead and behind us - and there was just a grey mist and the white crests of waves being whipped up by the wind. I checked that my swimming cap was in my pocket again. The Solent was said to be one of the busiest channels of boat traffic in the world. Or was that the English Channel? It was definitely usually busy, in any case, often with huge cruise liners.

"Are we nearly there?" I called out plaintively to Pete, who was steering at the back whilst I was tucked away at the bottom of the hull, fingering my swimming cap and trying to keep warm.

He shrugged his shoulders and shouted out over the sound of the sea, "About halfway, I reckon. Come and sit up here. You'll feel a lot better."

The swelling grey sea seemed to stretch forever. The freezing wind froze my fingers and my face. I decided I was better off hunkering down into the sleeping bag where, although I felt nauseous, I was at least warm. In those moments, if a proper boat had come along, I would happily have given up and been rescued. I thought of the migrants who regularly crossed the channel in tiny boats, not knowing what the future would hold.

An interminable two hours later, the mainland at last loomed up ahead. Pete called out, "Land Ahoy!" I cried with relief when Pete said it was safe to turn the engine on and we chugged into the watery reaches of Lymington. Climbing stiffly out of the boat, we hugged each other in silent relief.

Our first priority now was to find Fred and Henry2. It wasn't long before we discovered them standing immobile at the Ferry crossing gates surrounded by a bemused ferry crew and several small children. I wondered how they had managed it and whether a sixth sense had helped them mastermind the escape. There were no other robots in sight – that was a good thing. They were safe and so, hopefully, were we. Time would tell.

Chapter 40

Stanley called James and left a message asking him to call him urgently. When he finally got a reply, he was reassured by James' calm insistence that all would be well. He thought back to his father's sad funeral and to the last time he'd spoken properly with him. He remembered his father's words, "*Take care of your mother, please Stanley, whatever happens, she's not as tough as you think.*" He had agreed, feeling like full grown 'man of the world.' But he hadn't taken care of her, had he? He felt momentarily guilty but pushed those thoughts aside.

For James, it had been another tough day at the office with tempers fraying on all sides. Nobody could understand why the sudden closure of the island borders had happened, but it had caused chaos on the stock market. "Chaos on the stock market always means a lot of people losing money. We have been extremely careful and I'm delighted to say that we are not in that category," said James to those who had gathered in the Board Room for yet another emergency meeting.

"What do you mean?" asked Farmer who was becoming increasingly red-faced. "Care home shares are crashing everywhere." He was furious and so was his wife.

James nodded at him. "Yes, but we have made sure we were

ahead of the game and protected ourselves against the losses. You will have noticed that whilst the care home market and pensions schemes are all on edge and fragile, the technology and digital markets are sky high. So if you followed my advice then you should be fine." Stanley hadn't had an option but to put his faith in James but clearly the farmer had not followed his lead. It seemed likely he had left his money in his care home businesses.

James explained that he government was in disarray again with calls on all sides for resignations, especially for Shirley Harper Smith who was clearly taking the brunt of it, whilst the PM stood back. All the TV channels showed agonised interviews with distraught older people wringing their hands. Hospitals were no longer able to discharge older people to the island for rehabilitation and many closed their A&E departments refusing to take any new patients. Waiting lists were said to be shooting up yet again. There were also angry young people marching on Number 10 as the property market took an immediate hit and sales ground to a halt.

Stanley listened to all the chaos and wished again that he could talk to James the same way that he used to talk with his father. He missed having his father around, in so many ways. As soon as James had gone, Stanley left the office early. As he strode up the quiet, tree-lined Islington street towards home, he looked forward to a quiet drink in the garden, maybe even a barbecue if the rain held off. He glanced up at the rolling grey clouds moving rapidly across the sky. Cassie had called him to say there was a surprise for him at home. She wouldn't tell him what it was, just that he'd have to wait until he got there. Stanley smiled to himself, musing that it was probably a special project Troy had made at his nursery that morning.

As he neared the house, he was stunned to hear 'Amazing Grace' come flooding out from the open front door. He shivered, the last time he'd heard that had been at Dad's funeral. The words 'was blind and now I see' brought back the message that forgiveness and redemption are possible, regardless of the sins committed.

He came up to the front door and stopped; there, as it swung open, stood his mother.

Chapter 41

I stood in the doorway with a rueful smile and held out my arms to Stanley who exclaimed, rather rudely I thought, "Mum! What's happened? How on earth did you get here?"

"You mean what a lovely surprise Mum!" I laughed as I gave him a hug, "It's been so wonderful to finally meet Troy in person!! He reminds me so much of you when you were that age!!"

"Gosh, yes Mum, of course. It is lovely to see you again, we were so worried."

"Yes, Cassie told me you went to the island." I replied, "She's moved me back into my old bedroom. It's so good to be home again!" I added as he stood there looking disconcerted.

Troy came through the door, clapping his hands with delight at seeing his father. He called Henry2 to bring out his new bike which Henry had fitted with stabilisers. "Look, Dad, see how fast I can go!" He cried out as he spun off down the pavement.

"Please stop this minute and come back. Now!" Henry2 called out firmly and somewhat anxiously. "If you come inside, I can make you pancakes." When that had no impact he tried again, "Or we can do jigsaws. I know, I can teach you an old nursery rhyme – it's called 'Head and Shoulders, Knees and Toes.'"

Troy smiled at Henry2 and wheeled his bike back up the

pavement, "I know that one! And can you teach me jokes?"

"Yes! But only if you help," said Henry2. "And I might even laugh if you find out how to make me!"

Troy looked at him curiously before coming over to my side and putting his tiny warm hand in mine. "Granny, have you come for a sleepover?"

I replied, "Yes please, Troy."

Troy looked up at Henry2 with a broad smile on his face, "Can Henry2 have a sleepover too?"

"I'm sure he can – as long as you do jigsaws with Henry2, as well as make him laugh. Do you think you can do that?"

"Yes, I will try," said Troy determinedly. Then he paused, listening, "Granny, why are you making that funny noise?"

"What noise?" I asked.

Henry2 jumped in firmly saying, "Your grandmother is making a humming noise."

"What is humming?" asked Troy.

Henry2 went into auto mode. "Some people believe that humming is a psychological phenomenon that is heard worldwide. It is believed to emanate from the earth – possibly due to pollution. It happens in some special places."

"Why is Granny doing it?"

I laughed and shook my head, "Henry2, you've been on the internet again!" And to Troy, "Never mind, dear."

"Was the island a special place?" asked Troy again.

"Oh, yes," I laughed, "the island was, and still is, a very special place. One day I will take you there."

Henry2 chimed in. "The Isle of Wight is special for many reasons. There are several little-known facts about the island. First, it is one of the few remaining places where the red squirrel lives. The red squirrel is very rare now. The Isle of Wight is also home to the remarkable Leanam. The Leanam is a small slug-like creature that lives exclusively in the stretch of sea called The Solent that lies between the Isle of Wight and the mainland."

Troy looked puzzled, "Do the squirrels eat the Lee, Lean ... do they eat the slugs?"

"No!" I added hurriedly, "they eat nuts. Another notable fact is that your Grandfather Tom used to love the garlic which is a specialty on the island. There are lots of garlic farms on the island."

"What about Leeman?"

"Oh, it will survive for eons," I added, "although perhaps not with climate change."

"I don't think I like garlic. But I would like to see a Leanam." Troy replied.

"Henry2, I don't know what we'd do without you." I said, "You're such a mine of information. I'm just wondering, before it gets dark, if you could find Tom's old bicycle and pump the tires up? I fancy a spin around the square with my new grandson."

"I'm not new Granny, but I do like bike rides!" Troy replied.

Henry2 couldn't resist another educational input, "The bicycle wheels do not spin, they go in circular round movements."

Troy interrupted, singing his latest nursery rhyme, "The wheels on the bus go round and round ..."

Henry2 looked puzzled but picked up where he had been interrupted. "Anna, it is not safe for you to go on a bicycle ride until you are in better physical condition. Your body is still not fully recovered from the journey and your balance will not have sufficiently returned."

"But it's good for me! Even if I don't have that iDoc thing tracking my exercise, I need to have fun too. Please see what you can do."

Henry2 went reluctantly to get Tom's bicycle from the shed and returned 10 minutes later having welded metal stabilisers onto the back wheels. Whilst I laughed, he nodded approvingly at his own work. "Just like Troy's bicycle. You will be much steadier now! I went down the pavements and around the block with Troy by my side. It was a glorious moment of physical freedom, opening up future possibilities and fun with Troy, my new best friend singing away at my side. I felt safe, at home, and not alone anymore. The gardens we passed were beautiful and we even got a wave from a friendly neighbour I remembered from years ago.

Later that evening, when Cassie had put Troy to bed, we sat down together. Stanley was still recovering from the shock and wanted to go over the story again. "Mum, tell me what happened and what about your iDoc? You never told me why you had it? And why you got rid of it?"

"The iDoc was supposed to be a force for the good but I began to get this funny feeling that it was trying to tell me what to do. I wasn't sure if I could trust anyone anymore. I just wanted it out."

"That's when they found you trying to cut it out?" He winced.

I turned my wrist over, looked at the fading scar, and smiled as I remembered. "Henry2 was supposed to go off to the mainland but instead, they had kept him at the clinic as the back-up robot in case there was an emergency. Henry2 knew all along that I shouldn't be in the clinic and that he had to get me out of there. When he was helping me escape, he said, 'There are sometimes difficult judgements to be made between the good and the greater good.'

"How did Henry2 cotton on to the fact that the clinic was not a safe place for you?" Stanley asked.

"As you know, his guiding principle is to do no harm. When they tried to put me on the end-of-life care pathway after my ECT, Henry2 took executive action and removed me from the danger."

"So, he also knew that once he'd got you out, they'd try trace you and bring you back? 'For your own good' of course! They shouldn't have put that thing in you in the first place. Good for Henry2!"

"Yeeees," I said cautiously, "But I always got the feeling that you knew a bit more about what was going on than I did?"

"We were trying to solve a serious problem, Mum," said Stanley somewhat pompously. "You Baby Boomers were costing too much

276

as I've always said. The Isle of Wight seemed the best place to try out new projects and innovations. It was actually partly my idea!" Stanley said proudly.

I laughed, "Yes but your colleagues, the money makers – those venture capitalists – were part of the problem Stanley, not the solution!"

Stanley was about to remonstrate when Cassie put her hand on his arm and said. "We did worry about what was going on when we couldn't find you, didn't we Stan?"

I replied, "I'm worried about what's going on for the rest of them left on the island now. I just couldn't work out who was in charge, the venture capitalists, the Robot Network Programme, or the government?"

"Actually Mum," said Stanley, "I think that was part of the problem. No-one knew and we still don't, really. "

I recalled the voices in my dreams at the clinic and said,

"Someone does though and I have a feeling we will find out soon enough. Hopefully before too many more restrictions are forced through."

Stanley looked at me strangely and said firmly. "I'm sure we will work it out and what to do next, now that the borders are closed."

"Well, let me know if I can help!" I offered, half in jest, "I do know a bit about robots and even about growing older you know!"

Stanley changed the subject, "Whatever happened to Patrick?"

"Who? I don't know anyone called Patrick."

"He was your neighbour on the island. You used to talk about him a lot, but we never met him?"

I shook my head – should I know who this Patrick was? The name *did* sound vaguely familiar, but I had no recollection of anyone like that on the island. Just the old man who was looking after the house for Rose and he disappeared as soon as I took over. "Patrick was the name of Tom's younger brother – he died when you were little. I was very fond of him, he used to stick up for me and look after me when Tom was away. Why are you asking?"

Stanley shook his head and turned to Henry2 who was busy at the kitchen sink, "Henry2, you remember Patrick, don't you? What happened to him?"

Henry2 turned around and, polite as usual, said, "There was no one called Patrick. There was Peggie and Edward, and the angry man, Brian. There was Kevin, and Mrs Finlay. But there was no-one called Patrick." Either way, Patrick had gone and even if he had existed in my mind, he wasn't there anymore.

The next day I called Evelyn to tell her my news and put her on loudspeaker so we could all join in. She had quite a surprise for us too, "I'm coming to London!" she announced. "Andy's being sent on something called the 'Right Way' and I can't live in the middle of the Welsh mountains on my own anymore."

At the mention of 'Right Way' we all looked at each other in silent acknowledgement. "Oh goodness, Evie," I said, "that's awful about Andy, when is he going?"

Stanley grabbed the phone aghast, "You can't come here, there's no room!"

Cassie shook her head at him and took the phone away, "We're so sorry to hear about Andy. It'll be lovely to see you again after all this time. You're very welcome! What about Hugo and Matty?"

Evelyn replied, "Hugo will come too." Stanley snorted but Evelyn continued, "Matty just got into university to read Psychology, but I don't know where she'll be living because she's not speaking to me. I'm desperately worried about her."

Stanley groaned some more and Cassie tutted at him and said, "Stan, please can you move your things from your dad's study, we'll need the extra room for Evie now. And Hugo can move in with Troy for the time being."

Now that the house was going to be full again, there was one more thing I had to do before I could finally relax. After Sunday lunch, I got out my laptop and, humming happily, I googled 'safeguarding on the Isle of Wight.' The section on reporting abuse on the Isle of Wight Council website was clear. Reports could indeed be made retrospectively – for example if you suspected someone had died due to being abused by a family member. I looked down the different columns and, although I was tempted to tick all the boxes including the ones on sexual abuse, I stopped when I came to the box marked 'financial abuse' and filled in Brian's name as the financial abuser of Peggie and Edward. Smiling happily, I pressed the 'send' button.

Chapter 42

Cassie came into the sitting room after supper. Stanley was drafting something at his father's old desk in his study with the door open. When I asked what he was up to, he looked up, "It's something James has asked me to work on."

"Can I help at all?" I enquired.

"Not for the moment thanks, Mum. It's the next steps. A sort of backstop for the closure of the borders on the island. Now Generation Z are going to be taken over by Generation Alpha, we need to plan ahead. Of course, Troy will be one of them," Stanley smiled in wonder at the thought. "As a child of us Millennials, he will be the most digitally and technologically literate, so he'll accept robots as his friends and allies." He turned pompously back to his laptop as I shut the door quietly behind him.

On my way through to the sitting room, I stopped at the kitchen door and asked Henry2, who was polishing the glasses, "Henry2, do you think we've got it right now with the different generations all living together?"

Henry2 looked up and said, "Intergenerational families are recognised as the best way to bring up children and look after those who are growing older. It's the natural way."

"Thanks Henry2, well put. Perhaps you could explain that to

the government and to the venture capitalists?"

Henry2 returned to his chores, and I went through to the sitting room where the mirror on the mantel piece reflected the little crab apple tree that now stood a good ten feet tall. It was about to burst into bud ahead of the fruit that would hang in bunches from its branches. I was happy at last, sitting peacefully and quietly in front of the wood-burning stove with Cassie. I would miss the cottage, and my pond, and the wild garden. But maybe one day I could go back. She looked across at me and said, smiling, "Now tell me what *really* happened? How did you manage to make your escape with Henry2?!"

"Pour me another glass of wine and I'll tell you," I said happily. "It all happened so quickly at the end. My friend Pete had been trying to contact me whilst I was in the clinic and thank goodness, he didn't give up. Whilst I was in the hospital, Henry2 had kept an eye on my phone, and when he realised I was in real danger he contacted Fred." As she looked puzzled, I said, "Fred was Pete's robot."

Cassie looked non-plussed, "And what exactly was the danger?" she asked anxiously.

"The idiots mistook my recovery from ECT as me dying. Either that or it was intentional, I never trusted that Nurse Finlay even though she did rescue me from bleeding to death. Somehow, the system messed up but luckily Henry2 came to the rescue. I was terrified to discover that they'd started me on the new end-of-life care pathway, the 'Right Way.'" And then I added, "I'll never be entirely certain it was a genuine mistake ..."

"Thank goodness they didn't succeed. We had such a lovely surprise when you turned up on the doorstep!" Cassie said. "Now we can all live happily ever after in a multi-generational household just like it's supposed to be!"

"Well, let's just say it's our doorstep for now, shall we?" I said.

"Yes," Cassie laughed. I continued to tell the story of how Pete helped us to escape on his boat, and then Cassie asked, "What happened to your friends Pete and Fred?"

"Hopefully, they've reached Skye by now. It's where Pete was born. He only retired to the Isle of Wight because he thought it would be warmer there. The Isle of Skye is perfect now after climate change. I don't know what's happening to the others though. I do worry about Simon."

"What do you think the government will do next?"

"Who knows but there are a lot of lovely robots out there looking for good homes."

The next evening, there was yet another knock on the door. Stanley groaned again as he got up. When he opened the door, he found James Hillingdon on the doorstep. "Hello, there Stanley," James said smiling past him at me in the hallway, "I've come to take your mother out to dinner."

In the background there was a loud cackling noise as Troy discovered how to tickle Henry2 on his front screen.

THE END

Author Bio

Julia Ross has worked as a nurse, social worker and mediator, and has held the position of Director of Social Services in the London Borough of Barking and Dagenam for ten years. She worked for several years in the digital world learning about AI and predictive analytics before becoming Chair of the British Association of Social Workers (BASW) UK from 2022-2026.

Julia is passionate about writing and has published two books previously, *When People Die*, a book on death for children, and *Call the Social* a novel published in 2022.

Julia lives on the Isle of Wight where *The Lauging Robot* is set.